'Written with a deep love of rural France, for the countryside, the people, the way of life and the cuisine ... so pervasive and agreeable is the charm of this novel that it might even allow you to pass the time pleasantly as you wait in an airport departure lounge for your long-delayed holiday flight to France'     *Scotsman*

'Hugely enjoyable and absolutely gripping. Martin Walker has got off to a flying start in what promises to be a great series. Bruno will be the Maigret of the Dordogne'     Antony Beevor

'The pleasures of life in the Dordogne, distinctive well-rounded characters and an intriguing mystery are a winning combination ... Walker's relaxed style and good humour help to bring to life his engaging hero and his delightful home and make one of the most enjoyable books I've read in a long time'     *Sunday Telegraph*

'It's beguiling, evocative and utterly wonderful. It also made me very hungry; ideally one should read the book at the kitchen table while sipping a vin de noix and eating truffle pate. [He is] the Alexander McCall Smith of La France Profonde. No one should be allowed to go on holiday to France this summer without a copy'     Francis Wheen

'*Bruno, Chief of Police* has many of the characteristics of Golden Age novels, above all the apparently remote setting which reveals its involvement in wider events. Martin Walker's Dordogne is worth a visit'     *Times Literary Supplement*

'Martin Walker has not only written an engrossing roman policier, but has written a book that goes to the very heart of what France – rural, small-town France – is like. It's a thriller, and full of surprises, but it will also appeal to anybody who loves France ... by recreating the splendid complexities of French culture, history and life, and reminding us how different, how very different, it is from our own. *Bruno, Chief of Police* is a wonderful creation'     Michael Korda, author of *Charmed Lives* and *Queenie*

BRUNO, CHIEF OF POLICE

Martin Walker was educated at Balliol College, Oxford and Harvard. In twenty-five years with the *Guardian*, he served as Bureau Chief in Moscow and as European Editor and Assistant Editor in the US before becoming the Editor of United Press International. In addition to his prize-winning journalism, he wrote and presented the BBC series 'Martin Walker's Russia' and 'Clintonomics'. He has written several acclaimed works of non-fiction, including *The Cold War: A History*, and a historical novel, *The Caves of Périgord*, which reached No. 8 on the *Washington Post* bestseller list. He spends his summers in his house in the Dordogne.

# BRUNO, CHIEF OF POLICE

Martin Walker

Quercus

First published in Great Britain in 2008 by Quercus

This paperback edition first published in 2009 by

Quercus
21 Bloomsbury Square
London
WC1A 2NS

A CIP catalogue record for this book is available
from the British Library

ISBN 978 1 84724 598 4

10 9 8 7 6

Printed and bound in Great Britain by Clays Ltd, St Ives plc

*For Pierrot*

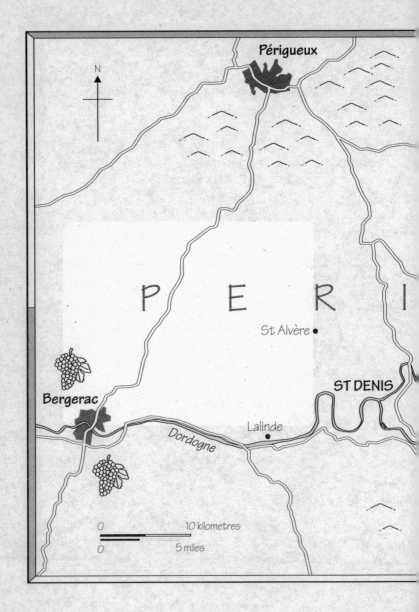

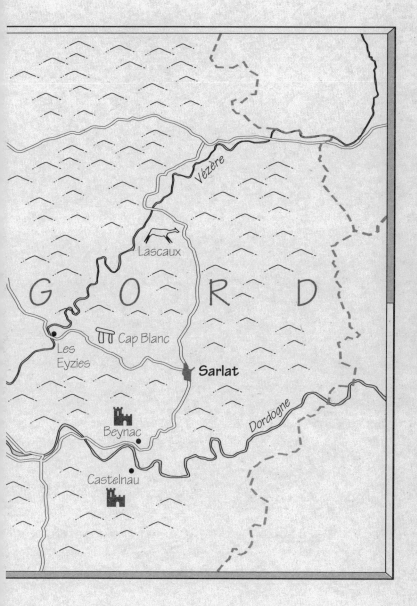

Police National
Place Dubernin
Périgueux

## INCIDENT REPORT
Dossier PN/24/MI/47398(P)

| | |
|---|---|
| Incident: | Unnatural death. |
| Cause of death: | Stab wounds, exsanguination. |
| Related incident: | Not known, no sign of robbery. |
| Date: | 11 May. |
| Location: | Commune de St Denis, Dordogne 24240. |
| Reporting Officer: | Chief of Police Municipale, Courrèges, Benoît. |
| Judge Magistrate: | To be appointed. |
| Case Officer: | Brigade Chief (Detectives) J-J Jalipeau. |
| Victim: | Hamid al-Bakr. |
| Date of Birth: | 14/7/1923 |
| Place of Birth: | Oran, Algeria. |
| Profession: | Retired Army sergeant, caretaker. Army number 47937692A. |
| Social Security number: | KV47/N/79457463/M. |
| Place of work: | (last known) Military School of Engineers, Lille. |
| Address: | La Bergerie, Chemin Communale 43, St Denis, 24240. |

## Report:
CoP Courrèges, accompanied by Gendarmerie Captain Duroc, Etienne, Post 24/37, were called to the remote country home of the deceased after a telephone call from the victim's grandson, Karim al-Bakr. Death was certified by Morisot, Albert, Fire Chief of St Denis. Death caused by blood loss after stab wounds to the trunk. Victim had been beaten and hands were bound. Scene of Crime team called from Bergerac.

**Note**: All reports to be copied to Office of Prefect, Périgueux.

# CHAPTER 1

On a bright May morning, so early that the last of the mist was still lingering low over the great bend in the river, a white van drew to a halt on the ridge over the small French town. A man emerged, strode to the edge of the road and stretched mightily as he admired the familiar view. He was still young, and evidently fit enough to be dapper and brisk in his movements, but as he relaxed he was sufficiently concerned about his love of food to tap his waist, gingerly probing for any sign of plumpness, always a threat in this springtime period between the end of the rugby season and the start of serious hunting. He wore what appeared to be half a uniform – a neatly ironed blue shirt with epaulettes, no tie, navy blue trousers and black boots. His thick, dark hair was crisply cut, his warm brown eyes had a twinkle and his generous mouth seemed always ready to break into a smile. On a badge on his chest, and on the side of his van, were the words *Police Municipale*. A rather dusty peaked cap lay on the passenger seat.

In the back of the van were a crowbar, a tangle of battery cables, one basket containing new-laid eggs, and another with his first spring peas of the season. Two tennis racquets, a pair of rugby boots, training shoes, and a large bag with various kinds of sports attire added to the jumble which tangled itself in a spare line from a fishing rod. Somewhere underneath all this were a first-aid kit, a small tool chest, a blanket, and a picnic hamper with plates and glasses, salt and pepper, a head of garlic and a Laguiole pocket knife with a horn handle and corkscrew. Tucked under the front seat was a bottle of not-quite-legal *eau de vie* from a friendly farmer. He would use this to make his private stock of *vin de noix* when the green walnuts were ready on the feast of St Catherine. Benoît Courrèges, Chief of Police for the small Commune of St Denis and its 2,900 souls, and universally known as Bruno, was always prepared for every eventuality.

Or almost always. He wore no heavy belt with its attachments of holster and pistol, handcuffs and flashlight, keys and notebook, and all the other burdens that generally weigh down every policeman in France. There would doubtless be a pair of ancient handcuffs somewhere in the jumble of his van, but Bruno had long forgotten where he had put the key. He did have a flashlight, and constantly reminded himself that one of these days he ought to buy some new batteries. The van's glove compartment held a notebook and some pens, but the notebook was currently full of various recipes, the minutes of the last tennis club meeting (which he had yet to type up on the temperamental old office computer that he distrusted) and a list of the names and phone numbers of the *minimes*, the young boys who had signed up for his rugby training class.

Bruno's gun, a rather elderly MAB 9mm semi-automatic, was locked in his safe in his office in the *Mairie*, and taken out once a year for his annual refresher course at the gendarmerie range in Périgueux. He had worn it on duty on three occasions in his eight years in the *Police Municipale*. The first was when a rabid dog had been sighted in a neighbouring Commune, and the police were put on alert. The second was when the President of France had driven through the Commune of St Denis on his way to see the celebrated cave paintings of Lascaux. He had stopped to visit an old friend, Gérard Mangin, who was the Mayor of St Denis and Bruno's employer. Bruno had saluted his nation's leader and proudly stood armed guard outside the *Mairie*, exchanging gossip with the far more thoroughly armed presidential bodyguard, one of whom turned out to be a former comrade from Bruno's army days. The third time was when the boxing kangaroo escaped from a local circus, but that was another story. On no occasion had Bruno's gun ever been used on duty, a fact of which he was extremely but privately proud. Of course, like most of the other men (and not a few women) of the Commune of St Denis, he shot almost daily in the hunting season and usually bagged his target, unless he was stalking the notoriously elusive *bécasse*, a bird whose taste he preferred above all others.

Bruno gazed contentedly down upon his town, which looked in the freshness of the early morning as if *le bon Dieu* had miraculously created it overnight. His eyes lingered on the way the early sunlight bounced and flickered off the eddies where the Vézère river ran under the arches of the old stone bridge. The place seemed alive with light, flashes of gold and red, as the sun magically concocted prisms in the grass beneath the willows, and danced along the honey-coloured façades of the ancient buildings along the river. There were glints from the weathercock on the church spire, from the eagle atop the town's war memorial where he had to attend that day's ceremony on the stroke of noon, from the windscreens and chrome of the cars and caravans parked behind the medical centre.

All looked peaceful as the business of the day began, with the first customers heading into Fauquet's café. Even from this high above the town he could hear the grating sound of the metal grille being raised to open Lespinasse's *tabac,* which sold fishing rods, guns and ammunition alongside the cigarettes. Very logical, thought Bruno, to group such lethal products together. He knew without looking that, while Madame Lespinasse was opening the shop, her husband would be heading to the café for the first of many little glasses of white wine that would keep him pleasantly plastered all day.

The staff of the *Mairie* would also be at Fauquet's, nibbling their croissants and taking their coffee and scanning the headlines of that morning's *Sud-Ouest*. Alongside them would be a knot of old men studying the racing form and enjoying their first *petit blanc* of the day. Bachelot the shoemender would take his morning glass at Fauquet's, while his neighbour and mortal enemy Jean-Pierre, who ran the bicycle shop, would start his day at Ivan's *Café de la Libération*. Their enmity went back to the days of the Resistance, when one of them had been in a Communist group and the other had joined de Gaulle's *Armée Secrète*, but Bruno could never remember which. He only knew that they had never spoken to one another since the war, had never allowed their families to speak beyond the frostiest '*bonjour*', and each man was said to have devoted many of the years since to discreet but determined efforts to seduce the other man's wife. The Mayor had once, over a convivial glass, told Bruno that he was convinced that each had attained his objective. But Bruno had been a policeman long enough to question most rumours of adulterous passion and, as a careful guardian of his own privacy in such tender matters, was content to allow others similar latitude.

These morning movements were rituals to be respected – rituals such as the devotion with which each family bought its daily bread only at a particular one of the town's four bakeries, except on those weeks of holidays when they were forced to patronise another, each time lamenting the change in taste and texture. These little ways of St Denis were as familiar to Bruno as his own morning routine on rising: his exercises while listening to Radio Périgord, his shower with his special shampoo to protect against the threat of baldness, the soap with the scent of green apples. Then he would feed his chickens while the coffee brewed and share the toasted slices of yesterday's baguette with his dog, Gigi.

Across the small stream that flowed into the main river, the caves in the limestone cliffs drew his eye. Dark but strangely inviting, the caves with their ancient engravings and paintings drew scholars and tourists to this valley. The tourist office called it 'The Cradle of Mankind'. It was, they said, the part of Europe that could claim the longest period of continual human habitation. Through ice ages and warming periods, floods and wars and famine, people had lived here for forty thousand years. Bruno, who reminded himself that there were still many caves and paintings that he really ought to visit, felt deep in his heart that he understood why.

Down at the riverbank, he saw that the mad Englishwoman was watering her horse after her morning ride. As always, she was correctly dressed in gleaming black boots, cream jodhpurs and a black jacket. Her auburn hair flared out behind her neat black riding hat like the tail of a fox. Idly, he wondered why they called her mad. She always seemed perfectly sane to him, and appeared to make a good business of running her small guest house. She even spoke comprehensible French, which was more than could be said of most of the English who had settled here. He looked further up the road that ran alongside the river, and saw several trucks bringing local farmers to the weekly market. It would soon be time for him to go on duty. He took out the one item of equipment that never left his side, his cell phone, and dialled the familiar number of the *Hôtel de la Gare*.

'Any sign of them, Marie?' he asked. 'They hit the market at St Alvère yesterday so they are in the region.'

'Not last night, Bruno. Just the usual guys staying from the museum project and a Spanish truck driver,' replied Marie, who ran the small hotel by the station. 'But remember, after last time they were here and found nothing, I heard them talking about renting a car in Périgueux to put you off the scent. Bloody Gestapo!'

Bruno, whose loyalty was to his local community and its mayor rather than to the nominal laws of France, particularly when they were really laws of Brussels, played a constant cat-and-mouse game with the inspectors from the European Union who were charged with enforcing EU hygiene rules on the markets of France. Hygiene was all very well, but the locals of the Commune of St Denis had been making their cheeses and their *pâté de foie gras* and their *rillettes de porc* for centuries before the EU was even heard of, and did not take kindly to foreign bureaucrats telling them what they could and could not sell. Along with other members of the *Police Municipale* in the region, Bruno had established a complex early warning scheme to alert the market vendors to their visits.

The inspectors, known as the Gestapo in a part of France that had taken very seriously its patriotic duties to resist the German occupation, had started their visits to the markets of Périgord in an official car with red Belgian licence plates. On their second visit, to Bruno's alarm, all the tyres had been slashed. Next time they came in a car from Paris, with the telltale number '75' on the licence plate. This car too had been given the Resistance treatment, and Bruno began to worry whether the local counter-measures were getting out of hand. He had a good idea who was behind the tyre-slashing, and had issued some private warnings that he hoped would calm things down. There was no point in violence if the intelligence system could ensure that the markets were clean before the inspectors arrived.

Then the inspectors had changed their tactics and come by train, staying at local station hotels. But that meant they were easily spotted by the hotel keepers who all had cousins or suppliers who made the *crottins* of goat cheese and the *foie gras*, the home-made jams, the oils flavoured with walnuts and truffles, and the *confits* that made this corner of France the very heart of the nation's gastronomic culture. Bruno, with the support of his boss, the Mayor of St Denis, and all the elected councillors of the Commune, even Montsouris the Communist, made it his duty to protect his neighbours and friends from the idiots of Brussels. Their idea of food stopped at *moules* and *pommes frites*, and even then they adulterated perfectly good potatoes with an industrial mayonnaise that they did not have the patience to make themselves.

So now the inspectors were trying a new tack, renting a car locally so that they might more easily stage their ambush and subsequent getaway with their tyres intact. They had succeeded in handing out four fines in St Alvère yesterday, but they would not succeed in St Denis, whose famous market went back more than seven hundred years. Not if Bruno had anything to do with it.

With one final gaze into the little corner of paradise that was entrusted to him, Bruno took a deep breath of his native air and braced himself for the day. As he climbed back into his van, he thought, as he always did on fine summer mornings, of a German saying some tourist had told him: that the very summit of happiness was 'to live like God in France'.

## CHAPTER 2

Bruno had never counted, but he probably kissed a hundred women and shook the hands of at least as many men each morning on market day. First this morning was Fat Jeanne, as the schoolboys called her. The French, who are more attuned to the magnificent mysteries of womanhood than most, may be the only people in the world to treasure the concept of the *jolie laide,* the plain or even ugly woman who is so comfortable within her own ample skin and so cheerful in her soul that she becomes lovely. And Fat Jeanne was a *jolie laide* of some fifty years and almost perfectly spherical in shape. She was not a beauty by any stretch of the imagination, but a cheerful woman at ease with herself. The old brown leather satchel in which she collected the modest fees that each stall holder paid for the privilege of selling in the market of St Denis thumped heavily against Bruno's thigh as Jeanne, squealing with pleasure to see him, turned with surprising speed and proffered her cheeks to be kissed in ritual greeting. Then she gave him a fresh strawberry from

Madame Verniet's stall, and Bruno broke away to kiss the roguish old farmer's widow on both wizened cheeks in greeting and gratitude.

'Here are the photos of the inspectors that Jo-Jo took in St Alvère yesterday,' Bruno said to Jeanne, taking some printouts from his breast pocket. He had driven over to his fellow municipal policeman the previous evening to collect them. They could have been emailed to the *Mairie*'s computer, but Bruno was a cautious man and thought it might be risky to leave an electronic trail of his discreet intelligence operation.

'If you see them, call me. And give copies to Ivan in the café and to Jeannot in the *bistro* and to Yvette in the *tabac* to show their customers. In the meantime, you go that way and warn the stall holders on the far side of the church. I'll take care of the ones towards the bridge.'

Every Tuesday since the year 1346, when the English had captured half the nobility of France at the Battle of Crécy and the grand Brillamont family had to raise money to pay the ransom for their Seigneur, the little Périgord town of St Denis has held a weekly market. The townspeople had raised the princely sum of fifty livres of silver for their feudal lord and, in return, they secured the right to hold the market on the canny understanding that this would guarantee a livelihood to the tiny community, happily situated where the stream of Le Mauzens ran into the river Vézère – just beyond the point where the remaining stumps of the old Roman bridge thrust from the flowing waters. A mere eleven years later, the chastened nobles and knights of France had once again spurred their lumbering horses against the English archers and their longbows and had been felled in droves. The Seigneur de Brillamont had to be ransomed from the victorious Englishmen all over again after the Battle of Poitiers, but by then the taxes on the market had raised sufficient funds for the old Roman bridge to be crudely restored. So, for another fifty livres, the townsfolk bought from the Brillamont family the right to charge a toll over the bridge and their town's fortunes were secured forever.

These had been early skirmishes in the age-old war between the French peasant and the tax collectors and enforcers of the power of the state. And now, the latest depredations of the inspectors (who were Frenchmen, but took their orders from Brussels) was simply the latest campaign in the endless struggle. Had the laws and regulations been entirely French, Bruno might have had some reservations about working so actively, and with such personal glee, to frustrate them. But they were not: these were Brussels laws from this distant European Union, which allowed young Danes and Portuguese and Irish to come and work on the camp sites and in the bars each summer, just as if they were French. His local farmers and their wives had their living to earn, and would be hard put to pay the inspectors' fines from the modest sums they made in the market. Above all, they were his friends and neighbours.

In truth, Bruno knew there were not many warnings to give. More and more of the market stalls these days were run by strangers from out of town who sold dresses and jeans and draperies, cheap sweaters and T-shirts and second-hand clothes. Two coal-black Senegalese sold colourful *dashikis*, leather belts and purses, and a couple of local potters displayed their wares. There was an organic bread stall and several local vintners sold their Bergerac, and the sweet Monbazillac dessert wine that the Good Lord in his wisdom had kindly provided to accompany *foie gras*. There was a knife-sharpener and an ironmonger, Diem the Vietnamese selling his *nems* – spring rolls – and Jules selling his nuts and olives while his wife tended a vast pot of steaming paella. The various stalls selling fruit and vegetables, herbs and tomato plants were all immune – so far – from the men from Brussels.

But at each stall where they sold home-made cheese and paté, or ducks and chickens that had been slaughtered on some battered old stump in the farmyard with the family axe rather than in a white-tiled abattoir by people in white coats and hairnets, Bruno delivered his warning. He helped the older women to pack up, piling the fresh-plucked chickens into cavernous cloth bags to take to the nearby office of Patrick's driving school for safe keeping. The richer farmers who could afford mobile cold cabinets were always ready to let *Tante* Marie and *Grande-mère* Colette put some of their less legal cheeses alongside their own. In the market, everyone was in on the secret.

Bruno's cell phone rang. 'The bastards are here,' said Jeanne, in what she must have thought was a whisper. 'They parked in front of the bank and Marie-Hélène recognised them from the photo I gave to Ivan. She saw it when she stopped for her *petit café*. She's sure it's them.'

'Did she see their car?' Bruno asked.

'A silver Renault Laguna, quite new.' Jeanne read out the number. Interesting, thought Bruno. It was a number for the *Departement* of the Corrèze. They would have taken the train to Brive and picked up the car there, outside the Dordogne. They must have realised that the local spy network was watching for them. Bruno walked out of the pedestrian zone and onto the main square by the old stone bridge, where the inspectors would have to come past him before they reached the market. He phoned his fellow municipal police chiefs in the other villages with markets that week and gave them the car and its number. His duty was done, or rather half his duty. He had protected his friends from the inspectors; now he had to protect them from themselves.

So he rang old Joe, who had for forty years been Bruno's predecessor as chief of police of St Denis. Now he spent his time visiting cronies in all the local markets, using as an excuse the occasional sale from a small stock of oversized

14

aprons and work coats that he kept in the back of his van. There was less selling done than meeting for the ritual glass, a *petit rouge*, but Joe had been a useful rugby player two generations ago and was still a pillar of the local club. He wore in his lapel the little red button that labelled him a member of the *Légion d'Honneur*, a reward for his boyhood service as a messenger in the real Resistance against the Germans. Bruno felt sure that Joe would know about the tyre-slashing, and had probably helped organise it. Joe knew everyone in the district, and was related to half of them, including most of St Denis's current crop of burly rugby forwards who were the terror of the local rugby league.

'Look, Joe,' Bruno began when the old man answered with his usual gruff bark, 'everything is fine with the inspectors. The market is clean and we know who they are. We don't want any trouble this time. It could make matters worse, you understand me?'

'You mean the car that's parked in front of the bank? The silver Laguna?' Joe said, in a deep and rasping voice that came from decades of Gauloises and the rough wine he made himself. 'Well, it's being taken care of. Don't you worry yourself, *petit* Bruno. The Gestapo can walk home today. Like last time.'

'Joe, this is going to get people into trouble,' Bruno said urgently, although he knew that he might as well argue with a brick wall. How the devil did Joe know about this already? He must have been in Ivan's café when Jeanne was showing the photos around. And he had probably heard about the car from Marie-Hélène in the bank, since she was married to his nephew.

'This could bring real trouble for us if we're not careful,' Bruno went on. 'So don't do anything that would force me to take action.'

He closed his phone with a snap. Scanning the people coming across the bridge, most of whom he knew, he kept watch for the inspectors. Then from the corner of his eye he saw a familiar car, a battered old Renault Twingo that the local gendarmes used when out of uniform, being driven by the new *Capitaine* he had not yet had time to get to know. From Normandy, they said, a dour and skinny type called Duroc who did everything by the book. Suddenly an alert went off in Bruno's mind and he called Joe again.

'Stop everything now. They must be expecting more trouble after last time. That new gendarme chief has just gone by in plain clothes, and they may have arranged for their car to be staked out. I've got a bad feeling about this.'

'*Merde*,' said Joe. 'We should have thought of that but we may be too late. I told Karim in the bar and he said he'd take care of it. I'll try and call him off.'

Bruno rang the *Café des Sports*, run by Karim and his wife, Rashida, very pretty though heavily pregnant. Rachida told him Karim had left the café already and she didn't think he had his mobile with him. *Putain*, thought Bruno. He started walking briskly across the narrow bridge, trying to get to the parking lot in front of the bank before Karim got into trouble.

He had known Karim since he first arrived in the town over a decade ago as a hulking and sullen Arab teenager, ready to fight any young Frenchman who dared take him on. Bruno had seen the type before, and had slowly taught Karim that he was enough of an athlete to take out his resentments on the rugby field. With rugby lessons twice a week and a match each Saturday, and tennis in the summer, Bruno had taught the lad to stay out of trouble. He got Karim onto the school team, then onto the local rugby team, and finally into a league big enough for him to make the money that enabled the giant young man to marry his Rashida and buy the café. Bruno had made a speech at their wedding. *Putain, putain, putain ...*

If Karim got into trouble over this it could turn very nasty. The inspectors would get their boss to put pressure on the Prefect, who would then put pressure on the *Police Nationale*, or maybe they would even get on to the Ministry of Defence and bring in the gendarmes who were supposed to deal with rural crime. If they leant on Karim and Rashida to start talking, there was no telling where it might end. Criminal damage to state property would mean an end to Karim's licence to sell tobacco, and the end of his café. He might not talk, but Rashida would be thinking of the baby and she might crack. That would lead them to old Joe and to the rest of the rugby team, and before you knew it the whole network of the quiet and peaceful town of St Denis would face charges and start to unravel. Bruno couldn't have that.

Bruno carefully slowed his pace as he turned the corner by the Commune notice board and past the war memorial into the ranks of cars that were drawn up like so many multi-coloured soldiers in front of the Crédit Agricole. He looked for the gendarme Twingo and then saw Duroc standing in the usual line in front of the bank's cash machine. Two places behind him was the looming figure of Karim, chatting pleasantly to Colette from the dry cleaning shop. Bruno closed his eyes in relief, and strode on towards the burly North African.

'Karim,' he said, and swiftly added '*Bonjour*, Colette,' kissing her cheeks, before turning back to Karim, saying, 'I need to talk to you about the match schedule for Sunday's game. Just a very little moment, it won't take long.' He grabbed him by the elbow, made his farewells to Colette, nodded at Duroc, and steered his reluctant quarry back to the bridge.

'I came to warn you. I think they may have the car staked out, maybe even tipped off the gendarmerie,' Bruno said. Karim stopped, and his face broke into a delighted smile.

18

'I thought of that myself, Bruno, then I saw that new gendarme standing in line for cash, but his eyes kept moving everywhere so I waited behind him. Anyway, it's done.'

'You did the tyres with Duroc standing there!?'

'Not at all.' Karim grinned. 'I told my nephew to take care of it with the other kids. They crept up and jammed a potato into the exhaust pipe while I was chatting to Colette and Duroc. That car won't make ten kilometres before the engine seizes.'

## CHAPTER 3

As the siren that sounded noon began its soaring whine over the town, Bruno stood to attention before the *Mairie* and wondered if this had been the same sound that had signalled the coming of the Germans. Images of ancient newsreels came to mind: diving Stukas, people dashing for aid raid shelters, the victorious Wehrmacht marching through the Arc de Triomphe in 1940 to stamp their jackboots on the Champs-Elysées and launch the conquest of Paris. Well, he thought, this was the day of revenge, the eighth of May, when France celebrated her eventual victory, and although some said it was old-fashioned and unfriendly in these days of Europe, the town of St Denis remembered the Liberation with an annual parade of its venerable veterans.

Bruno had posted the *Route Barrée* signs to block the side road and ensured that the floral wreaths had been delivered. He had donned his tie and polished his shoes and the peak of his cap. He had warned the old men in both cafés that the time was approaching and had brought up the flags from the cellar beneath the *Mairie*. The Mayor himself stood waiting, the sash of office across his chest and the little red rosette of the *Légion d'Honneur* in his lapel. The gendarmes were holding up the impatient traffic, while housewives grumbled that their bags were getting heavy and kept asking when they could cross the road.

Jean-Pierre of the bicycle shop carried the *tricolore* and his enemy Bachelot held the flag that bore the Cross of Lorraine, the emblem of General de Gaulle and Free France. Old Marie-Louise, who as a young girl had served as a courier for one of the Resistance groups and who had been taken off to Ravensbruck concentration camp and somehow survived, sported the flag of St Denis. Montsouris, the Communist councillor, carried a smaller flag of the Soviet Union, and old Monsieur Jackson – and Bruno was very proud of arranging this – held the flag of his native Britain. A retired schoolteacher, he had come to spend his declining years with his daughter who had married Pascal of the local insurance office. Monsieur Jackson had been an eighteen-year-old recruit in the last weeks of war in 1945 and was thus a fellow combatant, entitled to share the honour of the victory parade. One day, Bruno told himself, he would find a real American, but this time the Stars and Stripes were carried by young Karim as the star of the rugby team.

The Mayor gave the signal and the town band began to

21

play the *Marseillaise*. Jean-Pierre raised the flag of France, Bruno and the gendarmes saluted, and the small parade marched off across the bridge, their flags flapping bravely in the breeze. Following them were three lines of the men of St Denis who had performed their military service in peacetime but who turned out for this parade as a duty to their town as well as to their nation. Bruno noted that Karim's entire family had come to watch him carry a flag. At the back marched a host of small boys piping the words of the anthem. After the bridge, the parade turned left at the bank and marched through the car park to the memorial, a bronze figure of a French *poilu* of the Great War. The names of the fallen sons of St Denis took up three sides of the plinth beneath the figure. The bronze had darkened with the years, but the great eagle of victory that was perched, wings outstretched, on the soldier's shoulder gleamed golden with fresh polish. The Mayor had seen to that. The plinth's fourth side was more than sufficient for the dead of the Second World War, and the subsequent conflicts in Vietnam and Algeria. There were no names from Bruno's own brief experience of war in the Balkans. He always felt relieved by that, even as he marvelled that a Commune as small as St Denis could have lost over two hundred young men in the slaughterhouse of 1914–1918.

The schoolchildren of the town were lined up on each side of the memorial, the infants of the *Maternelle* in front sucking their thumbs and holding each other's hands.

Behind them, the slightly older ones in jeans and T-shirts were still young enough to be fascinated by this spectacle. Across from them, however, some of the teenagers of the *Collège* slouched, affecting sneers and a touch of bafflement that the new Europe they were inheriting could yet indulge in such antiquated celebrations of national pride. But Bruno noticed that most of the teenagers stood quietly, aware that they were in the presence of all that remained of their grandfathers and great-grandfathers, a list of names on a plinth that said something of their heritage and of the great mystery of war, and something of what France might one day again demand of her sons.

Jean-Pierre and Bachelot, who might not have spoken for fifty years but who knew the ritual of this annual moment, marched forward and lowered their flags in salute to the bronze soldier and his eagle. Montsouris dipped his red flag and Marie-Louise lowered hers so far it touched the ground. Belatedly, unsure of their timing, Karim and the English Monsieur Jackson followed suit. The Mayor walked solemnly forward and ascended the small dais that Bruno had placed before the memorial.

'*Français et Françaises*,' he declaimed, addressing the small crowd. 'Frenchmen and Frenchwomen, and the representatives of our brave allies. We are here to celebrate a day of victory that has also become a day of peace, the eighth of May that marks the end of Nazism and the beginning of Europe's reconciliation and her long, happy years of tranquillity. That peace was bought by the bravery of our sons of St Denis whose names are inscribed here, and by the old men and women who stand before you and who never bowed their heads to the rule of the invader. Whenever France has stood in mortal peril, the sons and daughters of St Denis have stood ready to answer the call, for France, and for the Liberty, Equality and Fraternity and the Rights of Man for which she stands.'

He stopped and nodded at Sylvie from the bakery. She pushed forward her small daughter, who carried the floral wreath. The little girl, in red skirt, blue top and long white socks, walked hesitantly towards the Mayor and offered him the wreath, looking quite alarmed as he bent to kiss her on both cheeks. The Mayor took the wreath and walked slowly to the memorial, leant it against the soldier's bronze leg, stood back, and called out, 'Vive la France, Vive la Republique.'

And with that Jean-Pierre and Bachelot, both old enough to be feeling the strain of the heavy flags, hauled them to an upright position of salute, and the band began to play Le Chant des Partisans, the old Resistance anthem. Tears began to roll down the cheeks of the two men, and old Marie-Louise broke down in sobs so that her flag wavered and all the children, even the teenagers, looked sobered, even touched, by this evidence of some great, unknowable trial that these old people had lived through.

As the music faded away, the flags of the three allies –

Soviet, British and American – were marched forward and raised in salute. Then came the surprise, a theatrical coup engineered by Bruno that he had arranged with the Mayor. This was a way for the old English enemy, who had fought France for a thousand years before being her ally for a brief century, to take her place on the day of victory.

Bruno watched as Monsieur Jackson's grandson, a lad of thirteen or so, marched forward from his place in the town band where he played the trumpet, his hand on a shiny brass bugle that was slung from a red sash around his shoulders. He reached the memorial, turned to salute the Mayor and, as the silent crowd exchanged glances at this novel addition to the ceremony, raised the bugle to his lips. As Bruno heard the first two long and haunting notes of the Last Post, tears came to his eyes. Through them he could see the shoulders of Monsieur Jackson shaking and the British flag trembled in his hands. The Mayor wiped away a tear as the last pure peals of the bugle died away, and the crowd remained absolutely silent until the boy put his bugle smartly to his side. Then, they exploded into applause and, as Karim went up and shook the boy's hand, his Stars and Stripes flag swirling briefly to tangle with the British and French flags, Bruno was aware of a sudden flare of camera flashes.

*Mon Dieu*, thought Bruno. That Last Post worked so well we'll have to make it part of the annual ceremony. He looked around at the crowd, beginning to drift away, and saw that young Philippe Delaron, who usually wrote the sports report for the *Sud-Ouest* newspaper, had his notebook out and was talking to Monsieur Jackson and his grandson. Well, a small notice in the newspaper about a genuine British ally taking part in the Victory parade could do no harm now that so many English were buying homes in the Commune. It might even encourage them to complain less about their various property taxes and the price of water for their swimming pools. Then he noticed something rather odd. After every previous parade, whether it was for the eighth of May, for the eleventh of November when the Great War ended, on the eighteenth of June when de Gaulle launched Free France, or the fourteenth of July when France celebrated her Revolution, Jean-Pierre and Bachelot would turn away from each other without so much as a nod and walk back separately to the Mairie to store the flags they carried. But this time they were standing still, staring fixedly at one another. Not talking, but somehow communicating. Amazing what one bugle call can do, thought Bruno. Maybe if I can get some Americans into the parade next year they might even start talking, and leave one another's wives alone. But now it was thirty minutes after midday and, like every good Frenchman, Bruno's thoughts turned to his lunch.

He walked back across the bridge with Marie-Louise, who was still weeping as he gently took her flag from her. The Mayor, and Monsieur Jackson and his daughter and grandson were close behind. Karim and his family walked ahead, and Jean-Pierre and Bachelot, with their almost identical wives, brought up the rear, marching in grim silence as the town band, without its best trumpeter, played another song from the war that had the power to melt Bruno: *J'attendrai*. It was the song of the women of France in 1940, as they watched their men march off to a war that turned into six weeks of disaster and five years of prison camps. '... day and night, I shall wait always, for your return.' The history of France was measured out in songs of war, he thought, many sad and some heroic, but each verse heavy with its weight of loss.

The crowd was thinning as they turned off to lunch, most of the mothers and children going home, but some families making an event of of the day and turning into Jeannot's bistro beyond the *Mairie*, or the pizza house beyond the bridge. Bruno would normally have gone with some friends to Ivan's café for his *plat du jour*, usually a *steak-frites* – except for the time when Ivan fell in love with a Belgian girl staying at a local camp site and, for three glorious and passionate months until she packed up and went back to Charleroi, *steak-frites* became *moules-frites*. Then there was no *plat du jour* at all for weeks until Bruno had taken the grieving Ivan out and got him heroically drunk.

But today was a special day, and so the Mayor had organised a *déjeuner d'honneur* for those who had played a part in the parade. Now they climbed the ancient stairs, bowed in the middle by centuries of feet, to the top floor of the *Mairie* which held the council chamber and, on occasions such as this, doubled as the banquet room. The town's treasure was a long and ancient table that served council and banquet alike, and was said to have been made for the grand hall of the chateau of the Brillamont family itself in those happier days before their Seigneur kept getting captured by the English. Bruno began counting; twenty places were laid for lunch. He scanned the room to see who his fellow diners might be.

There was the Mayor with his wife, and Jean-Pierre and Bachelot with their wives, who automatically went to opposite ends of the room. For the first time, Karim and his wife Rashida had been invited, and stood chatting to Montsouris the Communist and his dragon of a wife who was even more left-wing than her husband. Monsieur Jackson and Sylvie the baker and her son were talking to Rollo, the local headmaster, who sometimes played tennis with Bruno, and the music teacher, who was the conductor of the town band, and also the master of the church choir. He had expected to see the new captain of the local gendarmes, but there was no sign of the man. The plump and sleek Father Sentout, priest of the ancient church of St Denis who was aching to become a Monsignor, emerged puffing from the new elevator. He was pointedly not talking to his lift companion, the formidable Baron, a retired industrialist who was the main local landowner. Bruno nodded at him. He was a fervent atheist and also Bruno's regular tennis partner.

Fat Jeanne from the market appeared with a tray of champagne glasses, swiftly followed by young Claire, the Mayor's secretary, who carried an enormous tray of *amuse-bouches* that she had made herself. Claire had a *tendresse* for Bruno, and she'd talked to him of little else for weeks, leaving the Mayor's letters untyped as she thumbed through *Madame Figaro* and *Marie-Claire* to seek ideas and recipes. The result, thought Bruno as he surveyed the offerings of celery filled with cream cheese, olives stuffed with anchovies and slices of toast covered with chopped tomatoes, was uninspiring.

'They are Italian delicacies called bruschetta,' Claire told him, gazing deeply into Bruno's eyes. She was pretty enough although over-talkative, but Bruno had a firm rule about never playing on one's own doorstep. Juliette Binoche could have taken a job at the *Mairie* and Bruno would have restrained himself. But he knew that his reticence did not stop Claire and her mother, not to mention a few other mothers in St Denis, from referring to him as the town's most eligible bachelor. At just forty he thought he might have ceased being the object of this speculation, but no. The game of 'catching' Bruno had become one of the town's little rituals, a subject for gossip among the women and amusement among the married men, who saw Bruno as the valiant but ultimately doomed quarry of the huntresses. They teased him about it, but they approved of the discretion he brought to his private life and the polite skills with which he frustrated the town's mothers and maintained his freedom.

'Delicious,' said Bruno, limiting himself to an olive. 'Well done, Claire. All that planning really paid off.'

'Oh, Bruno,' she said, 'do you really think so?'

'Of course. The Mayor's wife looks hungry,' he said, scooping a glass of champagne from Fat Jeanne as she swept by. 'Perhaps you should start with her.' He steered Claire off to the window where the Mayor stood with his wife, and was suddenly aware of a tall and brooding presence at his shoulder.

'Well, Bruno,' boomed Montsouris, his loud voice more suited to bellowing fiery speeches to a crowd of striking workers, 'you have made the people's victory into a celebration of the British crown. Is that what you meant to do?'

'*Bonjour*, Yves,' grinned Bruno. 'Don't give me that people's victory crap. You and all the other Communists would be speaking German if it wasn't for the British and American armies.'

'Shame on you,' said Montsouris. 'Even the British would be speaking German if it wasn't for Stalin and the Red Army.'

'Yes, and if they'd had their way, we'd all be speaking Russian today and you'd be the Mayor.'

'Commissar, if you please,' replied Montsouris. Bruno knew that Montsouris was only a Communist because he was a *cheminot*, a railway worker, and the CGT labour union had those jobs sewn up for Party members. Other than his Party card and his campaigning before each election, most of Montsouris's political views were decidedly conservative. Sometimes Bruno wondered who Montsouris really voted for once he was away from his noisily radical wife and safe in the privacy of the voting booth.

'*Messieurs-Dames, à table*, if you please,' called the Mayor, adding, 'before the soup gets warm.'

Monsieur Jackson gave a hearty English laugh, but stopped when he realised nobody else was amused. Sylvie took his arm and guided him to his place. Bruno found himself sitting beside the priest, and bowed his head as Father Sentout delivered a brief grace. Bruno often found himself next to the priest on such occasions. As he turned his attention to the chilled vichyssoise, he wondered if Sentout would ask his usual question. He didn't have to wait long.

'Why does the Mayor never want me to say a small prayer at these public events like Victory Day?'

'It is a Republican celebration, Father,' Bruno explained, for perhaps the fourteenth time. 'You know the law of 1905, separation of church and state.'

'But most of those brave boys were good Catholics and they fell doing God's work and went to heaven.'

'I hope you are right, Father,' Bruno said kindly, 'but look on the bright side. At least you get invited to the lunch, *and* you get to bless the meal. Most mayors would not even allow that.'

'Ah yes, the Mayor's feast is a welcome treat after the purgatory that my housekeeper inflicts upon me. But she is a pious soul and does her best.'

Bruno, who had once been invited to a magnificent dinner at the priest's house in honour of some visiting church dignitary, raised his eyebrows silently, and then watched with satisfaction as Fat Jeanne whipped away his soup plate and replaced it with a healthy slice of *foie gras* and some of her own onion marmalade. To accompany it, Claire served him with a small glass of golden Monbazillac that he knew came from the vineyard of the Mayor's cousin. Toasts were raised, the boy bugler was singled out for praise, and the champagne and Monbazillac began their magic work of making a rather staid occasion convivial. After the dry white Bergerac that came with the trout and a well-chosen 2001 Pecharmant with the lamb, it became a thoroughly jolly luncheon.

'Is that Arab fellow a Muslim, do you know?' asked Father Sentout, with a deceptively casual air, waving his wine glass in Karim's direction.

'I never asked him,' said Bruno, wondering what the priest was up to. 'If he is, he's not very religious. He doesn't pray to Mecca and he'll cross himself before a big game, so he's probably a Christian. Besides, he was born here. He's as French as you or I.'

'He never comes to confession, though – just like you, Bruno. We only ever see you in church for baptisms, weddings and funerals.'

'And choir practice, and Christmas and Easter,' Bruno protested.

'Don't change the subject. I'm interested in Karim and his family, not in you.'

'Karim's religion I don't know about, and I don't think he really has one, but his father is most definitely an atheist and a rationalist. It comes from teaching mathematics.'

'Do you know the rest of the family?'

'I know Karim's wife, and his cousins, and some of the nephews who play with the *minimes*, and his niece Ragheda who has a chance to win the junior tennis championship. They're all good people.'

'Have you met the older generation?' the priest pressed.

Bruno turned patiently away from a perfectly good *tarte tatin* and looked the priest squarely in the eye.

'What is this about, Father? I met the old grandfather at Karim's wedding, which was held in the *Mairie* here without any priest or mullah in sight. Are you trying to tell me something or worm something out of me?'

'Heaven forbid,' said Father Sentout nervously. 'No, it is just that I met the old man by chance and he seemed interested in the church, so I just wondered ... He was sitting in the church, you see, while it was empty, and I think he was praying. So naturally, I wanted to know if he was a Muslim or not.'

'Did you ask him?'

'No, he scurried away as soon as I approached him. It was very odd. He wasn't even polite enough to greet me. I had hoped perhaps he might be interested in Catholicism.'

Bruno shrugged, not very interested in the religious curiosity of an old man. The Mayor tapped his glass with a knife and rose to make the usual short speech. As he listened dutifully, Bruno began to long for his after-lunch coffee, and then perhaps a little nap on the old couch in his office, to restore himself for a tiresome afternoon of administration at his desk.

## CHAPTER 4

Bruno always made it his business to establish good relations with the local gendarmes, who kept a station of six men and two women on the outskirts of town, in front of the small block of apartments where they lived. Since the station supervised several Communes in a large rural district in the largest Department of France, it was run by a Captain, in this case, Duroc. Right now, a very angry Duroc, dressed in full uniform, was leaning aggressively across Bruno's untidy desk and glowering at him.

'The Prefect himself has telephoned me about this. And then I got orders from the Ministry in Paris,' he snapped. 'Orders to stop this damned hooliganism. Stop it, arrest the criminals and make an example of them. The Prefect does not want embarrassing complaints from Brussels that we Frenchmen are behaving like a bunch of Europe-hating Englishmen. My boss in Paris wants no more destruction of the tyres of government inspectors who are simply doing their job and enforcing the law on public hygiene. Since I am reliably told that nothing takes place in this town without you hearing about it, my dear Chief of Police, I must formally demand your co-operation.'

He almost spat the final words and delivered 'Chief of Police' with a sneer. This Duroc was a most unappetising man, tall and thin to the point of gauntness, with a very prominent Adam's apple that poked out above his collar like some ominous growth. But, thought Bruno, one had better make allowances. Duroc was newly promoted, and evidently nervous about getting orders from high in his first posting as officer in charge. And since he would be here in St Denis for a couple of years at least, getting off on the wrong foot with him would be disastrous. In the best interests of St Denis, Bruno knew he had better be diplomatic, or he could forget his usual courteous requests to ensure that the traffic gendarmes stayed at home with their breathalysers on the night of the rugby club dance or the hunting club dinner. If the local sports-men couldn't have a few extra glasses of wine on a special night without getting stopped by the cops, he would never hear the end of it.

'I quite understand, *Capitaine*,' Bruno said emolliently. 'You're quite right and your orders are entirely proper. This hooliganism is a nasty blot on our reputation as a quiet and law abiding town, and we must work together on this. You will have my full cooperation.'

He beamed across his desk at Duroc, who now sported

two white, bloodless patches on his otherwise red face. Clearly, the Captain was very angry indeed.

'So, who is it?' Duroc demanded. 'I want to bring them in for questioning. Give me the names – you must know who's responsible.'

'No, I don't. I might make some guesses, but that's what they'd be. And guesses are not evidence.'

'I'll be the judge of that,' Duroc snapped. 'You wouldn't even know what evidence is. You're just a country copper with no more authority than a traffic warden. All you've got to offer is a bit of local knowledge, so you just stay out of it and leave it to the professionals. Give me the names and I'll take care of the evidence.'

'Evidence will not be easy to come by, not in a small town like this where most of the people think these European laws are quite mad,' Bruno said reasonably, shrugging off the insults. In time Duroc would discover how much he needed Bruno's local knowledge and, for his own good, he would have to cultivate the patience to teach his superior. 'The people round here tend to be very loyal to one another, at least in the face of outsiders,' he continued. 'They won't talk to you – at least, not if you go round hauling them in for tough questioning.'

Duroc made to interrupt, but Bruno rose, raised his hand to demand silence, and strolled across to the window.

'Look out there, my dear *Capitaine*, and let us think this through like reasonable men. Look at that scene: the river, those cliffs tumbling down to the willows where fisher-men sit for hours. Look at the old stone bridge built by Napoleon himself, and the square with the tables under the old church tower. It's a scene made for the TV cam-eras. They come and film here quite often, you know. From Paris. Foreign TV as well, sometimes. It's the image of France that we like to show off, the France we're proud of, and I'd hate to be the man who got blamed for spoiling it. If we do as you suggest, if we go in all heavy-handed and round up kids on suspicion, we'll have the whole town round our ears.'

'What do you mean, kids?' said Duroc, his brows knit-ted. 'It's the market types doing this stuff, grown-ups.'

'I don't think so,' Bruno said slowly. 'You ask for my local knowledge, and I'm pretty sure that a few kids are doing this. And if you start hauling in kids, you know what the outcome will be. Angry parents, protest marches, demonstrations outside the *Gendarmerie*. The teachers will probably go on strike in sympathy and the Mayor will have to take their side and back the parents. The press will descend, looking to embarrass the govern-ment, and the TV cameras will film newsworthy scenes of the heartland of France in revolt. It's a natural story for them – brutal police bullying children and oppressing good French citizens who are trying to protect their way of life against those heartless bureaucrats in Brussels. You know what the media are like. And then all of a sudden the Prefect would forget that he ever gave you any orders and your chief back in Paris would be unavailable and your career would be over.'

He turned back to Duroc, who was suddenly looking rather thoughtful, and said, 'And you want to risk all that mess just to arrest a couple of kids that you can't even take to court because they'd be too young?'

'Kids, you say?'

'Kids,' repeated Bruno. He hoped this wouldn't take too much longer. He had to do those amendments to the contract for the public fireworks for the Fourteenth of July, and he was due at the tennis club at six p.m.

'I know the kids in this town very well,' he went on. 'I teach them rugby and tennis and watch them grow up to play in the town teams. I'm pretty sure it's kids behind this, probably egged on by their parents, but still just kids. There'll be no arrests out of this, no examples of French justice to parade before Brussels. Just a very angry town and a lot of embarrassment for you.'

He walked across to the cupboard and took out two glasses and an ancient bottle.

'May I offer you a glass of my *vin de noix*, *Capitaine*? One of the many pleasures of this little corner of France. I make it myself. I hope you'll share a small aperitif in the name of our cooperation.' He poured two healthy tots and handed one to Duroc. 'Now,' he went on, 'I have a small idea that might help us avoid this unpleasantness.'

The Captain looked dubious, but his face had returned to a normal colour. Grudgingly he took the glass.

'Unless, of course, you want me to bring in the Mayor, and you can make your case to him,' Bruno said. 'And I suppose he could order me to bring in these children, but what with the parents being voters, and the elections on the horizon ...' He shrugged eloquently.

'You said you had an idea.' Duroc sniffed at his glass and took a small but evidently appreciative sip.

'Well, if I'm right and it's just some kids playing pranks, I could talk to them myself – and have a quiet word with the parents – and we can probably nip this thing in the bud. You can report back that it was a couple of underage kids and the matter has been dealt with. No fuss, no press, no TV. No nasty questions to your minister back in Paris.'

There was a long pause as the Captain stared hard at Bruno, then looked out of the window and took another thoughtful sip of his drink.

'Good stuff this. You make it yourself, you say?' He sipped again. 'I must introduce you to some of the Calvados I brought down with me from Normandy. Maybe you're right. No point stirring everything up if it's just some kids, just so long as no more tyres get slashed. Still, I'd better report something back to the Prefect tomorrow.'

Bruno said nothing, but smiled politely and raised his glass, hoping the inspectors had not yet found the potato.

'We cops have got to stick together, eh?' Duroc grinned

and leaned forward to clink his glass against Bruno's. At that moment, to Bruno's irritation, his mobile, lying on his desk, rang its familiar warbling version of the *Marseillaise*. With a sigh, he gave an apologetic shrug to Duroc and moved to pick it up.

It was Karim, breathing heavily, his voice shrill.

'Bruno, come quick,' he said. 'It's Grandpa, he's dead. I think – I think he's been murdered.' Bruno heard a sob.

'What do you mean? What's happened? Where are you?'

'At his place. I came up to fetch him for dinner. There's blood everywhere.'

'Don't touch anything. I'll be there as soon as I can.' He rang off and turned to Duroc. 'Well, we can forget about childish pranks, my friend. It looks like we have a real crime on our hands. Possibly a murder. We'll take my car. One minute, while I ring the *pompiers*.'

'*Pompiers*?' asked Duroc. 'Why do we need the firemen?'

'Round here they're the emergency service. It might be too late for an ambulance but that's the form and we had better do this by the book. And you'll want to tell your office. If this really is a murder, we'll need the *Police Nationale* from Périgueux.'

'Murder?' Duroc put his glass down. 'In St Denis?'

'That's what the call said.' Bruno rang the fire station and gave them directions, then grabbed his cap. 'Let's go. I'll drive, you ring your people.'

## CHAPTER 5

Karim was waiting for them at the door of the cottage, white-faced. He looked as if he had been sick. He stepped aside as Bruno and Duroc, still in his full-dress uniform, strode in.

The old man had been gutted. He lay bare-chested on the floor, intestines spilling out from a great gash in his belly. The place stank of them, and flies were already buzzing. There was indeed blood everywhere, including some thick pooling in regular lines on the chest of the old Arab.

'It seems to be some kind of pattern,' Bruno began, leaning closer but trying to keep his shoes out of the drying pools of blood around the body. It was not easy to make out. The old man was lying awkwardly, his back raised as though leaning on something that Bruno could not see for the blood.

'My God,' said Duroc, peering closely. 'It's a swastika. That's a swastika carved in the poor bugger's chest. This is a hate crime. A race crime.'

Bruno looked carefully around him. It was a small cottage – one bedroom, this main room with a big old stone fireplace which was kitchen, dining and sitting room all in one, and a tiny bathroom built onto the side. A meal had been interrupted; half a baguette and some sausage and cheese lay on a single plate on the table, alongside the remains of a bottle of red wine and a broken wine glass. Two chairs had been knocked over, and a photo of the French soccer team that had won the World Cup in 1998 hung askew on the wall. Bruno spotted a bundle of cloth tossed into a corner. He walked across and looked at it. It was a shirt, all its buttons now torn off as if the garment had been ripped from the old man. No blood on it, so somebody quite strong must have done it before starting to use the knife. Bruno sighed. He glanced into the bathroom and the tidy bedroom, but could see nothing out of place there.

'I don't see a mobile phone anywhere, or a wallet,' he said. 'It may be in his trouser pocket, but we'd better leave that until the scene-of-crime and forensic guys get here.'

'It'll be sodden with blood anyway,' said Duroc.

In the distance, they heard the fire engine's siren. Bruno went outside to see if his phone could get a signal this far from town. One bar of the four showed on the mobile's screen, just enough. He rang the Mayor to explain the situation, and then everything seemed to happen at once. The firemen arrived, bringing life support equipment, and

Duroc's deputy drove up in a big blue van with two more gendarmes, one of them with a large, rather old camera. The other carried a big roll of orange tape to mark out the crime scene. The place was suddenly crowded. Bruno went out to Karim, who was leaning wretchedly against the side of his car, his hand covering his eyes.

'When did you get here, Karim?'

'Just before I rang you. Maybe a minute before, not more.' Karim looked up, his cheeks wet with tears. 'Oh, *putain, putain*. Who could have done this, Bruno? The old man didn't have an enemy in the world. He was just looking forward to seeing his great-grandson. He'll never see him now.'

'Have you called Rashida?'

'Not yet. I just couldn't. She loved the old guy.'

'And Momu?' Karim's father was the maths teacher at the local school, a popular man who cooked enormous vats of couscous for the rugby dinners. His name was Mohammed but everyone called him Momu.

Karim shook his head. 'I only called you. I can't tell Papa, he was so devoted to him. We all were.'

'When did you last see your grandpa alive? Or speak to him?'

'Last night at Momu's. We had dinner. Momu drove him home and that was the last I saw of him. We sort of take it in turns to feed him and it was our turn tonight, which is why I came up to fetch him.'

'Did you touch anything?' This was Bruno's first murder, and as far as he knew the Commune's first as well. He had seen a lot of dead bodies. It was he who organised the funerals and dealt with grieving families, and he had coped with some bad car crashes so he was used to the sight of blood. But nothing like this.

'No. When I got here, I called out to Grandpa like I usually do and went in. The door was open like always and there he was. *Putain*, all that blood. And that smell. I couldn't touch him. Not like that. I've never seen anything like it.'

Karim turned away to retch again. Bruno swallowed hard. Duroc came out and told the other gendarme to start stringing the tape. He looked at Karim, still bent double and spitting the last of the bile from his mouth.

'Who's he?' Duroc asked.

'Grandson of the victim,' Bruno replied. 'He runs the *Café des Sports*. He's a good man, he's the one that rang me. I've talked to him. He touched nothing, rang me as soon as he got here.' Turning back to Karim, he said, 'Karim, where were you before you drove here to pick up your grandpa?'

'In the café, all afternoon. Ever since I saw you this morning.'

'Are you sure?' snapped Duroc. 'We can check that.'

'That's right, we can check that. Meantime, let's get him home,' Bruno said soothingly. 'He's in shock.'

45

'No, we'd better keep him here. I called the Brigade in Périgueux and they said they'd bring the *Police Nationale*. The detectives will want to talk to him.'

Albert, the chief *pompier*, came out, wiping his brow. He looked at Bruno and shook his head.

'Dead for a couple of hours or more,' he said. 'Come over here, Bruno. I need to talk to you.'

They walked down the drive and off to one side where the old man kept a small vegetable garden and a well-tended compost heap. It should have been a pleasant spot for an old man in retirement, the hill sloping away to the woods behind and the view from the house down the valley.

'You saw that thing on his chest?' Albert asked. Bruno nodded. 'Nasty stuff,' said Albert, 'and it gets worse. The poor old devil's hands were tied behind his back. That's why his body was arched like that. He would not have died quickly. But that swastika? I don't know. This is very bad, Bruno, it can't be anyone from round here. We all know Momu and Karim. They're like family.'

'Some nasty bastard didn't think so,' said Bruno. 'Not with that swastika. Dear God, it looks like a racist thing, a political killing. Here in St Denis.'

'You'll have to tell Momu. I don't envy you that.'

There was a shout from the cottage. Duroc was waving him over. Bruno shook hands with Albert and walked back.

'Do you keep a political list?' Duroc demanded. 'Fascists, Communists, Trots, *Front National* types, activists – all that?'

Bruno shrugged. 'No, never have and never had to. The Mayor usually knows how everyone votes, and they usually vote the same way they did last time, the same way their fathers did. He can usually tell you what the vote will be the day before the election and he's never wrong by more than a dozen or so.'

'Any *Front National* types that you know of? Skinheads? Fascists?'

'Le Pen usually gets a few votes, about fifty or sixty last time, I recall. But nobody is very active.'

'What about those *Front National* posters and the graffiti you see on the roads?' Duroc's face was getting red again. 'Half the road signs seem to have FN scrawled on them. Somebody must have done that.'

Bruno nodded. 'You're right. They suddenly appeared during the last election campaign, but nobody took them very seriously. You always get that kind of thing in elections, but there was no sign of who did it.'

'You're going to tell me that it was kids again?'

'No, I'm not, because I have no idea about this. What I can tell you is that there's no branch of the *Front National* here. They might get a few dozen votes but they've never elected a single councillor. They never even held a campaign rally in the last elections. I don't recall seeing any of their leaflets. Most people here vote either left or right or Green, except for the *Chasseurs*.'

'The what?'

'The political party for hunters and fishermen. That's their name. *Chasse, Pêche, Nature, Traditions*. It's like an alternative Green party for people who hate the real Greens as a bunch of city slicker *Ecolos* who don't know the first thing about the countryside. They get about fifteen percent of the vote here – when they stand, that is. Don't you have them in Normandy?'

Duroc shrugged. 'I don't know. I don't pay much attention to politics. I never had to before.'

'Grandpa voted for the *Chasse* party last time. He told me,' Karim said. 'He was a hunter and very strong on all that tradition stuff. You know he was a *Harki*? Got a *Croix de Guerre* in Vietnam, before the Algerian war. That's why he had to leave to come over here.'

Duroc looked blank.

'The *Harkis* were the Algerians who fought for us in the Algerian war, in the French Army,' Bruno explained. 'When we pulled out of Algeria, the ones we left behind were hunted down and killed as traitors by the new government. Some of the *Harkis* got out and came to France. Chirac made a big speech about them a few years ago, how badly they'd been treated even though they fought for France. It was like a formal apology to the *Harkis* from the President of the Republic.'

'Grandpa was there,' Karim said proudly. 'He was invited up to be in the parade for Chirac's speech. They paid his way, gave him a rail ticket and hotel and everything. He wore his *Croix de Guerre*. Always kept it on the wall.'

'A war hero. That's just what we need,' grunted Duroc. 'The press will be all over this.'

'Kept the medal on the wall?' said Bruno. 'I didn't see it. Come and show me where.'

They went back into the room that looked like a slaughterhouse and was beginning to smell like one. The *pompiers* were clearing up their equipment and the room kept flaring with light as the gendarme took photos. Karim kept his eyes firmly away from his grandfather's corpse and pointed to the wall by the side of the fireplace. There were two nails in the wall but nothing hanging on either one.

'It's gone.' Karim shook his head. 'That's where he kept it. He said he was saving it to give to his first grandson. The medal's gone. And the photo.'

'What photo?' Bruno asked.

'His football team, the one he played in back when he was young, in Marseilles.'

'When was this?'

'I don't know. Thirties or Forties, I suppose. He was in France then, as a young man.'

'During the war?'

'I don't know,' Karim shrugged. 'He never talked much about his youth, except to say he'd played a lot of football.'

'You said your grandpa was a hunter,' Duroc said. 'Did he have a gun?'

'Not that I ever saw. He hadn't hunted in years. Too old, he used to say. He still fished a lot, though. He was a good fisherman, and he and Momu used to go out early in the mornings before school.'

'If there's a gun, we'd better find it. Wait here,' Duroc instructed, and left the room. Bruno got out his phone again and rang Mireille at the *Mairie*, and asked her to check whether a hunting or fishing licence had been issued to the old man. He checked the name with Karim. Al-Bakr, Hamid Mustafa al-Bakr.

'Look under A for the al and B for the Bakr,' Bruno said. 'And if that doesn't find him, try H for Hamid and M for Mustafa.' He knew that filing was not Mireille's strong point. A widow, whose great skill in life was to make a magnificent *tête de veau*, the Mayor had taken her on as a clerk after her husband died young of a heart attack.

Duroc emerged from the house. 'Now we wait for the detectives. They'll probably take their own sweet time,' he said glumly. The *Gendarmerie* had little affection for the detectives of the *Police Nationale*. The gendarmes were part of the Ministry of Defence, but the *Police Nationale* came under the Ministry of the Interior and there was constant feuding between them over who did what. Bruno, with his own chain of command to the Mayor, was pleased not to be part of it.

'I'll go and see the neighbours,' said Bruno. 'We have to find out if they heard or saw anything.'

## CHAPTER 6

The nearest house was back towards the main road. It led to a gigantic cave, a source of great pride to the St Denis tourist office. Its stalagmites and stalactites had been artfully lit so that, with some imagination, the guides could convince tourists that this one was the Virgin Mary and that one was Charles de Gaulle. Bruno could never remember whether the stalactites grew up or down and thought they all looked like giant church organs, but he liked the place for the concerts, jazz and classical, that were held there in summer. And he relished the story that when the cave was first discovered, the intrepid explorer who was lowered in on a long rope found himself standing on a large heap of bones. They belonged to the victims of brigands who lay in wait to rob pilgrims who took this route from the shrines of Rocamadour and Cadouin to Compostela in distant Spain.

The house belonged to Yannick, the maintenance man for the cave, and his wife, who worked in the souvenir shop. They were away from home all day and their daughters were at the *lycée* in Sarlat, so Bruno did not expect much when he rang the doorbell. Nobody came, so he went round to the back, hoping that Yannick might be working in his well-tended garden. The tomatoes, onions, beans and lettuces stood in orderly rows, protected from rabbits by a stockade of chicken wire. There was no sign of Yannick. Bruno drove back to the main road and on to the nearest neighbour, the mad Englishwoman. Her house was a low hill and a valley away from the old Arab's cottage, but they used part of the same access road so she might have seen or heard something.

He slowed at the top of the rise and stopped to admire her property. Once an old farm, it boasted a small farmhouse, a couple of barns, stables and a pigeon tower, all built of honey-coloured local stone and arranged on three sides of a courtyard. There were two embracing wings of well-trimmed poplars set back from the house, sufficient to deflect the wind in winter but too far to cast a shade over the buildings or grounds. Ivy climbed up one side of the pigeon tower and a splendid burst of bright pink early roses covered the side by the old iron-studded door. In the middle of the courtyard stood a handsome old ash tree, and large terracotta pots filled with geraniums made splashes of colour against the gravel. Beside the largest barn was a vine-covered terrace with a long wooden table that looked a fine place to dine in summer. Off to its side was a vegetable garden, a greenhouse and a level area for parking. On the other side, behind a low fence covered in climbing roses, he saw the corner of a swimming pool.

From the top of the long gentle rise of the meadow, the property looked charming in the late afternoon sunlight, and Bruno drank in the sight. He had seen many a fine house and some handsome small chateaux in his many tours through his Commune, but he'd rarely seen a place that looked so completely at peace and welcoming. It came as a relief after the shock and horror of what he had found at Hamid's cottage, as if the two places, barely a kilometre apart, could not exist in the same universe. He felt calmer and more himself for seeing it, and was reminded that he had a job to do.

He drove slowly up the gravel road, lined on each side with young fruit trees that would form a handsome avenue some day, and stopped in the parking area. The mad Englishwoman's old blue Citroën was parked alongside a new VW Golf convertible with English number plates. He settled his cap on his head, switched off his engine, and heard the familiar plop-plop of a tennis ball. He strolled around to the back of the farmhouse, past an open barn where two horses were chewing at hay, and saw an old grass tennis court that he had never known was there.

Two women in short tennis dresses were playing with such concentration that they didn't notice his arrival. An enthusiastic but not very gifted player himself, Bruno watched with appreciation, for the women as much as for their play. They were both slim and lithe, their legs and arms graceful and already tanned against the white of their dresses. The mad Englishwoman – called Pamela Nelson, he had heard – had her auburn hair tied up in a ponytail, and her dark-haired opponent wore a white baseball cap. They were playing a steady and impressive baseline game. Watching the fluidity of her strokes, Bruno realised that the mad Englishwoman was rather younger than he'd thought. The grass court was not very fast and the surface was bumpy enough to make the bounce unpredictable, but it was freshly mowed and the white lines had been recently painted. It would be very pleasant to play here, Bruno thought, and the mad Englishwoman could evidently give him a good game.

In Bruno's view, anyone who could keep up a rally beyond half a dozen strokes was a decent player, and this one had already gone beyond ten strokes and showed no sign of stopping. The balls were hit deep, and were directed towards the other player rather than to the corners. They must be knocking up rather than playing a serious match, he thought. Then the mad Englishwoman hit the ball into the net. As her opponent turned to pick up some balls from the back of the court, Bruno called out, 'Madame, if you please?'

She turned, shading her eyes to see him against the

slanting sun that was sparkling golden lights in her hair. She walked to the side of the court, bent gracefully at the knees to put down her racquet, opened the gate and smiled at him. She was handsome rather than pretty, he thought, with regular features, a strong chin and good cheek bones. Her skin glowed from the tennis, and there was just enough sweat on her brow for some of her hair to stick there in charmingly curling tendrils.

'*Bonjour, Monsieur le Policier*. Is this a business call or can I offer you a drink?'

He walked down to her, shook her surprisingly strong hand, and removed his hat. Her eyes were a cool gray.

'I regret, Madame, this is very much business. A serious crime has been committed near here and we're asking all the neighbours if they've seen anything unusual in the course of the day.'

The other woman came to join them, said '*bonjour*' and shook Bruno's hand. Another English accent. The mad Englishwoman was the taller of the two but they were both attractive, with that clear English skin that Bruno had been told came from having to live in the perpetual damp of their foggy island. No wonder they came over to Périgord.

'A serious crime? Here, in St Denis? Excuse me, I'm forgetting my manners. I'm Pamela Nelson and this is Mademoiselle Christine Wyatt. Christine, this is our *Chef de Police* Courrèges. Look, we were just knocking a ball about and it's probably time for a drink. We shall certainly have one so may I offer you a *petit apéro*?'

'I'm afraid not this time, Madame. I'm on duty. It's about the old Arab gentleman, Monsieur Bakr, who lives in that small cottage near Yannick's house. Have you seen him today, or recently, or seen any visitors?'

'Hamid, you mean? That sweet old man who sometimes comes by to tell me I'm pruning my roses all wrong? No, I haven't seen him for a couple of days, but that's not unusual. He strolls by perhaps once a week and pays me pretty compliments about the property, except for the way I prune the roses. I last saw him in the café earlier this week, chatting with his grandson. What's happened? A burglary?'

Bruno deliberately ignored her question. 'Were you here all day today? Did you see or hear anything?' he asked.

'We were here until lunchtime. We lunched on the terrace and then Christine went into town to do some shopping while I cleaned the barn for some guests who arrive tomorrow. When Christine came back we played some tennis for an hour or so until you arrived. We've had no visitors except for the postman, who came at the usual time, about ten or so.'

'So you haven't left the property all day?' Bruno pressed, wondering why they were still knocking up after an hour rather than playing a game.

'No, except for my morning ride. But that takes me towards the river, away from Hamid's cottage. I went as far as the bridge, and then picked up some bread and the newspaper and some vegetables at the market and a roast chicken for lunch. I didn't notice anything out of the ordinary. But do tell me, is Hamid alright? Can I do anything to help?'

'Forgive me, Madame, but there is nothing you can do,' Bruno said. 'And you, Mademoiselle Wyatt? What time did you do your shopping?'

'I can't say exactly. I left after lunch, probably some time after two, and was back here soon after four.' She spoke perfectly grammatical French, but with that rather stiff accent the English had, as if they could not open their mouths properly. 'We had tea, and then came out to play tennis.'

'And you are one of the paying guests?' She had very fine dark eyes and carefully plucked eyebrows but wore no make-up. Her hands and nails, he noticed, were well cared for. No rings, and the only jewellery was a thin gold chain at her neck. They were two very attractive women, Bruno decided, and probably somewhere near his own age, although he reminded himself that you could never really tell with women.

'Not really, not like the people coming tomorrow. Pamela and I were at school together and we've been friends ever since, so I'm not renting but I do the shopping and buy the wine. I went to the supermarket and to that big wine *cave* at the bottom of the road. Then I stopped at the filling station and came back here.'

'So you're here on vacation, Mademoiselle?'

'Not exactly. I'm staying here while working on a book. I teach history at a university in England and I have this book to finish, so I worked all morning until lunchtime. I don't think I've met your Arab gentleman and I don't recall seeing another car, or anybody on the way to the supermarket and back.'

'Please tell me what's happened, Monsieur Courrèges,' said the mad Englishwoman, who was clearly not mad at all. 'Is it a burglary? Has Hamid been hurt?'

'I fear that I cannot say at this stage, I'm sure you understand,' he said, feeling slightly ridiculous as he usually did when required to play the formal role of policeman. He thought he'd better try to make up for it. 'Please call me Bruno. Everyone does. When I hear someone say Monsieur Courrèges I look around for an old man.'

'OK, Bruno, and you must call me Pamela. Are you sure I can't offer you a drink, some mineral water perhaps or a fruit juice? It's been a warm day.'

Bruno finally accepted, and they settled on some white metal chairs by the swimming pool. Pamela emerged with a refreshing jug of freshly made *citron pressé*, and Bruno leaned back to enjoy the moment. A cool drink in a delightful setting with not one but two charming and interesting women was a rare treat, and infinitely preferable to what would now be a madhouse of squabbling gendarmes and detectives and forensic specialists at Hamid's cottage. That brought the sobering thought that his next task would be to go and tell Momu of his father's death – if the Mayor hadn't beaten him to it – and arrange a formal identification. Wasn't there something special about Muslim burial rites? He'd have to check.

'I didn't know you had your own tennis court here,' he said. 'Is that why we never see you at the tennis club?' Bruno was proud of the club, with its three hard courts and its single covered court where they could play in winter, and the clubhouse with bathrooms and changing rooms, a bar and a big kitchen. The Mayor had used his political connections in Paris to get a government grant to pay for it.

'No, it's the concrete courts,' Pamela explained. 'I hurt my knee skiing some time ago and the hard court is bad for it.'

'But we have a covered court with a rubber surface. You could play there.'

'I get quite busy here in the summer when the guests start to come. Once I have all three of the *gîtes* filled, it takes most of my time. That's why it's such a treat to have Christine here and play some tennis with her. It's not a great court, hardly Wimbledon, but if you ever want to try a grass court just give me a call. My phone number is in the book under Nelson.'

'Like your famous Admiral Nelson of Trafalgar?'

'No relation, I'm afraid. It's quite a common name in England.'

'Well, Pamela, I shall certainly call you and see about a game on grass. Perhaps you'd like me to bring a friend and we could play mixed doubles.' He looked at Christine. 'Will you be here for long?'

'Till the end of the month, when Pamela has a full house. So I've got three more weeks here in the lovely Dordogne, then I go back to Bordeaux to do some more research in the archives, checking on footnotes.'

'It's the best time, before the tourists come in the school holidays and block the roads and markets,' said Pamela.

'I thought the national archives were in Paris,' Bruno said.

'They are. These are the regional archives and there's a specialist archive at the Centre Jean Moulin.'

'Jean Moulin the Resistance chief? The one who was killed by the Germans?' Bruno asked.

'Yes, it has one of the best archives on the Resistance and my book is about life in France under the Vichy regime.'

'Ah, that's why you speak such good French,' said Bruno. 'But a painful period to study, I think. Painful for France, and very controversial. There are still families here who never speak to each other because they were on opposite sides during the war – and I don't mean just the collaborators. You know old Jean-Pierre who runs the bicycle shop in town? He was in the Communist Resistance, the *Francs-Tireurs et Partisans*. Just across the road is Bachelot the shoe mender, who was in the *Armée Secrète*, the Gaullist Resistance. They were rivals then and they're rivals now. They go on the same parades and march side by side, even on the eighteenth of June, and they never speak. Yet it's been sixty years since it happened. Memories are long here.'

'What's so special about the eighteenth of June?' Pamela asked.

'It was the day in 1940 that de Gaulle appealed to France to fight on. He was speaking over the BBC,' said Christine. 'It's celebrated as the great day of the Resistance, when France recovered her honour and Free France declared that it would fight on.'

'"France has lost a battle, but she has not yet lost the war",' Bruno quoted from the de Gaulle speech. 'We all learn that in school.'

'Do they tell you that it's also the anniversary of Napoleon's defeat at the battle of Waterloo?' Christine asked teasingly, winking at Pamela.

'Napoleon defeated? Impossible!' Bruno grinned. 'Nobody who built our magnificent stone bridge here in St Denis could ever be defeated, least of all by the English of Perfidious Albion. Did we not drive you out of France in the Hundred Years War, starting here in the Dordogne under the great leadership of Joan of Arc?'

'But the English are back!' Christine said. 'That was a temporary setback, but it looks as if the English are taking France back again, house by house and village by village.'

'I think she's teasing you, Bruno,' said Pamela.

'Well, we're all Europeans now,' laughed Bruno. 'And a lot of us are quite glad the English come here and restore the ruined old farms and houses. The Mayor talks of it a lot. He says the whole *Departement* of the Dordogne would be in deep depression had it not been for the English and their tourism and the money they pour in to restore the places they buy. We lost the wine trade in the nineteenth century, and now we're losing the tobacco that replaced it and our small farmers can't compete with the big ranches up north. So you're welcome, Pamela, and I congratulate you on this place. You've made it very beautiful.'

'You might not say that if you came in midwinter and the gardens were bare, but thank you. I'm flattered that you approve and I'm very happy here,' Pamela said.

Bruno rose. 'Sadly, I must leave now and get on with my work.'

Pamela smiled at him and stood up. 'You must come again. I'll expect your call for that mixed doubles game. And if there's anything I can do for Hamid, perhaps take him something to eat, please let me know.'

'Indeed I shall. And thank you for your thoughtfulness.

63

But I think the authorities have matters in hand.' He realised he was sounding formal again.

'If there has been a burglary, should I take extra precautions?' she went on, not looking in the least concerned but obviously probing. 'I do always lock the doors and windows at night and set the alarm.'

'No, there's no reason to think you're in any danger,' Bruno said, but knew she would be sure to hear of the murder so he had better say something reassuring.

'You have an alarm, and here's my card with my mobile number. Feel free to call me at any time, day or night. And thank you for that refreshing drink. It's been a pleasure, Mesdames.' He laid his card on the table, bowed and walked back to his car, waving as he turned the corner by the horses. He felt much better – until he thought of the call he must pay on Momu.

## CHAPTER 7

Momu lived in a small modern house down by the river. It looked as if it had been built from one of the mass-produced kits that were springing up to provide cheap homes for locals who had been priced out of the market for older houses by the English with their strong currency. Like all the kit homes, it had two bedrooms, a sitting room, kitchen and bathroom side by side to share the plumbing, and all built on a concrete slab. The vaguely Mediterranean roof of rounded red tiles looked quite wrong in the Périgord, but maybe the Mediterranean look helped Momu feel more at home, Bruno thought charitably, as the house where he had spent several convivial evenings came into view. He sighed at the tangle of illegally parked cars that almost blocked the road. One of the most obstructive belonged to the Mayor, which was very unlike him. But the Mayor's presence was a relief – he would have told Momu. Bruno drove on for a hundred metres, parked legally and thought about what he had to say and do. First he would have to sort out the funeral arrangements and then try to reassure the family that Karim would be home soon, assuming the Mayor had taken care of the rest.

Bruno walked back to the house. Inside all the lights were blazing and he could hear the sound of a woman crying. He took off his hat as he entered and saw Momu slumped on the sofa, the Mayor's hand on his shoulder, but he rose to greet Bruno. Momu was a burly man, not as big as his son but barrel-chested and broad in the shoulders. His hands were big, and his wrists thick like a labourer's. Just the solid look of him was enough to keep order among his pupils, but they soon kept quiet from respect. Momu was a good teacher, they said, and made his maths classes interesting. Bruno had heard he made every class work out the combined weight of the local rugby team, and then of all the inhabitants of St Denis, and then of all the people in France, and then for the whole world. He had a deep, hearty voice, always heard at rugby matches on Sunday afternoons, cheering on his son. They touched cheeks and Momu asked for news. Bruno shook his head.

'I'm very sorry for your loss, Momu. The police won't rest until we find who did this, believe me,' Bruno said. He shook hands with the Mayor and the other men in the room, all Arabs except for Momu's boss, Rollo, the headmaster at the local school. Rollo held up a bottle of cognac and offered Bruno a glass, but he looked around to see what others were drinking and took an apple juice like the Arabs. This was their home, their time of grief, so he would abide by their rules. Anyway, he was on duty.

'I just came from the cottage,' he said. 'We're still waiting for the detectives and forensic men from Périgueux. Nothing more will happen until they arrive, and the police doctor releases the body. The gendarmes have sealed the place off, but when the detectives are done, I'll have to ask you to go up there and take a good look around to see if you notice anything missing or stolen. There were no obvious signs of a burglary or theft, except for a missing photo, but we have to check. When the police are through, they'll take the body to the funeral home but I need to know what you want to do then, Momu. I don't know if you have any religious rules or special customs.'

'My father gave up religion a long time ago,' Momu said solemnly. 'We'll bury him here in the town cemetery, in the usual way, as soon as we can. What about Karim? Is he still up there?'

Bruno nodded. 'Don't worry. It's routine. The detectives have to talk to the person who found the body but they probably won't keep him long. I just wanted to come and pay my condolences here and find out about the funeral and I'll go right back up there and keep an eye on Karim. He's had a very bad shock.'

When he had called back at Hamid's cottage, Bruno

had gone through another argument with Duroc who, between angry phone calls to demand why the *Police Nationale* were taking so long to get there, insisted on keeping Karim at the scene. That was about all the gendarme had done. It was left to Bruno to call the Public Works and arrange for a portable generator and lights to be taken up to the cottage, which had only basic electricity and no outdoor light. He also arranged for the local pizzeria to deliver some food and drink for the gendarmes, something Duroc should have thought of.

The sound of crying from the back room had stopped, and Bruno noticed Momu's wife peering round the door. Bruno had always seen her in Western dress, but today she wore a black scarf on her head which she held across her mouth as though it were a veil. Perhaps it was her mourning dress, he thought.

'What can you tell us?' Momu asked. 'All I know for sure is that the old man has been killed, but I still can't believe it.'

'That's all we know at this stage, until the forensics team do their work,' Bruno said.

'That's not what I heard at the fire station,' said Ahmed, one of the drivers for the Public Works, who also volunteered as a fireman. There were two professionals at the small local fire station and the rest were local volunteers like Ahmed, summoned as needed by the howl of the old wartime siren they kept on top of the *Mairie*. And since the

68

firemen were also the emergency medical team and the first people called out to any sudden death or crisis, it was impossible to keep anything quiet. The volunteers talked to their wives and the wives talked to each other and the whole town knew of fires or deaths or road accidents within hours.

'It was a brutal killing, a stabbing. That's all we really know so far,' said Bruno cautiously. He had a good idea of what Ahmed must have heard from the other firemen.

'It was racists, fascists,' Ahmed snapped. 'I heard what was carved on old Hamid's chest. It was those *Front National* swine, taking on a helpless old man.'

*Putain.* This bit of news had become public even faster than he had feared, and it would spread more poison as it travelled.

'I don't know what you heard, Ahmed, but I know what I saw, and I don't know if it was meant to be some kind of pattern or if they were wounds he received when he put up a fight,' he said levelly, looking Ahmed in the eye. 'Rumour has a way of exaggerating things. Let's stick with the facts for the moment.'

'Bruno is right,' said the Mayor quietly. A small, slim man whose mild-mannered looks were deceptive, he had a way of making himself heard. Gérard Mangin had been Mayor of St Denis long before Bruno had taken up his job a decade earlier. Mangin had been born in the town, into a family that had been there forever. He had won scholarships and competitive examinations and gone off to one of the *grandes écoles* in Paris where France educates its elite. He worked in the Finance Ministry while allying himself with a rising young star of the Gaullist party called Jacques Chirac and launching his own political career. He had been one of Chirac's political secretaries, and was then sent to Brussels as Chirac's eyes and ears in the European Commission, where he had learned the complex art of securing grants. Elected Mayor of St Denis in the 1970s, Mangin had run the party for Chirac in the Dordogne, and was rewarded with an appointment to the Senate to serve out the term of a man who had died in office. Thanks to his connections in Paris and Brussels, St Denis had thrived. The restored *Mairie* and the tennis club, the old folk's home and the small Industrial Zone, the camp sites, the swimming pool and the agricultural research centre had all been built with grants the Mayor had secured. His mastery of the planning and zoning codes had built the commercial centre with its new supermarket. Without the Mayor and his political connections, St Denis might well have died, like so many other small market towns of the Périgord.

'My friends, our Momu has suffered a great loss and we grieve with him. But we must not let that loss turn into anger before we know the facts,' the Mayor said in his precise way. He gripped Momu's hand and pulled the burly Arab to his side before looking round at Ahmed and

Momu's friends. 'We who are gathered here to share our friend's grief are all leaders of our community. And we all know that we have a responsibility here to ensure that the law takes its course, that we all give whatever help we can to the magistrates and the police, and that we stand guard together over the solidarity of our dear town of St Denis. I know I can count on you all in the days ahead. We have to face this together.'

He went first to Momu, and then shook hands with each of the others and gestured to Bruno to leave with him. As he reached the door, he turned and called out to the head teacher, 'Rollo, stay a while until I return to collect my wife.' Then, gently gripping Bruno's arm, he propelled him into the night, along the driveway and out of earshot of the house.

'What is this about a swastika?' he demanded.

'It isn't clear, but that's what the gendarmes and the firemen thought was carved into the guy's chest. They're probably right, but I told the truth in there. I can't be sure, not until the corpse is cleaned up. He was stabbed in the belly and then eviscerated. There could have been the *Mona Lisa* painted on that chest and I couldn't swear to it.' Bruno shook his head, squeezing his eyes to block out the dreadful image. The Mayor's grip tightened on his arm.

'It was a butchery,' Bruno went on after a moment. 'The old man's hands were tied behind his back. There were no signs of a robbery. It looked like he was interrupted while

71

having his lunch. Two things were missing, according to Karim. There was a *Croix de Guerre* he won while fighting for France as a *Harki*, and a photo of his old football team. The neighbours don't seem to have seen or heard anything unusual. That's all I know.'

'I don't think I ever met the old man, which probably makes him unique in this town,' said the Mayor. 'Did you know him?'

'Not really. I met him at Karim's just before he moved here. I never spoke with him beyond pleasantries and never got much sense of the man. He kept himself to himself, always seemed to eat on his own or with his family. I don't recall ever seeing him in the market or the bank or doing his shopping. He was a bit of a recluse in that little cottage way out in the woods. No TV and no car. He depended on Momu and Karim for everything.'

'That seems strange,' the Mayor mused. 'These Arab families tend to stay together – the old ones move in with their grown children. But a *Harki* and a war hero? Maybe he was worried about reprisals from some young immigrant hotheads. You know, these days they think of the *Harkis* as traitors to the Arab cause.'

'Maybe that's it. And because he wasn't religious perhaps some of these Islamic extremists could see him as a traitor to his faith,' Bruno said. Yet he didn't think Muslim extremists would want to carve a swastika into someone's chest. 'But we're just guessing, Sir. I'll have to talk to

Momu about it later. It must have been a chore for him and Karim, driving over every day to pick up the old man for his dinner and then taking him home again. Maybe there's more to Hamid than meets the eye, and perhaps you could ask Momu if he remembers any details about that old football team his father played in. Since the photograph has disappeared, it might be significant. I think they played in Marseilles back in the Thirties or Forties.'

'I'll do that, Bruno. Now I must go back inside and collect my wife.' The Mayor turned and held up a fist as he often did when he had prepared a mental list of what was to be done, unclenching a new finger to illustrate each different point. He always had at least two points to make but never more than four, probably because he would run out of fingers, thought Bruno, with a rush of affection for the old man. 'I know you understand how delicate this could be,' Mangin said. 'We'll probably have a lot of media attention, maybe some politicians posturing and making speeches and marches of solidarity and all that. Leave that side of it to me. I want you to stay on top of the investigation and keep me informed, and also let me know in good time if you hear of any trouble brewing or any likely arrests. Now, two final questions: first, do you know of any extreme right or racist types in our Commune who might conceivably have been guilty of this?'

'No, Sir, not one. Some *Front National* voters, of course, but that's all, and I don't think any of our usual petty criminals could have carried out an act of butchery like this.'

'Right. Second question. What can I do to help you?' The fourth finger snapped to attention.

'Two things.' Bruno tried to sound as efficient as his boss when he spoke to the Mayor, aware of a sense of both duty and affection as he did so. 'First, the *Police Nationale* will need somewhere to work, with phone lines and desks and chairs and plenty of space for computers. You might want to think about the top floor of the tourist centre where we hold the art exhibitions. There's no exhibition there yet, and it's big enough. If you call the Prefect in Périgueux tomorrow you can probably persuade him to pay some rent for the use of the space, and there's room for police vans too. It might be useful for people to see a reinforced police presence in the town. If we do that, they owe us. It's our town property so they're on our turf, which means they cannot bar us access.'

'And the second thing?'

'Most of all, I'll need your support to stay close to the case. It would help a great deal if you could call the Brigadier of the gendarmes in Périgueux and also the head of the *Police Nationale*, and ask them to order their men to keep me fully in the picture. There's good reason for it, with the political sensitivities and the prospect of demonstrations and tension in the town. You know our little *Police Municipale* does not rate very high in the hierarchy of our forces of order. Call me your personal liaison.'

'Right. You'll have it. Anything else?'

'You could probably get hold of the old man's military and civil records and the citation for his *Croix de Guerre* faster than I'll get them through the gendarmes. We know very little about the victim at this stage, not even whether he owned the cottage or rented it, what he lived on, how he got his pension, or whether he had a doctor.'

'You can check the civic records tomorrow. I'll call the Defence Minister's office – I knew her a bit when I was in Paris, and there's a chap in her cabinet who was at school with me. I'll have Hamid's file by the end of the day. Now, you go back up to the cottage and stay there until you can bring Karim back to his family. They're getting worried. Any trouble, just call me on the mobile, even if it means waking me up.'

Bruno went off comforted, feeling rather as he had in the Army when he had a good officer who knew what he was doing and trusted his men enough to bring out the best in them. It was a rare combination. Bruno acknowledged to himself, although he would never admit it to another soul, that Gérard Mangin had been one of the most important influences in his life. He had sought Bruno out on the recommendation of an old comrade in arms from that hideous business in Bosnia. The comrade happened to be the Mayor's son. Ever since, Bruno the orphan had felt for the first time in his life like a member of a family, and for that alone the Mayor had his complete loyalty. He got into his car and drove back up the long hill toward Hamid's cottage, wondering what arts of persuasion he might muster to prise poor Karim out of the custody of the tiresome Captain Duroc.

CHAPTER 8

The regional HQ of the *Police Nationale* had sent down their
new chief detective, Jean-Jacques Jalipeau, inevitably
known as J-J. Bruno had worked amicably with him once
before, on St Denis' only bank robbery. J-J had cleared that
up and even got some of the bank's money back, but that
had been two promotions ago. Now he had his own team,
including the first young woman Inspector that Bruno
had met. She wore a dark blue suit and a silk scarf at her
neck, and had the shortest hair he had ever seen on a
woman. She sat in front of a freshly installed computer in
the exhibition room, while around them other policemen
were plugging in phones, claiming desks, booting up
other computers and photocopiers and setting up the
murder board on the wall. Instead of the usual gentle
Périgord landscapes and water colours by local artists, the
room was now dominated by the long white board with its
grisly photos of the murder scene, including close-ups of
Hamid's bound hands and cleaned-up chest where the
swastika could clearly be seen.

'Okay, here we go. Our rogues' gallery of the extreme right. I hope your eyes are in good shape because we have got hundreds of snaps for you to view,' said young Inspector Perrault, who had told him with a briskly efficient smile to call her Isabelle. 'We'll start with the leaders and the known activists and then we'll go to the photos of their demonstrations. Just shout out if you recognise anyone.'

Bruno recognised the first three faces from TV, party leaders in publicity shots. Then he saw one of them again at a public rally, standing on a podium to address the crowd. Then came random photos of crowds: strangers, ordinary French men and women being addressed by party officials, each photo identified by the name and position of the official, including various *Departement* chairmen, secretaries and treasurers, regional chairmen, executive committee members, known activists and local councillors. They were old and young, plump and scrawny, attractive and lumpy – the kind of people he saw at the market or in the crowd at a rugby game. In fact he knew one tough-looking chap who had played rugby for Montpon, at the other end of the *Departement* on the way to Bordeaux.

'Just that one,' he said. 'I know him through rugby. He's played here once or twice.'

She made a note and they continued. Isabelle's short hair smelled of a sports shampoo he recognised from the tennis club. She looked fit, as though she ran or worked out every day. Her legs were long and slim and her shoes looked too flimsy for a police officer and far too expensive, even on an Inspector's salary.

'Who collected all these pictures?' he asked, looking at her hands, nails cut short but her fingers long and elegant as they danced over the computer keys.

'We get them different places,' she said. She had no regional accent, but was well spoken, sounding cool but affable, a bit like a TV news announcer. 'Some from their websites, election leaflets, press photos and TV footage. Then there are some from the *Renseignements Généraux* that we're not supposed to know about, but you know how computer security is these days. We take photos of their marches and rallies, just so we know who they are. We do the same for the far left. It seems only fair.'

She was screening images of what looked like a pre-election rally in the main square of Périgueux, shot after shot of the crowd, taken from a balcony. There were dozens of faces in each shot and Bruno tried to scan them conscientiously. He stopped at one face, but realised it was only a reporter he knew from *Sud-Ouest*, standing to the side of the rally squinting against the smoke from his cigarette, and holding a notebook and pencil. He rubbed his eyes and signalled Isabelle to continue.

'You sure you don't want to take a break, Bruno?' she asked. 'It can send you crazy, staring at these screens all the time, especially if you're not used to it.'

'I'm not,' he said. 'We don't have much use for computers

down here. I don't really know how to use them beyond typing and emails.'

She stopped, told him to look out of the window to rest his eyes and came back with some sludgy coffee from the hotplate they had rigged up in the corner. 'Here,' she said, handing him a plastic cup and juggling her own as she fished one-handed for a cigarette and lit a Royale.

'This coffee's terrible,' said Bruno. 'But thanks for the thought. If we can spare five minutes there's a café on the next corner.'

'You must have forgotten what a slave-driver J-J can be,' she smiled. 'When I first started working for him I didn't even dare go to the toilet. I'd go in the morning and then just wait. I'll probably pay for it when I'm older.'

'Well, this is St Denis. Everything stops for lunch. It's the law,' Bruno said, wondering if she would take this as an invitation. He wasn't sure that he had enough cash in his wallet to pay for them both.

'I think we're too pressed for time,' she said kindly, and turned back to the screen.

This time the photos, of the same event in the same square, had been taken from another vantage point. Again, Bruno tried to look at each face. Nothing, nothing – then he stopped. There was a face he knew, a central heating salesman from St Cyprien to whom he had once given a ticket for obstruction. Again, Isabelle made a note then went on scrolling. The same rally, yet another vantage point, but no face he recognised except those that he'd seen in the previous photos.

'Right, that's the Périgueux rally. On to the one in Sarlat,' said Isabelle, clicking her way expertly through the computer screens. She probably used these machines every day. The only computers they had in the *Mairie* were the big ones used for local taxes and social security and the one he shared with the Mayor's secretary. In Sarlat the rally was smaller. Again, he saw a couple of people he knew from rugby, and one from a tennis tournament, but nobody from St Denis. Then she brought up the photos from a campaign meeting in Bergerac, and at the third shot he gave a small gasp.

'Seen someone? I can blow the faces up a bit if you want.'

'I'm not sure. It's that group of young people there.'

She enlarged the image but the angles were wrong, and she scanned through the rest of photos, looking for shots from a different viewpoint. And there, close to the stage, were two youngsters he knew well. The first was a pretty blonde girl from Lalinde, about twenty kilometres away, who had reached the semi-finals of the St Denis tennis tournament last summer. And the boy with her, looking at her rather than at the stage, was Richard Gelletreau, the only son of a local doctor in St Denis.

'We may get lucky here,' Isabelle said, when she had printed out the photos and scribbled down Richard's name. 'The Party branch in Bergerac is two doors down from a bank, and it has a security camera. Don't ask me how, but somehow the *RG* got hold of the tape and made some mug shots of everyone coming in and going out during the campaign.'

'Is that legal?'

She shrugged. 'Who knows? It's not the kind of stuff that can be used in court, but for an investigation ... well, it's just the way it is. If you think this is something, wait till you see the stuff the *RG* has on the Communists and the left – archives going back to before the war.'

The *Renseignements Généraux* was the intelligence arm of the French police, part of the Ministry of the Interior, and had been collecting information on threats to the French state, to its good order and prosperity, since 1907. They had a formidable, if shadowy, reputation, and Bruno had never come across their work before. He was impressed, even though the shots of the people entering and leaving the *FN* office were not very good. It was too far for a clear focus, but he could pick out young Richard easily enough, holding hands with the girl as they went in, putting his arm protectively around her waist when they left.

They went through the rest of Isabelle's mug shots, but Richard Gelletreau provided the only clear connection to St Denis.

'What can you tell me about the boy?' she said, swivelling her chair and picking up a notepad from the desk.

'He's the son of the chief doctor at the clinic here, and they live in one of the big houses on the hill. The father is a pillar of the community, been here all his life, and the mother used to be a pharmacist. I think she still owns half of the big pharmacy by the supermarket. The girl is from Lalinde. She played tennis here last year and I can get her name from the club easily enough. The boy went to the usual schools here and has just finished his first year at the *lycée* in Périgueux. He stays there in the week and comes home for weekends. He'll be about seventeen by now, a normal kid, good at tennis, not much involved in rugby. His parents are well-heeled so they'd go skiing. And of course he was in the mathematics class with Momu – that's the teacher who is the son of the dead man.'

'Local knowledge is a wonderful thing. I don't know what we'd do without it.' Isabelle smiled at him. 'Thanks, Bruno. Just hang on here and I'll go and tell J-J. It may be nothing, just coincidence, but so far it's the only lead we have.'

The forensics team were still working, and the finger-prints report had yet to come in, but the preliminary report that lay on Isabelle's desk was clear enough. Hamid had been hit hard in the face, probably to stun him, and then tied up for some time. The weals on his wrists where he had tried to work loose the rough red twine that farmers use were a clear indication that he had been alive and working on his bonds for more than a few minutes. He had been stabbed deep into the lower belly by a long, sharp knife, which was then pulled up and across 'like a Japanese ritual suicide' said the report. There was no sign of a gag, and screams would have been likely from the victim, the report went on. Traces of red wine were found in his eyes and his thinning hair, as though someone had thrown a glass of it in his face. The time of death was put between midday and two p.m., most probably around one o'clock. Indications were that the swastika had been scored into his chest postmortem. Bruno took some small relief from that.

There was no sign of a theft. Hamid's wallet was found in the back pocket of his trousers. It contained forty euros, an ID card, a newspaper photo of himself standing in a parade by the Arc de Triomphe in Paris, and another of Karim scoring a try in a rugby match. Apart from some old bills and postage stamps, that was it. There was a cheque book from Crédit Agricole in a drawer with some pension slips, and some previously unopened mail from the bank, mainly showing deposits from a military pension. The old man had over 20,000 euros in the bank. Bruno raised an eyebrow at that. He knew from the *Mairie*'s records that Momu and his father had bought the small cottage two years ago for 78,000 euros in cash, which was not a bad deal given the predatory way the local agencies were pricing up every tumbledown ruin to sell to the English and the Dutch.

The old man had had no luxuries in the cottage, not even a refrigerator. He kept his supplies in a small cupboard – wine, paté, cheese, fruit and several bags of nuts. There were two litre bottles of cheap *vin ordinaire*, and one very good bottle of a Chateau Cantemerle '98. At least sometimes the old man had cared about what he drank. There was cheap ground coffee in an unsealed bag on the shelf above the small stove which was fuelled, like the hot water, by gas canisters. This was routine in rural homes; Bruno cooked and heated his own water in the same way. He continued to run his eye down the list: Hamid had no gun and no hunting licence, but he did have an up-to-date fishing licence and an expensive fishing rod. No TV, just a cheap battery radio tuned to France Inter. No newspapers or magazines, but a shelf of war and history books whose titles were listed in the report. There were books on de Gaulle, on the Algerian War, the French war in Vietnam, World War II and the Resistance. And two books on the OAS, the underground army of the French Algerians who had tried to assassinate de Gaulle for giving the colony its independence. That might be significant, Bruno thought, although he could see no connection to a swastika. Apart from the money, and the medal and photo that had disappeared, there was not a lot of evidence of what seemed to have been a rather lonely and even primitive life.

At the back of the file, Bruno found a new printout showing details from the pensions computer. Until almost two years ago, Hamid had been living up in the north, over twenty years at the same address in Soissons, until his wife Allida died. Then he moved to the Dordogne. Bruno did the calculation. The old man had come here the month after Karim's marriage, probably to be with the only family he had left. His profession was listed as *gardien*, or caretaker. Bruno scanned the pension printout. He had worked at the military academy, where he'd had a small service flat. Yes, they'd do that for an old comrade with a *Croix de Guerre*. And with a service flat, he'd have paid no rent, which would account for the savings. There was no sign on the pension form of any medical problem, and no doctor was listed.

That reminded him. He rang Mireille at the *Mairie* to see if the Ministry of Defence information had arrived yet. No, but she could tell him that Hamid was not named on any local doctor's lists, nor at the clinic, nor with any of the pharmacies in town, and no medical claims were registered on the social security computer. Evidently he was a healthy person, probably thanks to having been a footballer. Why had that photo disappeared along with the medal?

'Hey, Bruno. Robbed any good banks lately?' grinned J-J, striding into the room with Isabelle at his heels. 'I always thought you must have been the brains behind that job. It was too smart for those idiots we put away.'

'It's good to see you, J-J.' Bruno smiled with genuine pleasure as they shook hands. They had been taken to a magnificent celebration dinner at *Le Centenaire* in Les Eyzies at the end of the case by the bank's regional manager. Two Michelin stars, a couple of bottles a head of some of the best wine Bruno had ever tasted, and a chauffeur to take him home again. He'd had to stay off work the next day. 'I see you're a big shot now, top cop in the *Departement*.'

'And there's not a day goes by that I don't sit back and feel a twinge of envy for the life you have here, Bruno.' J-J gave him an affectionate slap on the back. 'That's what intrigues me about this vicious little murder – it's so out of character for this place. Isabelle tells me you think we might have a lead in this doctor's son.'

'I'm not sure I'd call it much of a lead, but he's the only local from St Denis that I recognised in the photos. This is a weekday. He should be at school in Périgueux.'

Isabelle shook her head. 'I just checked. He didn't turn up on Monday. He reported sick, and they got a note signed by his dad the doctor.'

'Gelletreau writing a sick note for his son? I think we'd better verify that,' said Bruno, impressed at her speed of action but wary that she'd gone elsewhere to make the calls rather than do so in his presence. Not quite a team player, this Isabelle. 'He doesn't like writing sick notes at all, old Gelletreau. He accuses half his patients of malingering. He told me I just had a cold once, and it turned into pneumonia. And doctors are notoriously tough on their own families.' He reached for the phone.

'You see why I like this guy?' J-J said to Isabelle. 'Local knowledge. That's real policing for you. Not all this computer crap.'

'Madame Gelletreau?' Bruno said into his phone. If Isabelle could move fast, so could he. 'Could I speak to Richard, please? It's Bruno about the tennis, or is he too sick? He's at school in Périgueux, you say. Oh, my mistake, I'd heard he was at home sick. Very well, it's not urgent.' He rang off.

'This looks a little more serious,' said J-J. 'A false note to school, and he's at neither place.'

Bruno drove down to the tennis club with Isabelle and checked the records. The semi-finalist from Lalinde was named Jacqueline Courtemine. Bruno rang his counterpart in Lalinde, a young ex-serviceman called Quatremer whom he knew only slightly and asked for an address and some information about the family. In return, Bruno explained that they were looking for a young man who might be in her company, and that Quatremer might want to keep an eye on the house until the *Police Nationale* turned up in force.

Then he called Quatremer's predecessor, an old hunting friend named René who had retired the previous year, put the same question and elicited a volley of information. Jacqueline's parents were separated, perhaps divorced. The mother was living in Paris on money from the wealthy father, who had inherited a family furniture store and expanded it into a profitable chain that now stretched across the region. Between his business and his mistresses he was rarely at home, and Jacqueline had the large house on the outskirts of town pretty much to herself, as well as her own car. René thought she would be going to university in the fall and, he said, she had a reputation as a wild one. Bruno scribbled quick notes on how to find the house while Isabelle called J-J, and then warned his old friend that Quatremer might need some support and advice. 'And warn your Mayor,' Bruno added, before ringing off.

Isabelle was already waiting in her car. She drove down to the main road leading to Bergerac and pulled in to wait for J-J. She fished in the back seat for the magnetic blue light, and as she clamped it onto her roof J-J's big black Citroën drew up, flashing its lights, with another police car close behind. They joined the small convoy and raced towards Lalinde.

## CHAPTER 9

The police convoy drew up to a large, detached house that stood on the low hill that rose above Lalinde with a sweeping view of the river Dordogne. The river was wide and shallow here, on its descent from the high plateau and into the flat farmlands that had for a century produced tobacco to make the dark Gauloises cigarettes. Designed in the traditional Périgord style, with a steep tile roof, tall chimneys and turrets like witches' hats, the house gleamed with a brightness of stone that showed it had been newly built. Four cars, a motorbike and two small scooters called *mobylettes* were parked untidily on the broad gravel forecourt. Behind the house was a large garden, and then the land rose gently again to the hill that stretched all the way to Bergerac. Noisy rock music came from the open windows, and an empty bottle of wine lay on its side in the hallway.

'Very welcoming,' said J-J. 'A wide-open door and the smell of grass – so we can hold her on a possession charge if we have to.' He directed the second carload of detectives to go round to the back, knocked quietly on the open wooden door, waited for a moment and strode in.

Several teenagers wearing vacant expressions were sprawled around a table in the big dining room that opened onto a patio and swimming pool at the rear. A large bar ran along the side of the room. Cans of beer and bottles of wine stood on the table, along with dirty plates, a cheese board and a bowl of fruit. Through the window, Bruno could see three young men with shaven heads and tattoos playing in the pool with two bare-breasted girls. J-J went over to the impressive stereo and pressed a button. The music whined to a blessed halt. Bruno could see no sign of Richard Gelletreau at the table or in the pool.

'Mademoiselle Courtemine?' J-J asked. Silence. He repeated her name. The silence lengthened. 'Is Mademoiselle Courtemine or the owner of this property present? This is a police inquiry.'

One of the girls at the table put her hand to her mouth and glanced at the wide staircase. J-J gestured with his head and Isabelle went quickly up the stairs.

'Seize that,' J-J told another detective, gesturing to the bag of grass and rolling papers on the table. 'Then get all their names and ID. Bring that local copper in from the front gate. He should know most of them. What's his name again, Bruno?'

'Quatremer.'

'Good, now we'll try again,' said J-J, facing the young

people round the table. 'I'm looking for Richard Gelletreau.'

No response. The girls in the pool had their hands over their breasts. The lads were looking round, probably considering running for it, Bruno thought, but at that moment more police came round from the side of the house. Bruno tried to focus on the faces, to see if he recognised any of the young people. The youths in the pool looked vaguely familiar, perhaps from the surveillance photos he had seen. His eyes kept drifting back to the half-naked girls. His own teenage years had never been like this. If they had been, who knows what strange political group he might have been ready to join.

'J-J,' called Isabelle from upstairs. 'Here.'

J-J motioned Bruno to come with him. They walked side by side up the wide and handsome staircase. The landing above was the size of an average living room. Straight ahead was a corridor with a series of closed doors onto rooms that would have faced the town. They followed the sound of Isabelle's voice to a second wing that must have stretched towards the garden. They walked into a large room that would have been bright and airy had the curtains been open, but was now dark but for some low lighting and the flickering of a TV. On the tangled bed were two young people, hauling themselves from sleep. The girl was trying to pull the sheet up to cover them. She was wearing a black bra, and a black peaked cap lay on her pillow. The boy, who was naked, could not move. His wrists and ankles were bound to the bedposts with scarves.

Bruno raised his eyes from the couple on the bed to two posters on the wall. One was of Jean-Marie Le Pen, leader of the *Front National*; the other was what looked like an original cinema placard for the film *The Battle of Algiers*. Above the bed various objects hung on the wall, forming a tableau that included bayonets, daggers and a German Wehrmacht helmet. The boy on the bed turned his head away from the sudden light and groaned. It was Richard. He looked around, recognised Bruno, and groaned again.

'Who the fuck are you?' the girl spat. 'Get out.'

'Check out the TV, J-J,' said Isabelle. 'Nazi porn.'

And it was. Two men in black uniforms with swastika armbands and SS lapel flashes were being serviced by two young women, one white and blonde and evidently willing, one black and in manacles.

J-J moved very fast as the girl squirmed to the side of the bed. He caught her wrist in his strong hand and yanked it behind her back as she yelped. He held her firmly while he looked at the bedside table for which she had been reaching. A razor blade lay next to a small mirror on which sat some grains of white powder.

'You've been a naughty girl,' J-J said, still holding her firmly. 'Cocaine. That's three years, right there.' He took a pen from his pocket and poked the lid of a small box beside the mirror. He shook his head at the pile of small white pills inside and then looked at the girl, who was now silent. She had stopped squirming and the bed sheets had fallen away to reveal that she was wearing black stockings, supported by a black suspender belt over a shaven pubis.

'All this and Ecstasy too,' said J-J quietly. It appeared to Bruno that J-J looked genuinely shocked. 'I think we have enough here for trafficking charges. That could be ten years in prison, Mademoiselle. I hope you enjoy the company of tough old lesbians. You are going to be spending a lot of time with them.'

He turned to Isabelle. 'Put the cuffs on this young lady of the house, and then let's take our own photos of this scene. I want another forensics team to go through this room and check out every knife in the house. The Périgueux boys are still at St Denis so you may have to call more in from Bergerac, and we'll also have the narcotics lads in. We could do with some extra manpower for the search. It's a big property.'

He looked at Bruno. 'Bruno, we must track down the owner of the house and this girl's parents. They'll have to be informed, and you'd better do the same with the boy's father. Then tell my boys to organise a search of the premises as soon as they have all the young thugs downstairs arrested, charged with possession of illegal drugs and in police cells where we can question them. I take it this is indeed the young Richard?' Bruno nodded. 'He looks very like his photo. Isabelle, I want a lot of shots of the pair of them and make sure you get the focus just right. Then you can start checking out all the other videos and films in Mademoiselle Courtemine's collection.'

'Including her own,' Isabelle said drily, pointing at the back wall. Neither Bruno nor J-J had yet noticed the small video camera on its tripod that pointed at the bed, a red light on its side still blinking.

As evening began to fall, more carloads of police arrived, along with two vans to take away a total of eight young people. Jacqueline waited in handcuffs; Richard was finally untied once the police photographers had finished with the bedroom and the forensics team had taken their samples. He and Jacqueline were then each given a set of the plastic white overalls the forensics team used, handcuffed again and taken to police HQ in Périgueux. Bruno had tracked down the families. Jacqueline's father was on a business trip to Finland and would fly home the next day. The mother was driving down from Paris. Richard's father would meet them in Périgueux. Lawyers had been arranged, but the search had already found four shoe boxes of what the narcotics boys said were Ecstasy pills in one of the outbuildings.

'Street value of twenty thousand euros, they tell me,' said J-J, lighting an American cigarette. He and Bruno were standing on the wide terrace in front of the house that looked down to the small town of Lalinde and the broad Dordogne river. 'They just found another shoe box in her car, hidden under the spare wheels. Lots of fingerprints. She can't talk her way out of it. And those tattoo-covered louts in the pool turn out to be members of the *Front*'s *Service d'Ordre*, its own private security guard. They had photos of themselves with Le Pen at some party rally. Drugs in their cars and very large amounts of cash in their wallets.'

'Have you told Paris yet?' asked Bruno. 'The politicians will love that. *Front National* types involved in a drug-running gang, perverting our French youth.'

'Sure, sure,' said J-J, 'but it's the murderer I'm after. I don't much care about the politics, except that I hate that Nazi stuff. My God, after what this country went through in the war, to see these young kids getting caught up in that filth ... that, and drugs and the kinky sex. Whatever happened to this generation, Bruno? Do you have kids?'

'No kids, J-J, and no wife as yet,' said Bruno, surprising himself with the note of sadness he heard in his own voice. Where had that come from? He changed the subject. 'And straight sex was always good enough for me. If I came across a woman dressed in that Nazi way and wanting to tie me up, I think I'd be laughing too much to do her justice.'

'Well, I certainly can't say that porno film turned me on,' said J-J. 'Mind you, at my age there's not much that does light my fire.'

'Yet in the old days, there wasn't much that didn't get you going. Your reputation still goes ahead of you, J-J. I'm surprised that little Isabelle isn't wearing armour.'

'Not necessary with these new regulations, Bruno. Sexual harassment, rights of women – you're lucky to be out it, down here in your little Commune. They can fire you these days if you so much as look at a woman colleague.'

'We have that as well. It's everywhere. We aren't insulated from what goes on everywhere else,' said Bruno. 'Maybe I was fooling myself when I thought we were different down here, with our little weekly markets and all the kids playing sports and staying out of trouble. A good place to raise a family, you'd think, and now this. You know, J-J, this is my first murder.'

'So when do your start on your own family, Bruno? You aren't getting any younger. Or do you have your own little harem among the farmers' wives?'

Bruno grinned. 'I wish. Have you seen the farmers' fists?'

'No, and I haven't seen the farmers' wives either,' laughed J-J. 'But seriously, aren't you planning to settle down? You'd make a good father.'

'I haven't found the right woman,' shrugged Bruno, and embarked on the usual half-truth that he deployed to keep his privacy, and to damp down the memory of the woman he had loved and lost, rescued and then failed to save. It was nobody's business but his own. 'I suppose I came close to it a couple of times, but then I didn't feel quite ready, or I got nervous, or she lost patience and moved away.'

'I remember that pretty brunette who worked for the railway – Josette. You were seeing her when we worked together.'

'She went away when they did the cutbacks. They moved her up north to Calais to work on the Eurotunnel service because she spoke good English. I miss her,' said Bruno. 'We got together once in Paris for a weekend, but somehow it wasn't the same.'

J-J grunted, a sound that seemed to acknowledge many things, from the power of women to the corrosive effects of time and the inability of men to ever quite explain or comprehend them. As darkness spread over the river below them, they stood in silence for a moment.

'I guess I'm lucky, really, having something close to an ordinary family life,' said J-J. 'Most cops' marriages don't work out, what with the strange hours and the things you can't talk about, and it's not easy making friends outside the police. Civilians get nervous around us. But you know that – or maybe it's different down here for you, a country copper in a small town where everybody knows you and likes you and you know everybody's name.'

This time it was Bruno's turn to grunt. He did think it was different in St Denis, at least for him, but he was sure J-J did not want to hear that.

'The only thing she gives me grief about now is grandchildren,' J-J went on. 'She goes on and on about why our kids aren't married and breeding.' He sighed. 'I suppose your folks are getting at you about the same thing.'

'Not really,' Bruno said shortly. No, he couldn't leave it there. 'I thought you knew I was an orphan.'

'I'm sorry, Bruno. I didn't mean—' J-J turned away from the view to scrutinise him. 'I remember somebody telling me that, but it slipped my mind.'

'I never knew them,' Bruno said levelly, not looking at J-J. 'I know nothing of my father, and my mother left me in a church when I was a baby. It was the priest who christened me Benoît, the blessed one. You can understand why I call myself Bruno instead.'

'Jesus, Bruno. I'm really sorry.'

'I was in a church orphanage until I was five, and then my mother committed suicide up in Paris. But first she wrote a note to her cousin down in Bergerac naming the church where she'd left me. The Bergerac cousins raised me, but it wasn't easy because they never had much money. That's why I went off to the Army as soon as I left school. It wasn't a very happy childhood but they're the nearest to a family I've got, and they have five kids of their own so there's no pressure on me.'

'Do you still see them?'

'Weddings and funerals, mostly. There's a lad I'm close to because he plays rugby. I've taken him out hunting a few times, and tried to talk him out of going into the Army. He sort of listened; joined the Air Force instead.'

'I thought you enjoyed your time in the service? I remember you telling some stories, that night we went out to dinner.'

'Bits of it were fine. Most of it, really. But I don't tend to talk about the bad times. I'd rather forget them.'

'You mean Bosnia?'

Yes, he meant Bosnia. He'd been there with the UN peacekeepers, but he quickly found there wasn't much peace to be kept. They'd lost over a hundred dead, a thousand wounded, but nobody remembered that any more. They barely even noticed at the time. They were being hit by snipers and mortars from all sides, Serbs, Muslims and Croats. He'd lost friends, but the UN orders were they were not to fight back, hardly even to defend themselves. Not a glorious chapter. This was partly why he'd chosen to come and live here, in the quiet heart of rural France. At least it used to be quiet before they got a dead Arab with a swastika carved in his chest. He told J-J some of this, but not all.

'Well, you turned out okay, despite everything. The orphanage, Bosnia, all that,' J-J said finally. 'And I'm a prying old busybody. I suppose it goes with the job. Still, I meant it about my wife, she's a good woman. I'm lucky.' J-J paused. 'You know she's got me playing golf?'

'She never has,' laughed Bruno, grateful for the change of subject, and of mood.

'She started playing with a couple of her girlfriends, then she insisted I take some lessons, said we had to have some common interests for when I retire,' J-J said. 'I quite enjoy it; a nice stroll in the open air, a couple of drinks after, some decent types in the club house. We're planning on going down to Spain this summer on one of those special golfing vacations – play every day, get some lessons. Look, bugger this, I need a drink. Stay here. I'll be right back.'

Bruno turned and looked back at the house. All the lights were on and white-garbed figures crossed back and forth behind the windows. The last time he had seen this many police was in the passing-out parade from his training course. He thought he knew what J-J was building up to say. This was going to be a very messy case, with politics and media and national interest, and he'd want Bruno out of it. That would be fine with Bruno, except that his job was to look after the interests of the people of St Denis, and he had no idea how to do that.

'Well, it looks like we have our chief suspect for the poor old Arab.' J-J's silhouette loomed out of the light in the house, offering him a glass. A Ricard, mixed just right, not too much ice. The furniture tycoon would hardly miss a couple of drinks.

'It's circumstantial, unless forensics come up with some traces or we find the weapon,' Bruno said.

'One of those Nazi daggers on the wall, if you ask me. I told forensics to take special care with them.'

'You know you're going to lose control of this case once Paris gets involved. There's too much politics.'

'That's why I want to wrap it up fast,' said J-J. 'They're sending down a *Juge-magistrat* from Paris, along with something they call a media coordinator to handle the press. They'll be spinning everything for the evening news and the Minister's presidential ambitions. I'd be surprised if he doesn't come down here himself, maybe even for the funeral.'

'The Mayor is already worried enough about the impact on tourism this summer without having ministers making headlines. I can just see it now.' Bruno shook his head. 'St Denis: the little town of hate.'

'In your shoes, I'd try to keep out of the way. Let the big boys do their thing and then try and sweep up the broken crockery when they go. That's the way it works.'

'Not with my Mayor, it doesn't,' said Bruno. 'Don't forget he used to be on Chirac's staff up in Paris. Anybody who worked for a president of the Republic can play politics with the best of them. And he's my boss.'

'Well, they can't fire you.'

'It's not that,' said Bruno. 'He's been good to me – helped me, taught me a lot. I don't want to let him down.'

'You mean, like the father you never had?'

Speechless for a moment, Bruno stared intently at J-J then took a deep breath and told himself to relax. 'You must have been reading some paperback on psychology,' he said, more curtly than he had intended.

'*Merde*, Bruno, I didn't mean anything by it.' J-J leaned forward and gave him a soft punch on the arm. 'I was just talking, you know ...?'

'Forget it, maybe you're right,' Bruno said. 'He *has* been like a father to me. But it's not just the Mayor. It's the town itself and the damage all this mess could do. It's my home, and it's my job to defend it.'

# CHAPTER 10

It was raining, not the hard driving downpour of a summer thunderstorm but a thin persistent drizzle that would last for a couple of hours, so the four men hurried across the wet grass to the covered court of which Bruno was rather proud. It looked like a disused hangar on an old airfield, with a corrugated roof in translucent plastic and tarpaulins for walls. But the court was sound inside, and boasted an umpire's chair, a scoreboard, and benches for spectators. An array of small placards, advertising local businesses and the *Sud-Ouest* newspaper, hung on the metal frame

Bruno partnered with the Baron, who was not a real baron but, as the main landowner in the district and a man of sometimes imperious habits, was widely known by the nickname and openly rejoiced in it. Xavier and Michel took the other side, as they usually did, and they began to knock up, not too hard and none too skilfully, for the pleasure of the game and of the weekly ritual. When Bruno took the ball to serve, the Baron stayed alongside him at the back of the court. He preferred playing the back court, letting 'young Bruno' take the volleys at the net. As always, each man was allowed to have his first serve as many times as he required to get the ball in. And, as usual, Bruno's hard first serve went long but his second was decently placed. Xavier played it back to the Baron, who returned one of his deceptive drop shots. Michel was the better player, but the men played together so often they knew each other's game and limitations. After a double fault, a missed volley and one accidentally excellent serve that made Bruno think he might one day be able to play this game, they changed ends.

'Have you caught the bastard yet?' Michel asked as they passed each other at the net. He ran the local public works department. Sixteen men served under him and he supervised a motor pool of trucks, ditch-diggers and a small bulldozer. He was a powerful man physically though not tall, and compact with a small but firm paunch. He was even more powerful in the life of the town and his signature was needed on any planning permission. He came from Toulon, where he had served twenty years in the Navy engineers.

Bruno shrugged. 'It's out of my hands. The *Police Nationale* are running the show, and Paris has got involved. I don't know much more than you do, and if I did, you know I couldn't talk about it.'

He knew that his companions wouldn't let him get

away with that. These four were the town's shadow government. The Baron owned the land, and was rich enough to make the discreet donations that helped the tennis and rugby clubs to keep functioning as they did. Michel was a man of real influence and Xavier was the *Maire-adjoint*, the deputy who did most of the administrative work and ran the day-to-day business of the *Mairie*. He had worked in the sub-Prefecture in Sarlat until he came home to St Denis, where his father ran the Renault dealership and his father-in-law owned the big local sawmill. Along with Bruno and the Mayor, these men ran the business of the town. They had learned to be discreet and they expected Bruno to keep them informed, above all at these ritual Friday meetings.

Michel had a classic serve, a high toss of the ball and good follow-through, and his first service went in. Bruno's forehand return hit the lip of the net, and rolled over to win the point.

'Sorry,' he called, and Michel waved acknowledgement then bounced the ball to serve again. When they reached deuce, which they called *egalité*, two men entered the court, shaking the raindrops from their faces. Rollo from the school always arrived a little late. He waved a greeting, and he and Dougal, a Scotsman who was the Baron's neighbour and drinking chum, sat on the bench to watch the end of the set. It was not long before Rollo and Dougal rose to take their turn. This was the usual rule. One set, and then the extra men played the losers. Bruno and the Baron sat down to watch. Rollo played with more enthusiasm than skill and loved to attack the net, but Dougal had once been a useful club player and his ground shots were always a pleasure to watch.

'I suppose you can't say much,' the Baron began, in what he thought was a low voice.

'Not a thing,' replied Bruno. 'You understand.'

'It's just I heard there were some arrests over in Lalinde last night and that you were involved. A chum of mine saw you there. I just want to know if there was a connection to our Arab.'

'Our Arab, is he now?' Bruno asked. 'I suppose he is, in a way. He lived here, died here.'

'Our Arab I said, and I mean it. I know Momu and Karim as well as you do. I know the old man was a *Harki*, and I have a very special feeling for the *Harkis*. I commanded a platoon of them in the Algerian war. I spent the first month wondering when one of them would shoot me in the back, and the rest of the war they saved my neck on a regular basis.'

Bruno turned and looked at the Baron curiously. In the town, he had a reputation as a real right-winger, and it was said that only his devotion to the memory of Charles de Gaulle kept the Baron from voting for the *Front National*.

'I thought you were against all this immigration from

North Africa,' Bruno said, breaking off to applaud as Michel served an ace.

'I am. What is it now, six million, seven million Arabs and Muslims over here, swamping the place? You can't recognise Paris any more. But *Harkis* are different. They fought for us and we owed them – and we left too damn many of them behind to have their throats cut because we wouldn't take them in. Men who fought for France.'

'Yes, the old man was a *Harki*. More than that, he got a medal. He fought for us in Vietnam too, that's where he won it.'

'In that case, he wasn't a *Harki*. They were irregulars. He sounds like he was in the regular Army, probably a *Zouave* or a *Tirailleur*. That's what most of their regiments were called. They were allowed back into France when it was over, but most of the *Harkis* were refused entry and got their throats slit. And most of the ones who made it to France were put in camps. It was a shameful time. Some of us did what we could. I managed to bring some of my lads back on the troopship, but it meant leaving their families, so the bulk of them decided to stay and take their chances. Most of them paid the price.'

'How did you find out that they had been killed?' Bruno wanted to know.

'I stayed in touch with the lads I brought over, helped them get jobs, that sort of thing. I took some of them on in my business. They had ways of keeping contact through their families. You know I'm not much of a churchgoing type, but every time I heard one of my *Harkis* had been killed, I used to go and light a candle.' He stopped, looked down at his feet. 'It was all I could do,' he murmured. He cleared his throat and sat up. 'So tell me about our Arab, a good soldier of France. Do you know who killed him?'

'No. Our enquiries continue, just like the police spokesmen say. We're just at the start of the case and I'm not even really involved. As I said, the *Police Nationale* are handling it. They've set up a temporary office in the exhibition rooms.'

'What about Lalinde?'

'There may not even be a connection. It seems to have been more of a drugs bust,' Bruno said, careful not to tell his friend an outright lie.

The Baron nodded, his eyes still fixed on the game. Rollo had just served two double faults in a row.

'Did I ever tell you about how we left Algeria?' he asked suddenly. Bruno shook his head.

'We were in Oran, at the harbour. Chaos it was. De Gaulle had signed the peace deal at Evian and then the Paras and half the army in Algeria launched that crazy *coup d'état*. I was the only officer in my unit who refused to join and I would have done, except that I wouldn't go against de Gaulle. Anyway, my lads would never have joined in. I was running a platoon of conscripts by then, young Frenchmen, and they all had those new-fangled little transistor radios from Japan so they could listen to their rock music. But what they also got on their radios at that time was de Gaulle, telling them to disobey any officer who wanted them to take up arms against the Republic, against him, against France. So the conscripts stayed in their barracks and wouldn't move – that's what stopped the coup. They stayed there until the troopships came in to take us home.'

'This was that time in '61?' Bruno asked. 'General Salan and those people who went on to start the OAS, the ones who tried to assassinate de Gaulle?'

'That's right,' said the Baron grimly. 'Anyway, I got our unit down to the troopship, and on the way we picked up those of my old *Harkis* that we could find, or who were smart enough to know they had better get out fast. My sergeant had been with me all through the war and he liked the *Harkis*, so he helped. We scrounged some uniforms – no shortage of them – and we just let them board with us. There were no lists, nothing organised because there were so few officers, so I just bullied them all aboard.'

'And when you got to France?' Bruno asked. 'How did you get them ashore?'

'They couldn't put us all into the naval base at Toulon, where at least they had some kind of control system, so we docked at Marseilles, at the commercial port, and the Army laid on dozens of trucks to drive us to the nearest bases. But there was no system for which unit went to which base, so the sergeant and I told my lads to go home for a few days and as long as they reported back within a week I'd make sure it was OK. We all just rushed off the ship, boarded any old truck, and lads, including my *Harkis*, were dropping over the tailboard at every corner. We had raided the kitbags in the ship's hold and got them some civilian clothes and a few francs. Apart from that, all they had was my name and address.'

'It sounds crazy,' said Bruno. 'I knew the Algerian war ended in a mess, but I didn't know about that.' Vaguely, he heard Dougal call out 'five-fou' in his funny accent and the four men were changing ends. It looked as if the set was almost over. He had barely noticed.

'You have to remember, in those days there were no computers,' the Baron went on. 'There were just lists on paper. We lost ours in the chaos, and the troopship was too crowded for any proper roll-calls. What wasn't lost was burned by me and the sergeant when we got back to the regimental base at Fréjus. Remember, I was the only officer who had stayed loyal, so they were not going to give me a hard time. The Colonel even congratulated me for getting the men back at all.'

'Game and set,' called Dougal, and on the court they began collecting the tennis balls.

'The thing I remember best,' said the Baron, 'was the very last moment. I stayed at the foot of the gangplank, trying to be sure I had all my men. I was one of the last aboard. And one of the Algerian dockworkers was standing there by the bollard, ready to cast off the ship's rope. He looked me straight in the eye, and he said, "Next time, we invade you." Just like that. And he kept his eyes fixed on me until I turned and boarded the ship. I'll never forget it. And when I look at France these days, I know he was right.'

As always after their game, the group of men walked back to the clubhouse, slowly this time since the rain had eased. They showered and then brought in the ingredients of their ceremonial Friday lunch from their cars. Bruno provided the eggs from his hens and the herbs from his garden. In early spring, he picked *boutons de pissenlit*, the tiny green buds of the dandelion, but now it was young garlic and flat-leaved parsley, and some of his own truffles that he had stored in oil since the winter. Michel brought his own paté and *rillettes*, made from the pig they had gathered to slaughter in February, in happy defiance of the European Union regulations. Dougal supplied the bread and the cheese and the bottle of scotch whisky that they took as an aperitif after their first, thirst-quenching beers from the tap at the clubhouse bar. Rollo brought the beefsteaks and Xavier the salad and the *tarte aux pommes*, and the Baron provided the wine, a St Emilion '98 that was tasted and judged to be at its best.

Bruno cooked, as he always did, and when they had set the table and prepared the salad the men gathered at the hatch between the kitchen and the bar. Usually they joked and gossiped, but this time there was only one topic on their minds.

'All I can say is that we don't yet have any firm evidence, and so no obvious suspect,' Bruno told them as he broke the dozen eggs, lit the grill for the steaks, and threw a stick of unsalted butter into the frying pan. He began to slice the truffle very thin. 'We have some leads that we're following. Some point one way and some another, and some of them I don't know about because I am on the fringes of this investigation. That's all I can say.'

'The doctor's son has been arrested, along with a bunch of *Front National* thugs,' said Xavier. 'That we know.'

'It may not be connected,' said Bruno.

'It looks connected,' said Michel. '*Front National* thugs and a swastika carved into the poor old bastard's chest. Who else would do that?'

'Maybe the murderer did that to cast suspicion elsewhere,' said Bruno. 'Have you thought of that?'

'Which doctor's son?' asked Rollo.

'Gelletreau,' said Xavier.

'Young Richard?' said Rollo, startled. 'He's still at the *lycée*.'

'He was playing truant from his *lycée* this week. He forged a note from his dad,' said Bruno, tossing the whipped eggs into the sizzling butter and the fresh garlic. As the base of the omelette began to cook, he threw in the sliced truffle and twirled the pan.

'In the *Front National*? Richard?' Rollo repeated, disbelief in his voice. 'I never had any idea when he was at the college here. Well, he was younger then.' He paused. 'Well, I suppose there was one thing, a fight with one of Momu's nephews, but nothing too serious. Two bloody noses and some name-calling, the usual thing. I suspended them both from school for a day and sent a note to the parents.'

'A fight with an Arab? With one of Momu's nephews, and then Momu's dad gets killed?' said the Baron. 'That sounds significant. What was the name-calling? *Sale beur* – dirty Arab, that kind of thing?'

'Something like that,' Rollo said stiffly. 'Look, I didn't mean ... it was just one of those tussles that boys get into. It happens all the time, we know that. I should never have mentioned it.'

They fell into a silence, all eyes on Bruno as he lifted and tilted the heavy iron pan, gave two strategic pushes with his wooden spoon and tossed the herbs into the runny mix before folding the giant omelette over onto itself. Without a word, they all trooped to the table and sat. The Baron poured the wine and Bruno served the perfect omelette, the earthy scent of the truffle just beginning to percolate as he divided it onto six plates.

'One of your best, Bruno,' said the Baron, slicing the big country loaf against his chest with the *Laguiole* knife he took from the pouch at his belt. He was not trying to change the subject, since all the men understood that something significant had been said and the matter could not be allowed to rest.

'But you did mention it, my dear Rollo,' the Baron went on, reverting to the topic. 'And now you must satisfy not just our curiosity but the judicial questions this must raise. Our friend Bruno may be too delicate to insist, but you understand what is at issue here.'

'It was just boys,' Rollo said. 'You know how they are. One gets a bloody nose, the other gets a black eye and then they're the best of friends.' He looked from one to the other, but none was meeting Rollo's eye.

'Well, were they?' asked Michel.

'Were they what?' snapped Rollo. Bruno could see he hated the way this was going.

'Did they become the best of friends?'

'They didn't fight again.'

'Friends?'

'No, but that doesn't mean anything. They got on. Momu even invited the boy back to his home, sat him down to dinner with the family so he could see for himself they were just another French family. No difference. Momu told me he liked the boy. He was bright, respectful. He took flowers when he went.'

'That would have been his mother's idea,' said Xavier.

'She's on the left, isn't she?' Michel asked.

'Green,' said Xavier, who followed such allegiances closely. 'She got involved in that campaign against the pollution from the sawmill. Thirty jobs at stake and those daft *Ecolos* want to close it down.'

'What I mean is that Richard wouldn't have heard any of this anti-immigrant stuff at home. His mother is a Green and the doctor doesn't seem to have any politics,' Michel continued. 'So where did he pick it up?'

'In bed, I think,' said Bruno. 'I think he fell for that girl from Lalinde who got to the tennis semi-finals last year, and she was in the *Front* pretty deep. She's a pretty thing and he was besotted with her.'

'That can't be right,' said Rollo. 'This fight took place three years ago, when they were at the college here. They'd have been thirteen or so. And young Richard didn't meet the girl until the tournament last summer.' He took his glass as if he were about to gulp the wine, but remembered himself and took an appreciative sniff of the St Emilion and then a sip. 'When he left my care, he was a fine boy, a good pupil, a credit to the town. I thought he might go on to Paris, the *Sciences-Po* or the *Polytechnique*.'

'Instead, it looks like it could be prison for your fine boy,' said the Baron, using a chunk of bread to mop up every last trace of buttery egg from his plate.

CHAPTER 11

Bruno did not normally drink in the mornings, but Saturday was the exception. It was the day of the small market of St Denis, usually limited to the open space beneath the *Mairie* where the stall holders set out their fruit and vegetables, their homemade breads and their cheeses between the ancient stone pillars. Stéphane, a dairy farmer from the rolling country up the river, parked his custom-made van in the car park to sell his milk and butter and cheeses. He always arranged a small *casse-croûte*, a breaking of the crust, at about nine a.m., an hour after the market opened. For Stéphane, who rose at five to tend his cows, it was like a mid-morning snack, but for Bruno it was always the first bite of his Saturdays, and he took a small glass of red wine with the thick hunk of bread stuffed with Stéphane's rabbit pâté. The wine came from young Raoul, who had taken over his father's business selling wines at the various local markets. This day he had brought along a young Côtes de Duras, best known for its whites, but he thought this red was special. It was certainly an improvement on the Bergerac Bruno normally drank on Saturday mornings.

'What does that one sell for?' he asked.

'Normally five euros, but I can let you have a case for fifty, and you should keep it three or four years,' said Raoul.

Bruno had to be careful with his money, since his pay was almost as modest as his needs. When he bought a wine to store it was usually to share with friends on some special occasion, so he preferred to stay with the classic vintages that his chums would know. Mostly he bought a share of a barrel with the Baron from a small winemaker they knew in Lalande de Pomerol, and they bottled the three hundred litres themselves, a well-lubricated day to which they both looked forward and which, inevitably, by evening became a large party for half the village at the Baron's chateau.

'Have you seen the doctor?' Stéphane asked.

'Not yet,' said Bruno. 'It's out of my hands. The *Police Nationale* are involved and everything is being handled over in Périgueux.'

'He's one of us, though,' Stéphane said, avoiding Bruno's eye and taking a large bite of his bread and pâté.

'Yes, and so are Karim and Momu,' Bruno said firmly.

'Not quite the same way,' said Raoul. 'The doctor's family has been here forever and he delivered half the babies in town, me and Stéphane included.'

'I know that, but even if the boy is not involved in the

murder, there's still a serious drugs case being investigated,' said Bruno. 'And it's not just some weed, there are pills and hard drugs – the kind of things we want to keep out of St Denis.'

Bruno felt uneasy about the spreading word of mouth. Half the town seemed to know about young Richard Gelletreau's arrest, and everybody knew the doctor and his wife. There were not many secrets in St Denis, which was usually a good thing for police work, but not this time. Naturally people would talk about the arrest of a schoolboy, the son of a prominent neighbour, but there were layers to this rumour, about Arabs and Islam, that were something new both for him and for St Denis. Bruno read his morning newspaper and watched the TV and listened to France-Inter when he worked in his garden. He knew there were supposed to be six million Muslims in a France of sixty million people, that most of them came from North Africa and too few of them had jobs, probably through no fault of their own. He knew about the riots and the car burnings in Paris and the big cities, about the votes that the *Front National* had won in the last elections, but he had always felt that was something remote from St Denis. There were fewer Arabs in the Dordogne than in any other department of France, and those in St Denis were like Momu and Karim: good citizens with jobs and families and responsibilities. The women did not wear the veil and the nearest mosque was in Périgueux. When they married, they performed the ceremony in the *Mairie* like good republicans.

'I'll tell you what we also want to keep out of St Denis,' said Raoul, 'and that's the Arabs. There are too many here already.'

'What, half a dozen families, including old Momu who taught your kids to count?'

'Thin end of the wedge,' said Raoul. 'Look at the size of the families they have – six kids, seven sometimes. Two or three generations of that and we'll be outnumbered. They'll turn Notre-Dame into a mosque.'

Bruno put his glass down on the small table behind Stéphane's van, and wondered how best to handle this without getting into a row in the middle of the market.

'Look, Raoul. Your grandmother had six kids, or was it eight? And your mother had four, and you have two. That's the way it goes, and it will be the same for the Arabs. Birth rates fall, just as soon as the women start to get an education. Look at Momu – he only has two kids.'

'That's just it. Momu is one of us. He lives like us, works like us, likes his rugby,' replied Raoul. 'But you look at some of the rest of them, six and seven kids, and the girls don't even go to school half the time. When I was a lad there were no Arabs here. Not one. And now there's what, forty or fifty, and more arriving and being born every year. And they all seem to have first call on the public housing. With prices the way they are now I don't know how my own youngsters will ever get a start in life and be able to afford their own house. And for our family, this is our country, Bruno. We've been here forever, and I'm very careful about who I want to share it with.'

'You want to know why the *Front National* gets the vote it does?' chimed in Stéphane. 'Just open your eyes. It's not just the immigrants, it's the way the usual parties have let us down. It's been coming for years, that's why so many people vote for the Greens or for the *Chasse* party. Don't get me wrong, Bruno. I'm not against the Arabs, and I'm not against immigrants; not when my own wife is the daughter of a Portuguese who immigrated here back before the war. But they are like us. They are white and European and Christian, and we all know the Arabs are something different.'

Bruno shook his head. In one part of his mind he knew that there was some truth in this, but in another he knew that it was all totally, dangerously wrong. But most of all he knew that this kind of conversation, this kind of sentiment, had been threatening to come, even to quiet little St Denis, for a long time. Finally it was here.

'You know me,' he said after a pause. 'I'm a simple man – simple tastes, simple pleasures – but I follow the law because it's my job. And the law says anybody who is born here is French, whether they are white or black or brown or purple. And if they're French, they're just the same as everybody else in the eyes of the law, and that means in my eyes. And if we stop believing that, then we are in for real trouble in this country.'

'We already have trouble. We've got a murdered Arab and one of our own lads under arrest, and now a load of drugs floating around,' said Raoul flatly. 'Nobody is talking about anything else.'

Bruno bought some butter and some of the garlic-flavoured *Aillou* cheese from Stéphane, a pannier of strawberries, and a big country loaf from the organic baker in the market and took them up the stairs to his office in the *Mairie* before going along the hall to the Mayor's office. His secretary didn't work Saturdays, but the Mayor was usually in, smoking the big pipe his wife wouldn't allow around the house and working on his hobby, a history of the town of St Denis. It had been under way for fifteen years already, never seemed to make much progress, and he was usually glad of an interruption.

'Ah, my dear Bruno,' Gérard Mangin said, rising and moving across the thick Persian rug that glowed in soft reds against the dark wooden floorboards to the small corner cupboard where he kept his drink. 'A pleasure to see you on this fine morning. Let us share a small glass and you can tell me your news.'

'Not very much news, Sir, just what J-J could tell me on the phone this morning. And just a very small glass, please, I have to drive home and see to the garden. You know young Gelletreau was arrested, and he has a lawyer; so does the young girl from Lalinde. So far they are saying very little except that they know nothing at all about the killing of Hamid. We're still waiting for the forensics, but there's nothing obvious to connect them. No fingerprints, no blood traces.'

The Mayor nodded grimly. 'I had hoped everything might be settled quickly, even if it meant one of our local boys is responsible. But if this business is going to go on without any obvious result, the mood will turn sour very fast. I'm not sure which is worse. I just wish there was something we could do to speed things up – ah yes, and that reminds me.' He picked up a sheet of notepaper from his desk. 'You asked me about the old man's photograph of his soccer team. Momu remembers it well. It was an amateur team that played in a youth league in Marseilles and all the players were young North Africans. They had a coach, a former professional player for Marseilles called Villanova, and he was in the photo along with the rest of the team. They won the league championship in 1940. Momu remembers that because his father held a soccer ball in the photo with the words Champions, 1940 painted in white. But that's all he remembers.'

'Well, it's a start, but it doesn't tell us why the killer might want to take the photo away, or the medal,' said Bruno. 'By the way, I had to tell J-J about the fight that Gelletreau got into with Momu's nephew, which is probably meaningless but it is a connection. Of course the boy is still in big trouble because of the drugs and the politics, and J-J says he expects Paris to send down some big shot to make a big political case of it to discredit the *Front*.'

The Mayor handed Bruno a small glass of his own *vin de noix*, which Bruno had to admit was probably just a little better than his, but then Mangin had had more practice. The Mayor perched on the edge of his large wooden desk, piled high with books, files bound with red ribbon, and with an elderly black telephone on the corner. Neither a computer nor even a typewriter graced the remaining space, only an old fountain pen, neatly capped and resting on the page of notes he had been taking.

'I also heard from Paris today, from an old friend in the Justice Ministry and then from a former colleague in the *Elysée*, and they said much the same thing,' the Mayor told Bruno. The *Elysée* Palace was the official home, as well as the personal office, of the President of France. 'They see some political opportunities in our misfortune, and I have to say that, in their place, I might look at things the same way.'

'But you're not in their place, Sir. And in St Denis we have a great embarrassment on our hands that could do a lot of damage,' said Bruno.

'Well, I used to be in their place when I was young and ambitious so I understand their motives and their concerns. But you're right, we have to consider what is best for St Denis.' He turned to his window that overlooked the small market square and the old stone bridge. 'If this thing drags on and becomes a nasty confrontation between Arabs and whites and the extreme right, we will get lots of publicity and we are likely to have a lot of bitterness that could last for years. And, of course, we would stand to lose a good deal of this year's tourist season.'

'But the law must take its course,' said Bruno. He had been worried about the same things, and the Mayor's responsibilities were far greater: he had a duty to almost three thousand souls, and to a history that went back centuries and had built this *Mairie* and the serene old room where they now talked. Bruno remembered his first visit, to be interviewed by this same man, who still had a political career and a seat in the Senate at the time. Bruno's only recommendation had been a letter from the Mayor's son, Captain Mangin, the best officer he had ever known in the Army, and the man who pulled the unit through that bastard of a mission in Sarajevo. He owed a lot to the Mangins, father and son, two men who had given him their trust. He had been awed then, in his first meeting with the Mayor, by the heavy dark beams on the ceiling and the wood panelling on the walls, the rich rugs, and the desk that seemed made for the governance of a town far grander than St Denis. But that had been before Bruno came to know it and make it his home.

'Indeed the law must do as it must, and for the moment the course of the law seems to be based in Périgueux, and in Lalinde, our sister town,' the Mayor said. 'So if there is to be trouble, I would much rather it took place in Périgueux and Lalinde rather than here. You understand me, Bruno? It won't be easy to deflect attention from our little town, but we must do what we can. I told Paris that they might want to focus on Périgueux rather than here, but I'm not sure they quite got the point. Or maybe they got it too well.'

He sighed, and continued. 'There's another problem that will certainly concern you. I've just been advised that my dear colleague Montsouris is planning to hold a small demonstration here at lunchtime on Monday. A march of solidarity, he calls it.' The Mayor's lip curled a trifle and Bruno was left in no doubt of his irritation. 'France in support of her Arab brethren under the red flag seems to be his idea. He has asked for my support with Rollo to get the school children marching against racial hatred and extremism. What do you think?'

Bruno weighed the issue quickly, calculating how many people might be involved and what the route might be, and wondering whether he would have to block the road. In the back of his mind, he remembered the conversation he had just had in the market with Stéphane and Raoul. A march of solidarity might not be altogether popular given the current mood of the town.

'We certainly can't stop it, so we may have to go along with it and keep it as low-key as possible,' he said.

'Don't tell me you don't know Montsouris and his wife and how they operate? They'll call all the newspapers and TV and get some of the trade unions involved – all the publicity that we don't need.'

'Well, I think it might be better if we are known as a town that stands up for racial harmony than if we get stuck with the label of a centre of race hatred,' said Bruno. 'You know what the Americans say: if they give you lemons, make lemonade. And if we have to have such a march, it might be better that it takes place with you at the head and the moderates, rather than leave it to the red flags.'

'You could be right.' The Mayor was grudging.

'If you take charge, Sir, and set the route, perhaps we could limit it? Just make it from the *Mairie* to the war memorial, because old Hamid was a veteran and a war hero,' said Bruno, suddenly seeing a way through this potential political mess. 'You remember I told you he won the *Croix de Guerre*, so you could make it a patriotic march, nothing to do with Arabs and the extreme right, but the town commemorating the tragic death of a brave soldier of France.' He paused, then added quietly, 'It has the merit of being true.'

'You're becoming quite a canny politician.' In the Mayor's terms, if not in Bruno's, this was a compliment.

'It must be your influence, Sir,' he said, and they smiled at one another with genuine affection. The Mayor raised his glass and they drank.

Suddenly their calm mood was shattered by the braying sound of the *Gendarmerie* van. The sound grew, and then stayed, as if right beneath the window. The two men looked at each other and moved as one towards the window and saw blue uniforms and grey suits scrambling amid the market stalls. They were closing in upon an agile boy who was darting between them and ducking beneath the stalls, delaying the inevitable moment of his capture.

'*Merde*,' said Bruno. 'That's Karim's nephew.' And he dashed for the stairs.

By the time Bruno reached the covered market, the boy had been caught and his arm was held firmly by a self-congratulatory Captain Duroc. The two men in grey suits, whose faces Bruno recognised, were the hygiene inspectors from Brussels, civil servants who should never have been working on a Saturday. One of them held a large potato above his head in triumph.

'This is the rascal,' declared the other grey suit. 'We caught him red-handed.'

'And this is the potato, just like the one he used on our car on Tuesday,' piped up the one holding it.

'Leave this to me, gentlemen,' said Duroc very loudly, and glanced triumphantly around at his audience of market people and shoppers who were gathering round to enjoy the scene. 'This young devil is going to the cells.'

'*Mon Capitaine*, perhaps it would help if I came along,'

said Bruno, surprising himself with the smoothness of his voice, since he was churning inside with anger, directed mainly against himself. If only he had thought ahead and made sure this nonsense of slashing tyres and immobilising cars had been stopped; if only he had not stayed for that ridiculous self-congratulatory drink with the Mayor; if only he had remembered to talk to Karim ... But of course he couldn't raise it with Karim, not with his grandfather just murdered, and now he had to make sure that Karim's young nephew didn't bring down a lot more trouble on everyone else. Think, Bruno!

'I can ensure that we inform the parents, *mon Capitaine*,' he said. 'You know the regulations about minors, and I think I have their number in my phone. You can take the statements of complaint of these two gentlemen at the *Gendarmerie* while I contact the boy's family.'

Duroc paused, and pursed his lips. 'Ah, yes. Of course.' He turned to glower at the two civil servants. 'You know how to find the *Gendarmerie*?'

'What about my eggs?' shrilled old Mother Vignier, pointing to the mess of shells and yolks on the ground beside her overturned stall. 'Who's going to pay for that?'

One of the inspectors bent down to retrieve a shell, and came up with a nasty look of triumph.

'No date stamp on this egg, Madame. You know it's strictly against the regulations? Such eggs may be consumed for private use but it is an offence under the Food Hygiene law to sell them for gain.' He turned to Captain Duroc. 'We have here another offence in this market, officer.'

'Well, you had better find a witness that these eggs were being sold,' said Bruno. 'Madame Vignier is known for her generosity, and makes a regular donation of her surplus eggs to the poor. And if she has any left over after the Saturday market, she gives them to the church. Is that not so, Madame?' he said courteously, turning to the old hag who was staring at him, her mouth agape. But her brain moved fast enough for her to nod assent.

Everybody knew the old woman was poor as a church mouse since her husband drank the farm away. She bought the cheapest eggs at the local supermarket, scraped off the date stamps, rolled them in straw and chicken-shit and sold them to tourists as farm-laid for a euro a piece. No local ever bought anything from her except her *eau de vie* since her one useful legacy from her drunk of a husband had been his ancestral right to eight litres a year – and she naturally made a very great deal more than that.

'Shall I summon the local priest to testify to Madame Vignier's good character?' Bruno went on. 'You may not yet have had the time to make the acquaintance of our learned Father Sentout, a very important man of the church who is soon, I gather, to be made a Monsignor.'

'A Monsignor?' said Duroc suspiciously, as if he had never heard the word.

'No, no,' said the inspector. 'We need not bother the good Father with this minor matter of the eggs. The lady may go. We are only concerned with this boy and his damage to state property, namely, our automobile.'

'You saw him damage your car today?' enquired Bruno politely. He was damned if these two grey men were going to get away with this.

'Not exactly,' said the inspector. 'But we saw him hanging around our car and we called the gendarmes, and when we pounced he had a potato in his hand.'

'Forgive me, but this is a vegetable market with hundreds of potatoes on sale. What's so unusual about a boy holding a potato?'

'He used a potato to immobilise our car at the Tuesday market. That's what. The engine seized up on the road to Périgueux.'

'Somebody threw a potato at your car. Was the windscreen broken?' Bruno was beginning to enjoy this.

'No, no. The potato was stuffed into the exhaust pipe to block the escaping gases, and the engine died. It was quite badly damaged and we had to wait for two hours for a breakdown truck.'

'Did you see this boy do this on Tuesday?'

'Not exactly, but *Capitaine* Duroc told us when we complained that he thought it must have been some boy, and so we came back today to see if we could see one – and we caught him.'

'You are on duty today, on a Saturday?' Bruno pressed.

'Not exactly,' he repeated, 'but since our duties bring us to the Dordogne this week and next, we decided to stay over and make a weekend of it in your delightful part of the country,' he added ingratiatingly. 'So much history ...' His voice trailed off as he saw the coldness in Bruno's expression.

'So, you are "not exactly" on duty today. Yes or no?'

'Er, no.'

'Let me get this clear, Monsieur,' said Bruno. 'Your car was allegedly damaged by a person or persons unknown on Tuesday, and it is not yet established that any damage was caused by the potato rather than by other causes. And now because you find a boy holding a potato, in a vegetable market, somewhere near your unharmed car of today – a day when you are not on duty and thus I presume not empowered to enforce the hygiene rules that you tried to deploy against the kindly Madame Vignier – you are now proposing to take the very serious step of arresting and bringing charges against a minor?'

'Well, yes.'

Bruno drew himself up to his full height, frowned and assumed his most formal tone of voice.

'I suggest that while I telephone the boy's parents to inform them of the forcible detention of their son for being in suspicious possession of a potato ...' he paused to let the absurdity of this sink in, 'I am also bound as an officer of the law to inform the parents of their right to file a formal complaint against persons responsible for what may be the wrongful arrest of a minor. So, at this time I would advise that you might want to contact your own superiors in order to establish what exactly is your personal authority and responsibility in such matters, and whether your department will defray any legal expenses that you are likely to incur. This will include any liability that you may have unfortunately brought upon the gendarmes if unlawful arrest is indeed established. I'm sure that you would not want to implicate *Capitaine* Duroc and his men, who clearly acted in the finest and most efficient traditions of the *Gendarmerie*, if such is the case.'

Somebody in the crowd let out a long, appreciative whistle for his performance, and Bruno then solemnly opened his shirt pocket and drew out the pencil and notepad on which he had written his morning shopping list. 'I had better make a formal record of this notification,' he said. 'So, gentlemen, might I see your identity cards, please, along with any documents that testify to your lawful authority? – oh, and *Capitaine* Duroc,' he went on, 'we shall obviously need a camera to take photographs of that young boy's arm and shoulder where you have been gripping so tightly. Just a formality, you understand, to protect you personally against any malicious charges of ill-treatment as a result of your being suborned into what seems very likely to be a case of wrongful arrest.'

There was a long silence, and then the Captain let go of the boy's arm. The lad burst into tears, scurried over to Bruno and buried his face in the policeman's freshly laundered shirt.

'Well, we may have been a little hasty ...' began the more grey of the two grey men. 'But the damage to our car is a serious matter.'

'Indeed it is, Sir, which is why we should proceed according to the letter of the law,' said Bruno. 'We will all go to the *Gendarmerie* where you will file your complaint, and I shall bring the parents, and probably their legal representative, and there will be no need for further witnesses since the Mayor and I saw the arrest and forcible seizure of this young boy from the window of the Mayor's office.'

'My chief of police is absolutely right,' said the Mayor from behind Bruno's shoulder. 'We saw the whole thing, and I must state that I am deeply disturbed that an underage member of our community can be seized in this way on what seems the flimsiest of evidence. As Mayor of St Denis and a senator of the Republic, I reserve the right to bring this matter to the attention of your superiors.'

'But unless we file charges, we'll be liable for the damage to the car,' bleated the younger grey man.

'Shut up, you fool,' hissed his partner, who had been visibly jolted when the Mayor mentioned that he was also a senator, and he turned towards Bruno and Mangin. *'Monsieur le Maire, Monsieur le Chef de Police, mon Capitaine,* allow me to congratulate you on the efficiency and good sense you have brought to ease this little misunderstanding. I think it might be advisable for all of us to let this matter rest, and we shall continue our duties elsewhere in the region.'

He bowed slightly, took his companion firmly by the elbow and beat a hasty but still dignified retreat from the market.

'Bloody Gestapo,' said the Mayor, and Duroc's eyes widened.

Bruno leaned down and ruffled the boy's hair. 'Where did you learn that trick with the potato?' he asked.

'From my great-grandpa. He told me it was what they used to do to the German trucks in the Resistance.'

Bruno's garden had been planned with decades in mind. The first time the Mayor had shown him the small stone cottage, its roof just beginning to collapse, with its sheltering trees on the hill above and the great sweep of the view to the south across the plateau, Bruno had known that this place would suit him well. The old shepherd who had lived here had died almost a decade earlier. His heirs, who had gone away to Paris, had neglected to pay the modest taxes so it had fallen into the hands of the Commune, which meant into the disposition of the Mayor. They had walked over the wide stretch of rough turf that would become Bruno's lawn and his terrace, poked around the overgrown vegetable garden and the collapsed hen house, and carefully lifted the rotting wooden cover from the well. The stone work was still sound and the water fresh. The beams of the old barn behind the cottage were solid chestnut and would last forever, and the cart track from the road up to the cottage, although rutted and overgrown, was easily passable. They had paced out the dimensions, twelve metres long and eight deep. Inside, there was one large room and two small, and the remains of a ladder that went up to the attic beneath the roof.

'It comes with four hectares but it will take a lot of work,' the Mayor had said.

'I'll have the time,' Bruno had replied, already imagining how it could be and wondering whether his Army gratuity would be sufficient to buy this home of his own. Not a countryman born, he had little idea what four hectares of land would be.

'The land stretches to the brow of the hill behind, in those woods, about a hundred metres to the right and down to the stream below us,' the Mayor explained. 'We cannot legally sell the place unless it is habitable, which means that the Commune would have to instal electricity but you would have to fix the roof and put in some windows before we can make a contract. That's your risk. If I'm voted out of office in the elections, you might have done the work for nothing. I cannot promise that my successor would honour the deal, but we might be able to reach a long leasehold agreement, tied to the post of *Chef de Police*.'

Bruno, just a few months into the job as the Municipal Policeman of St Denis, was confident that the Mayor would be re-elected in St Denis so long as he was breathing, and probably even if he were not, so they shook hands on the bargain and he set to work. It was springtime, so to save his rent money Bruno moved into the barn with a camp bed, a sleeping bag and a camping stove, and came to relish the briskness of his morning shower – a bucket of water from the well poured over his head, a quick soaping, and then another bucket to rinse himself off. It was the way he and his unit had kept clean on manoeuvres. He spent his first days off and all his evenings clearing the old vegetable garden and building a new fence of chicken wire to keep out the rabbits. Then, with a happy sense of mission, he began planting potatoes, courgettes, onions, lettuce, tomatoes and herbs.

He explored the copse of trees behind the vegetable garden and found wild garlic. Later, in the autumn, he discovered the big brown *cep* mushrooms, and under one of the white oaks he saw the darting movement of the tiny fly that signalled the presence of truffles on his land. Below the turf that stretched out generously to the front of his new home were hedges of raspberries and blackcurrants, and three old and distinguished walnut trees.

By the time the electricity was connected, he had put new lathes and tiles on the cottage roof and installed insulation. He had bought ready-made windows from *Bricomarché*, making them fit by building his own wooden frames. The doorway was of an unusual size, so he built his own door of planks and beams, and to fulfil a longstanding fancy of his own ever since he had first seen a

138

horse staring curiously over a half-door in the cavalry stables at Saumur, he made the door so that the top half
could open separately, and he could lean on the sill of the
half-door inside the cottage and gaze out at his property.
Michel from the public works depot had brought up a
mechanical digger to repair the old car track, dig a hole
for the septic tank and lay trenches for the pipes. Michel
stayed to help instal the electricity circuit and run cables
to the barn. René from the tennis club had put in the
plumbing, and old Joe had brought his cement mixer up
the newly levelled track to help him lay a new floor, and
then showed him how to make foundations for the addi-
tions that Bruno was planning – a large bedroom and
bathroom. Without really thinking about it, Bruno
assumed that someday there would be a wife here and a
family to house.

By the end of the summer, the foundations of the new
wing were laid and Bruno had moved out of the barn and
into the big room of the cottage with its view over the
plateau. He could take a hot shower in his own bathroom
with water from the gas heater, fuelled by the big blue
containers that Jean-Louis sold at the garage. He had a gas
cooker, a refrigerator, a sink with hot and cold running
water, wooden floors, and a very large bill at the
*Bricomarché* that he would be paying off with one fifth of
his monthly paycheck for the next two years.

He signed the contract of sale in the Mayor's office, the

town *notaire* on hand to ensure that all was legal. There was enough of his Army gratuity left to pay the first year of property taxes and to buy a good wood-burning stove, a lamb and a hundred litres of good Bergerac wine, and throw himself a housewarming party. He dug the pit for the fire that would roast the lamb and borrowed the giant *fait-tout* enamel pot from the tennis club to make his couscous. He added trestle tables and benches from the rugby club, feasted all his new friends, showed off his house and became an established man of property.

What he had not expected were the gifts. His colleagues at the *Mairie* had clubbed together to buy him a washing machine, and Joe brought him a cockerel and half a dozen hens. It seemed that every housewife in St Denis had prepared him jars of homemade pâté or preserved vegetables and jams, salamis and *rillettes*. Not a pig had been killed in St Denis over the past year but some of it ended in Bruno's larder. The tennis club brought him a set of cutlery and the rugby club brought him crockery. The staff of the medical clinic gave him a mirror for his bathroom and a cupboard with a first-aid kit that could have equipped a small surgery. Fat Jeanne from the market gave him a mixed set of wine and water glasses that she had picked up at the last *vide-grenier* jumble sale, and even the staff at *Bricomarché* had donated a set of cooking pots. Michel and the lads from the public works depot made him a gift of some old spades and garden tools that they had managed to replace by juggling next year's budget. The gendarmes bought him a big radio, and the *pompiers* gave him a shotgun and a hunting licence. The *minimes*, the children of the tennis and rugby clubs whom he taught to play, had put together their centimes and bought him a young apple tree, and everyone who came to his housewarming brought him a bottle of good wine to lay down in the cellar that he and Joe had built under the new wing.

As the night wore on, Bruno had felt compelled to take a small toast with every one of his guests. Finally, when wine and good fellowship overcame him sometime towards dawn, he fell asleep with his head on one of the trestle tables. The friends who had stayed the course carried him into his house, took off his shoes, laid him on the big new bed that René had built and covered him with the quilt that the *pompiers*' wives had sewn.

But Bruno had one more gift. It was curled up peacefully asleep on an expanse of old newspaper, and, as Bruno rose with an aching head, it woke up and came across to lick his feet and then scrambled up into his lap to burrow into the warmth and gaze at its new master with intelligent and adoring eyes. This was the Mayor's gift, a basset hound from the litter of his own renowned hunting dog, and Bruno decided to name him Gitane, or gypsy. But by the end of the day, when Bruno had already come to delight in his puppy's long, velvet ears, outsized feet and seductive ways, it had been shortened to Gigi. For

Bruno it had been the most memorable evening of his life – his formal baptism into the fraternity of the Commune of St Denis.

Dressed in shorts and sandals, Bruno was staking his young tomato plants when he heard a car labouring up the track and one of the celebrants from that first happy night came into view. But there was no cheer in Doctor Gelletreau as he levered himself from the elderly Mercedes, patted the welcoming Gigi, and lumbered up the path to the terrace. Bruno rinsed his hands under the garden tap and went to welcome his unexpected guest.

'I called at your house earlier, but there was no-one there,' Bruno told him.

'Yes, thanks, Bruno. I found your note on the door. We were in Périgueux, with the lawyer and then at the police station,' said the doctor, who had taped Bruno's broken ribs after a rugby game, tended his influenza and signed his annual certificate of health after a casual glance up and down the policeman's healthy frame. Gelletreau was overweight and far too red in the face for comfort, a man who ignored the sound advice he gave to his patients. With his white hair and heavy moustache, he looked almost too old to have a teenage son but there was a daughter even younger.

'Any news?' Bruno asked.

'No, the damn fool boy is being held pending drugs

charges, which the lawyer says may not stand since he was under – er – restraint when the police arrived.' The doctor was visibly embarrassed, and Bruno resisted the temptation to grin. 'But it's the murder they are interested in,' Gelletreau said.

'I can't talk about that, Doctor, not with you,' said Bruno, as Gigi came to nuzzle his leg. Automatically, he reached down to scratch behind his dog's ears.

'Yes, yes, I understand that. I just wanted you to know that I strongly, thoroughly believe him to be innocent of this crime. He's my son, and I'm bound to say that, but I believe it with all my heart and soul. There's no cruelty in the boy, Bruno, you know that. You have known him long enough.'

Bruno nodded. He had known young Richard since he was little more than a toddler, taught him to hold a tennis racquet, and then how to serve and hit a ball with topspin. Richard was a careful player rather than an aggressive one, and if Bruno were any judge of human nature, he doubted the lad had anything of the killer about him. But who knew what people could do under the sway of drugs or passion or political fervour?

'Have you seen Richard?'

'They gave us ten minutes with him, just us and our lawyer. The Mayor recommended some bright young fellow called Dumesnier from Périgueux so we engaged him. Apparently they didn't even have to let us see him, but the lawyer fixed it. They let us give him a change of clothes, after they searched every seam,' he said heavily. 'He's terrified – and ashamed and confused. You can imagine. But he says he knows nothing of the killing. And he keeps on asking after that damn Jacqueline. He's besotted with her.'

'His first girlfriend,' said Bruno, with understanding.

'She's his first lover, his first sex, and she's a pretty little thing. Pure poison, but certainly pretty. He's seventeen this week, you know. You remember how we were at that age, all those hormones raging. She's all he can think about. He's infatuated.'

'I understand.'

'Can you tell them that?' Gelletreau asked eagerly. 'Can you speak for him, just to explain that? I know you aren't running this business, Bruno, but they'll listen to you.'

'Doctor, sit down, and let me get you a glass. It's hot and I need a beer and you can join me.' He steered Gelletreau to one of the green plastic chairs on his terrace and went inside to get two cans from the refrigerator and two glasses. When he emerged he was surprised to see the doctor drawing on a yellow Gitane.

'You made me give those things up,' Bruno said, pouring the beers.

'I know, I know. I haven't smoked in years, but you know how it is.'

They raised their glasses to one another and drank in silence.

'You have made it very pleasant here, Bruno.'

'You said that when you were here last year for the barbecue, Doctor. I think you're changing the subject. Let
me try to answer what you said before.' Bruno put his
glass down and leaned forward, his elbows on the green
table.

'I'm not really part of the case,' he began. 'It's a matter
for the *Police Nationale*, but they consult me whenever they
want some local knowledge. I haven't seen all the evidence. I haven't seen the full forensic report on the
murder, or on the house where Richard was arrested, and
they probably won't show them to me. But I can tell you
that the detective running the investigation is a decent
sort and he'll go with the evidence. In a case like this, he'll
want to be sure that the evidence is very clear before he
makes any recommendation to the *Juge-magistrat*. I would-
n't be surprised if they send some ambitious hotshot
down from Paris because of the politics that are mixed up
in this affair. This is the sort of case that can make or
break a career, and the *Juge-magistrat* will want to be very
certain before he lays formal charges. If Richard is innocent, I'm very confident that he'll be cleared.'

'The Mayor just told me the same thing.'

'Well, he's right. And you have to concentrate on being
a support for your wife and family, and for Richard. You've
got a good lawyer, which is the most important thing at
this stage. Other than that, what you have to focus on is

telling Richard you love him and believe in him. He needs that right now.'

Gelletreau nodded. 'We'll give him all the support we can, you know that, but the question I keep asking myself is whether I really know my son as I thought I did. I can't get this dreadful *Front National* business out of my head. We had no idea he was getting involved like that. He never showed any interest in politics.'

'It may have been the girl who drew him in. That's one of the things the detectives are looking at. They'll get to the bottom of it, Doctor. And I don't know about you, but at that age if my first lover had been a raging Commie I'd have carried a red flag and marched wherever she asked me to.' Bruno emptied his glass. 'Another beer?'

'No thanks. I haven't finished this one. And you don't want to have a second after being out in this sun.' Gelletreau managed a wan smile. 'That's your doctor speaking.'

'There's one more thing.' Bruno twirled his empty glass, wondering how best to put this. 'You'd better start thinking about what to do if and when he's cleared and released. It wouldn't be a good idea to keep him at school locally. It would be difficult, with the gossip and the relatives of the old man. You should send him away to stay with a relative or think about a boarding school; maybe even send him abroad where he can make a fresh start and put all this behind him. Perhaps you could even suggest that he goes into the military for a while. It did me no harm, and it would be the kind of clean break the boy will need.'

'It did me no harm either, although I just did three years as a medical orderly in West Africa, enough to save me a year of medical school. But I don't think the boy is cut out for that kind of life, that kind of discipline. Maybe that's the problem,' said the doctor with a sigh. 'Still, he respects the military. He said how could anyone think he would kill someone who'd won a *Croix de Guerre*. But getting him out of here when all this is done is a good thought, Bruno. Thanks for the advice.'

As the good doctor drove away, Bruno began to wonder how on earth the boy had known about the *Croix de Guerre* ...

## CHAPTER 13

Less than an hour later, with the sun sinking fast and the heat easing so that he had donned a T-shirt, Bruno was watering the garden when he heard another vehicle lumbering up the track. He turned, just in time to catch a glimpse of a strange car and some unknown young man with short hair staring intently at the track. Then the hedge rose again and blocked his view. He emptied the watering can and turned again, at which point he recognised the car. It was Inspector Isabelle in her unmarked car; her short hair had fooled him. She got out, waved, and opened the rear door to bring out a supermarket bag.

'Hi, Bruno. I came to invite you to supper, unless you have plans.'

'It looks like you made the plans already, Isabelle,' he said, coming forward to push the enthusiastic Gigi out of the way and kiss the young woman on both cheeks. She was looking carefree and casual and distinctly appealing in her jeans and red polo shirt, with a brown leather jacket slung loosely over her shoulders. In her trainers, she stood just a fraction below his height.

'Pâté, beefsteak, baguette and cheese,' she said, standing back to brandish her bag. 'That's what J-J said you liked to eat. And wine, of course. What a wonderful dog – is this the great hunting dog J-J told me about?'

'J-J asked you to come?' She was not the first woman to come here alone bearing food, but she was the first to descend upon him uninvited, and he was old-fashioned enough to be disconcerted by her arrival. He decided he had better approach this unexpected evening as if she were here as a professional colleague, just another police chum. At least he had no inquisitive neighbours to start a new episode of the St Denis soap opera that he privately dubbed *Catching Bruno*.

'Not exactly,' said Isabelle, down on her knees and making much of the enchanted Gigi, who always liked women. 'Can basset hounds really hunt wild boar?'

'That's what they were bred for, supposedly by St Hubert himself. They aren't fast but they can run all day and never tire so they exhaust the boar. Then one hound goes in from each side and grabs a foreleg and pulls and the boar just sprawls flat, immobilised until the hunter comes. But I use this one mainly to hunt *bécasse*. He has a very gentle mouth.'

'J-J said I should brief you on the day's developments,' she said, prising herself free from the dog's attentions. 'He left me in charge at the murder room here, but all the action has moved to Périgueux and I got bored and lonely, so I thought I'd pay you a visit. It was another time J-J told me what you liked to eat, as if I couldn't guess.'

'Well, I'm curious to know the latest and you are most welcome. And congratulations on finding the house.'

'Oh, that was easy,' she said. 'I just asked the woman in the *Maison de la Presse* when I went to pick up *Le Monde*. They have a small piece about a racist murder in the Périgord, with the *Front National* involved. Half of the Paris press corps will be down here by Monday.'

And with Dominique in the *Maison de la Presse*, the whole of St Denis would know by now that Bruno had a new lady friend. They'd be staking out the bottom of the road to see if she left at a decent hour. He resolved privately that she would.

'He's called Gigi,' said Bruno, as his dog signalled complete devotion by rolling onto his back and baring his tummy to be scratched.

'Short for Gitane. J-J told me. He's a great fan of yours and he told me all about you on our first drive down here.'

'He's a good man and a fine detective,' said Bruno. 'Hand me that bag and come and sit down. What would you like to drink?'

'A *petit* Ricard for me, lots of water, please, and then can you show me round? J-J said you'd been in the engineers in the army and you built the whole place yourself.'

She was trying very hard to please, thought Bruno, but he smiled and invited her through the main door and into the living room with the large fireplace he had built last winter. They went into the kitchen where he made the drinks while she leaned against the high counter where he normally sat for his solitary meals. He poured four careful centimetres of Ricard into each tall glass, tossed in an ice cube and filled the glasses from a jug of cold water from the refrigerator. He handed one to Isabelle, raised his glass in salute, sipped and turned to work.

He unwrapped the beefsteak she had brought and made a swift marinade of red wine, mustard and garlic, salt and pepper. Then he took the flat of a cleaver and hammered the steaks until they were the thinness he liked, and put them in the marinade.

'Your own water?' she enquired.

'We put an electric pump in the well. It takes it up to a water tank and it tastes good, I had it tested. I said we. My friends from the town built this place more than I did – the plumbing, electricity, foundations, all the real stuff. I was just the unskilled labourer. Come on, there's not much more to see.'

He showed her his boot room by the door, where he kept the washing machine and an old sink, his boots and coats, fishing rod and gun, and the ammunition, all locked away. She hung her leather jacket on a spare hook and he showed her the big bedroom he had built and the smaller spare room that he used as a study. He watched her make a fast appraisal of the double bed with its plain white sheets and duvet, the bedside reading lamp and the shelf of books. A copy of *Le Soleil d'Austerlitz*, one of Max Gallo's histories of Napoleon, lay half open by the bed, and she moved closer to look at the other books. She ran a finger gently down the spine of his copy of Baudelaire's poems and turned to raise a speculative eyebrow at him. He half-smiled, half-shrugged, but said nothing, and kept silent when she turned to him again after studying the print of Douanier Rousseau's *Soir de Carneval* on the wall opposite the bed. He bit his lip when he saw her looking at the framed photographs he kept on the chest of drawers. There were a couple of happy scenes of tennis club dinners, one of him scoring a try at a rugby game, and a group photo of men in uniform around an armoured car, Bruno and Captain Félix Mangin with their arms around each other's shoulders. Then, inevitably, she focused on the photograph of Bruno, in uniform and laughing and lounging on an anonymous riverbank with a happy Katarina, pushing her long fair hair back from her usually sad eyes. It was the only picture he had of her. Isabelle said nothing but brushed past him and looked into the spartan bathroom.

'You're very neat,' she said. 'It's almost too clean for a bachelor.'

'That's only because you caught me on cleaning day,' he

grinned, spreading his hands in innocence. So now she knows there was a woman in my life, he thought. So what? It was a long time ago, and the ache had dulled.

'Where does Gigi sleep?'

'Outside. He's a hunting dog and supposed to be a watchdog.'

'What's that hole in the ceiling?'

'My next project, when I get round to it. I'm going to put a staircase and a couple of windows in the roof, and make an extra bedroom or two up there.'

'There's no TV,' she said.

'I have a radio,' he said flatly. 'Come and see the outside and I'll make a barbecue for the steak.'

She admired the workshop he had made at one end of the barn, the tools all hanging on a pegboard on the wall, and the jars of pâté and preserves standing in military ranks on the shelves. He showed her the chicken run, where a couple of geese had joined the descendants of Joe's original gift of chickens, and she counted the numbers of tomato plants and the rows of vegetables.

'Do you eat all that in a year?'

'A lot of it, and we have dinners and lunches down at the tennis club. Any extra I can always give away. I put some into cans for the winter.'

He picked up a stack of dried branches from last year's grapevine and stacked them in the brick barbecue, then he shook a bag of wood charcoal onto the top, thrust a sheet of old newspaper underneath and lit it. Back in the kitchen, he put plates, glasses and cutlery on a tray and opened her wine, a decent *cru bourgeois* from the Médoc. He opened the jar of venison pâté she had brought, put it on a plate with some cornichons and arranged the wedge of Brie on a wooden board.

'Let's eat outside,' he said, taking the tray. 'You can make the salad while I do the steak, but we have time to enjoy our drinks before the barbecue is ready.'

'There's no sign of a woman here,' Isabelle remarked, when they had sat down at the green plastic table on his terrace and were watching Gigi licking his lips in anticipation. The dog knew what it meant when the barbecue was lit.

'Not at the moment,' said Bruno.

'No woman, no TV, no pictures on your walls except photos of sports teams. No family photos, no pictures of adoring girlfriends, except that one when you were in the army. Your house is impeccable – and impersonal – and your books are all non-fiction. I deduce that you are a very self-controlled and organised man.'

'You haven't seen the inside of my car,' he smiled, deflecting her comment. 'It's a mess.'

'That's your public life, your work. This home is the private Bruno, and very anonymous it is, except for the books, and even they are classics, the kind of works you might expect to find in the house of an educated man.'

'I'm not an educated man,' he said. 'I left school at sixteen.'

'And went into the Army youth battalion,' she said. 'Yes, I know. And then into the combat engineers, and you did paratroop training and were promoted. You served in some special operations with the Legion in Africa before you went to Bosnia and won a medal for hauling some wounded men from a burning armoured car. They wanted to make you an officer but you refused. And then you were shot by a sniper when you were trying to stop some Serb paramilitaries from burning a Bosnian village, and they flew you back to France for treatment.'

'So – you've read my Army file. Did you make enquiries with the *Renseignements Généraux*?' Privately, he thought how little the official files really knew. He wondered if she had made the connection between the name of his captain in Bosnia, Félix Mangin, who wrote that approving report and carefully avoided explaining why Bruno had tried to save that particular Bosnian village, and the name of Mayor Mangin in St Denis.

Félix had been with him when they first found the ramshackle old motel that the Serbs had turned into a brothel for their troops, and had rescued the Bosnian women who had been forced to service them. Rescued them, then moved them into what was supposed to be a safe house in a secure Bosnian village and brought in *Médecins Sans Frontières* to treat the women and try to help them recover from the nightmare. No, the official files never had the full story, and dry prose never explained all the human decisions and accidents of life that made up reality.

'No, I did not ask for your file. J-J got hold of it on the day after the arrests at Lalinde when we realised that this was going to blow up into a political matter. It was routine, the kind of standard background check we'd do on anybody mixed up in something as sensitive as this. He showed it to me. I was impressed. I just hope my superiors write equally good things about me in my performance reviews,' she smiled. 'The *RG* files cover everything: credit cards, subscriptions, your surprisingly poor scores on the *Gendarmerie* pistol range given that your army file rated you as a marksman, your healthy savings account.'

'I'm not rich, but I don't have much to spend my salary on,' he said, as if that might explain something.

'Except in friends and reputation,' she said, and finished her Ricard. 'I am not here as a cop, Bruno, just as an amiable colleague who is far from home and with not much to do on the rare evening I get time off. I'm not probing, but naturally I'm curious about the woman in the photo.'

He said nothing. She picked up the wine and poured herself a glass, twirled it and sniffed.

'This is the wine J-J ordered when he took me to lunch when I first came down here,' she said. He nodded, still with most of his Ricard to finish.

'And what did J-J tell you to brief me about?' he asked, determined to shift the conversation back onto safe ground.

'He hasn't got very far. No fingerprints and no forensics that put the boy or the girl anywhere inside Hamid's cottage, nor any of the other young fascists we found at her house. They both deny knowing him or ever visiting him, and there's no blood on those daggers on her wall. So all we have so far is the drugs and the politics, and while we can convict the girl on the drugs, the boy was tied up. A lawyer can say that makes him non-complicit, and since he's under eighteen he counts as a juvenile.'

'That sex looked pretty consensual to me,' said Bruno.

'Yes,' she said briskly. 'I suppose it was, but that was the sex, which is not illegal, even for juveniles, and it's not evidence of drug use. We may have to release the boy. If it had been down to me and what I learned in Paris, I'd have put pressure on the boy through the girl. Call it a hunch, but I feel sure they have some involvement in the murder, even though there's no forensic evidence. She's certainly going down on drugs charges and the boy is evidently obsessed with her, keeps asking about her. We might have got an admission on the drugs out of him and used that as a lever to get some more information. But J-J does not play it that way, as you know.'

'Justice is alive and well and living in Pèrigord,' said Bruno drily. He glanced behind him at the embers. Not ready yet. He finished his Ricard and Isabelle poured him a glass of Médoc.

'There's one new development, from that patch of mud on the track that leads to the cottage,' she said. 'We took casts of the tyre prints, and there's one set that could match Jacqueline's car – except that they're Michelins, and they match thousands of cars on the road.'

'Yes, and the track leads to several houses.'

'True. And some ambitious young *Juge-magistrat* arrives from Paris on Monday to take over the case, at which point we simply become the investigators following the leads he chooses. My friends in Paris say there's some political jockeying over who gets the job, but so far J-J stays in charge of the case, probably because there's so little evidence. If we were close to proving anything, some Paris brigadier would have been down to take the credit. Now I'll make the salad.'

He rose to join her, turning on the terrace light as he passed. In the kitchen he took some slightly wilted lettuce from the refrigerator and pointed her to the olive oil and the wine vinegar. He put a pot of water on to boil and began to peel and slice some potatoes, then he flattened some cloves of garlic, took a frying pan and splashed in some oil. When the water boiled, he tipped in the sliced potatoes, aware that she was watching, and turned over his egg timer, a miniature hourglass, to blanch them for three minutes.

'When the timer goes, drain them, dry them on a bit of kitchen paper and fry them in the oil for a few minutes with the crushed garlic. Add salt and pepper – it's over there – and bring it all out,' he said. 'Thanks. I'll go and do the steaks.'

The embers were just right, a fine grey ash over the fierce red. He put the grill close to the coals, arranged the steaks, and then under his breath sang the *Marseillaise*, which he knew from long practice took him exactly forty-five seconds. He turned the steaks, dribbled some of the marinade on top of the charred side, and sang it again. This time he turned the steaks for ten seconds, pouring on more of the marinade, and then another ten seconds. Now he took them off the coals and put them on the plates he'd left to warm on the bricks that formed the side of the grill. Soon Isabelle appeared, the frying pan in one hand and the salad in the other, and he brought the steaks to the table.

'You waited,' she said. 'Another man would have come in to see that I was doing it *his* way.'

Bruno shrugged, handed her her plate and said, '*Bon appetit*.' She shared out the potatoes and left the salad in the bowl. Good. He liked to soak up the juices from the meat in his potatoes rather than mix them with the oil and vinegar of the salad.

'The potatoes are perfect,' he said.

'So is the steak.'

'There's one thing that nags at me,' said Bruno. 'I saw Richard's father, and somehow the boy knew that old Hamid had won the *Croix de Guerre*. Now unless you or J-J told him that during the questioning, I don't know how he would have known about it if he hadn't seen it on the wall or been in the cottage. Were you in on all the interrogation sessions?'

'No. J-J did that in Périgueux. But the sessions are all on tape so we can check. I don't think J-J would have tripped up like that. Is it something he could have heard at school from one of Hamid's relatives?'

'Possibly, but as I told you, he didn't get on too well with them. There was that fight in the playground.'

'Too long ago to mean much.' He watched with approval as she wiped the juices from her plate with a piece of bread and then helped herself to salad and cheese. 'That steak was just right.'

'Yes, well, the credit is all yours, and thank you for bringing dinner, and the wine.' He thought he ought to keep the conversation on the case, but there was not much new to say. 'The boy's father says he's absolutely sure Richard didn't do it.'

'What a surprise!' she said. 'Don't you have a candle, Bruno? With this electric light, I won't be able to see the stars, and they must be brilliant here.'

'I know the boy too, and I think the father may be right.' Bruno went into his boot room and brought out a small oil lamp. He took off the glass case, lit the wick, replaced the glass, and only then turned off the terrace light.

'That would mean we have no suspect at all,' she said. 'And the press and politicians baying at our heels.'

'Hang on a moment,' he said. He went into the house for a sweater, and came back with her leather jacket and his mobile phone. 'In case you get cold,' he said, giving her the jacket and thumbing in a number.

'Momu,' he said. 'Sorry to bother you, but it's Bruno. Something has come up in the case. You remember when young Richard had that fight in the playground and you had him home to dinner to teach him some manners and show him how French and normal you all were? You remember that?'

Isabelle watched Bruno as he spoke on the phone. Without looking in her direction, he knew that she was appraising him. The call ended, but he held the phone to his ear and delayed returning to the table, trying to fathom her intentions. He assumed that she liked him, and she was bored in St Denis just as she was bored in Périgueux. She probably thought he might make an amusing diversion. But she was out of her depth here in the country. Had this been Paris, she would have known the ways to signal whether or not she was ready to stay, but she was smart enough to understand that the social codes were different here, the mating rituals more stately, more hesitant. She would probably find that interesting in itself, to flirt a while with a stranger in this strange land they called *la France profonde*, deepest France, and probably eat some excellent meals along the way.

Bruno imagined her telling herself that the food alone would be worth the detour. Well, she would have to learn that he was nobody's temporary plaything. She would have to wait for the end of his phone call and then go back to her modest room in the *Hôtel de la Gare*, listen to the music on her iPod and muse about a man who grew his own food, built his own house, did not have a TV set, and wasn't even looking at her as he turned off his phone. A man who was very far from sure he even wanted a dalliance with a young woman as clearly clever and ambitious as Isabelle.

'Another dead end,' said Bruno. 'Momu – that's the son of the murdered man – had your chief suspect round to dinner when he was thirteen years old, and told him how proud the family was that his father had won the *Croix de Guerre* fighting for France. That's how Richard knew about the medal.' He sank down on his chair, and seemed to collect himself. 'Some coffee, Isabelle?'

'No thanks. I'd never sleep, and I have to get up early to make sure the murder book is up to date and check on those tyre tracks. J-J will be coming down tomorrow to make sure everything is in order for the guy from Paris.'

He nodded. 'By the way, there's some demonstration

being arranged for Monday at noon, a march of solidarity organised by our Communist councillor, but the Mayor will probably lead it. I don't expect many people, mainly schoolchildren.'

'I'll tell J-J, make sure the *RG* are there with their cameras,' she said, with a nervous laugh, and stood, suddenly hesitant, uncertain how best to take her departure. 'Just for the files,' she added. 'But I think we both know how much the official files can never know and explain.'

'Thank you for giving me such an unexpected and pleasant evening, and Gigi thanks for you for the dinner he's making from the scraps. I'll see you to your car.' He walked round the table, walked on past her to her car, and held open the car door for her. She kissed him briefly on both cheeks, but before she could close her door Gigi darted past Bruno's legs and put his paws on her thighs and licked her face. She gave a start, then laughed, and Bruno pulled his dog away.

'Thank you, Bruno,' she said sincerely. 'I enjoyed the evening. It's lovely here. I hope you'll let me come again.'

'Of course,' he said, with a kind of courteous neutrality that he knew she would find very hard to read. He wondered if she felt disappointed to be leaving. 'It would be my pleasure,' he added, and was surprised by the brilliant smile she gave him in return, a smile that seemed to transform her face.

Isabelle closed the door, started the engine and

reversed back down to the track. She turned, then looked in the mirror to see him standing there and waving farewell, Gigi at his knee. As the lights of her car disappeared he looked up and gazed at the great sweep of the stars twinkling in the black night above him.

## CHAPTER 14

After considerable thought while he washed the dishes from supper and fed Gigi what few scraps remained, Bruno concluded that, of all his friends, the Baron would be the most suitable partner to play mixed doubles with the mad Englishwoman and her friend. He caught himself; with Pamela and Christine. He said them aloud, enjoying the soft sounds they made, thinking they were names to be murmured in gentle intimacy. He liked both names, just as he liked the name Isabelle, another soft sibilant, to be breathed gently into a lover's ear. He dragged his thoughts back to the delicate question of a partner for the mixed doubles. The Baron was old enough to be reassuring, socially at ease, and a character, with a touch of eccentricity unusual in a Frenchman. It was a well-known fact, established in all French school textbooks, that the English liked eccentrics.

Bruno rather liked them too, and sometimes wished he had a touch more eccentricity himself. He relished the moments when he had stepped out of his placid and careful character and taken risks and sought adventure. He turned that word around in his mouth for a long moment: adventure – the word still inspired him. It still triggered boyhood dreams of travel to mysterious places and daring challenges, dreams of drama and passion of an intensity that a quiet country policeman seldom knew. But then he had become a country policeman because that kind of intensity had battered him so badly when he had tasted it in Bosnia. His hand strayed to the old scar just above his hip, and he felt again the sudden confusion of memories, of noise and flames, the world spinning as he fell, the glare of headlamps and blood on the snow. It was a sequence he could never get straight in his mind, the events and images all jumbled. Only the soundtrack remained clear – a symphony of helicopter blades in low rhythm against the counterpoint chatter of a machine gun, the slam of grenades, the squealing clatter of tank tracks. Bruno felt a kind of self-pity begin to steal over him and mentally shook himself for being so foolish, and so self-absorbed that he was almost forgetting the drama on his own doorstep. A country policeman seldom had to deal with murder, drugs and bizarre sex games all in a single week.

Having stacked the dishes carefully in their rack to drain and set out his cup, plate and knife for breakfast, he knelt to caress Gigi, who was snuffling amiably at his feet, hoping that perhaps not all the scraps from dinner had gone. He cradled the dog's head in his hands, scratching those soft spots behind its ears, then bent his own head so that their foreheads met and he made an affectionate noise deep in his throat, hearing its echo as his dog responded. There ought to be a word for that deep and loving sound a dog could make – had Gigi been a cat, Bruno would have said it purred – for this was not a growl, a word that carried a hint of menace. Gigi twisted his head to lick Bruno's face, clambering up so that his front paws rested on his master's shoulders, the better to lick his ears and nuzzle into his neck. Bruno relished the contact and the affection, and hugged his dog before patting its shoulders and getting to his feet. Time for bed, he told Gigi, for both of us.

What I am trying to do now is distract myself from the subject that really occupies my mind, Bruno admitted to himself as he led Gigi out to the kennel. He took a last attentive look at the fence around his hen house, and heard an owl hooting far off in the woods. He checked that nothing was left on the table and splashed water on the ashes in the barbecue. He knew he was trying to avoid the moment of introspection and self-doubt that was upon him. The fact was that he now deeply regretted his tame acceptance of Isabelle's departure.

Was that it, he asked himself, looking up to the great blaze of stars and the distant moving lights of airliners. Had he merely acquiesced in Isabelle's decision to return to her hotel, or had he, by his own timidity, given the impression that her company was not desired? A bolder Bruno would have taken her decisively in his arms under the night sky, and embarked on the great adventure of a new affair with a lithe and distinctly modern young woman of intelligence and ambition.

Come on, Bruno, he told himself as he brushed his teeth. Don't demean yourself or understate your value. You built your house with your own hands. You've taught yourself to be a gardener who can feed himself and his friends, and you've become a countryman who understands the feel of the soil and the rhythms of the seasons, and the old sweet ways of rural France. You're a man of duty and responsibility to yourself and your community. You've seen foreign lands, you've known love and war and wounds and battle, and that was more than enough adventure for anyone. Adventure meant risk and danger, and he'd seen his share of both. He would not willingly seek them out again. The sudden image of the bomb-shattered French light tank at Sarajevo airport flooded into his mind, the torn bodies of men he had trained with, eaten with, fought beside. That had been adventure, and praise be to *le bon Dieu* that it was over.

He picked up the photograph of himself with Katarina, taken in that glorious Bosnian summer not long after they had become lovers, and before the winter came with the snow that gave cover to the Serb raiding party and the sniper who had shot him. He had been a man of great vigour and passion then, and able to carry out the violent acts that were part of his duty. He put down the photograph and pulled out the thin volume of Baudelaire she had given him, opening it to read her inscription to him and to stare at her flowing signature. He could also hear her voice again, reading the poems aloud to him in that curiously liquid French that she had taught her schoolchildren before the war came. He was almost wholly glad those days were long gone but then, as he slipped between the cool sheets and turned out the light, he thought, you're also a man whose bed has been empty too long and who seems to have got out of the way of enticing attractive women into it.

Then a more cheerful idea emerged, as it usually did when he had been unduly hard on himself. He had recently met three attractive and unattached women. First, Isabelle, who in the absence of an obvious suspect would be here in St Denis for some time. Then there was Pamela the mad Englishwoman, who lived here and whom he found interesting. And there was her friend Christine, here only briefly but she seemed a forthright and enterprising woman, and was in some ways the prettiest of the three. And he would be playing tennis with them both tomorrow, with only his friend the Baron as rival for their company.

It promised to be entertaining. The Baron was an

inveterate competitor. He hated to lose, hated even more to lose to a woman, and above all could not abide losing to the English. And from what Bruno had seen of their play, Christine and Pamela were likely to trounce them on an unpredictable grass court. The silent struggle between the Baron's fury at defeat and his innate and chivalrous courtesy would be an entertainment in itself. With a smile of affection for his friend, and a glow of satisfaction at having steered his own thoughts from gloomy introspection into more agreeable paths, Bruno drifted into an untroubled sleep.

It was a lovely May morning as they drove in the Baron's big old Citroën up the track beside Yannick's house, past the turnoff to Hamid's lonely cottage, and over the rise to the beguiling setting of Pamela's farmhouse. The Baron slowed his car to a halt, and gazed at the scene in solemn approval, then climbed out to stand and take a longer look. Bruno opened his door and joined him, enjoying the Baron's reaction to the surroundings and pleased that it matched his own. They looked in silence, until a drumming noise came from behind them and they turned to see two horsewomen, their hair flowing free, cantering along the ridge towards them and spurring into a near gallop as they saw the car and the two men.

Unlike for Pamela's usual trips into town, there was no riding cap or neat black riding coat for this morning's ride. She was wearing a white shirt open at the neck, with a green silk scarf that flowed into her auburn hair, and some old trousers stuffed into her riding boots. The Baron let out a low whistle of appreciation that only Bruno could hear, and raised his hand in salute.

'We'll just be a moment, Bruno. And welcome to your friend,' called Pamela as she reined in her snorting brown mare to a quick trot. Christine rode on at speed, lifting a hand briefly in greeting before bending back over her horse's neck and racing on down the slope. Pamela gazed enviously after her, but turned back to shout, 'We'll take the saddles off and change and see you on the court. You can use the *cabane* by the swimming pool to change.'

Those last words almost disappeared into the wind as she took off again, cantering over the turf to follow Christine back towards the house, taking the long way round the back of the property rather than having to dismount and deal with gates and fences.

'Two handsome women riding fast on horseback. *Mon Dieu*, but that's a magnificent sight,' exclaimed the Baron, and Bruno knew that whatever happened on the tennis court, the day would be a success.

He had warned the Baron that the two women played in tennis dresses, so both men wore white shorts and T-shirts. It struck Bruno that their four white-clad figures looked almost formal as they met on the court and made introductions. The Baron bowed as he presented Pamela with a bottle of champagne 'to toast your victory, Mesdames'. She took it quickly to the *cabane*, where an ancient refrigerator purred noisily, and by the time she rejoined them, the Baron had invited Christine to be his partner and Bruno was sending forehands over the net to each of them in turn.

'It looks like you're stuck with me,' he said as Pamela came onto the court, bringing another can of tennis balls.

'I always prefer to have the law on my side, Bruno,' she smiled, and they began to knock up seriously, two balls in play, with Bruno sending his to Christine and the Baron playing with Pamela. The women played well and with careful control, placing each ball deep, and Bruno found himself responding in kind and getting into a rhythm of forehand after forehand. It was a satisfying routine after his more usual knock-up style that sent half the balls into the net.

The first set went with serve to four all, although Bruno had to fight back from fifteen-forty down. Pamela and Christine knew the court and the strange ways of grass, and used their experience to position themselves while Bruno and the Baron tired themselves scrambling to try and anticipate each wayward bounce. The women still looked cool and fresh and in control, while the men were mopping their brows and flapping the fronts of their shirts.

At set point, Bruno waited for the crucial serve, swaying gently on the balls of his feet, knowing the Baron's game well enough to expect a slice. But the Baron fooled him, serving a fast ball to his forehand, and Bruno played it down the line back to Christine. She returned it to him, and he played the same shot back to her from the baseline. The rhythm was back. Five strokes, six and then eight, and the rally was still going strong when Christine suddenly changed tactics and hit her next forehand hard to Pamela. She played it back to the Baron, and it was their turn to exchange strokes from the baseline. Then Pamela's sixth shot hit some oddity on the grass surface and the ball bounced high and wide. The Baron barely scrambled it back, saw it hit the top of the net and drop forlornly onto his side of the court. Game and set.

'What a magnificent rally,' called Pamela, with an enthusiasm so warm that Bruno could not think it quite genuine. 'Well done, Baron, and hard luck on that very unfair last bounce. I think you had us but for that.'

'I need a drink,' said Christine, running forward to shake Bruno's hand and then going back to kiss the Baron on both cheeks. 'And I need a shower,' laughed Pamela, 'and then a drink. And thank you for the game and that last rally. I can't think when I played a rally that lasted so long.'

Bruno admired the easy skill of the women in soothing bruised male egos. He and the Baron had been outplayed. Dripping with sweat, they looked as if they had been through a long hard game instead of a single set of mixed doubles. The Baron, usually grim faced and tight of lip when he had lost a game, was almost purring with pleasure at their attention.

'You'll find a shower and towels in the *cabane*,' Pamela told them. 'We'll take our showers inside and see you out here in ten minutes for the champagne. Meanwhile, there are bottles of water in the refrigerator. Help yourselves.'

Bruno mopped his neck with his towel, and put away his racquet as the Baron limped up smiling.

'What charming girls,' he said.

Bruno grinned a weary assent. They were indeed charming, and yes, they were also girlish, and if they could twist the cynical old Baron around their little fingers so easily, they were two very formidable women. After he had drunk a litre of water, showered and changed, he sauntered out to the table by the pool, where four champagne flutes and an ice bucket stood ready, beside a bottle of dark purple cassis. He looked discreetly at the label. It was a bottle of the real stuff from the Bourgogne, not the industrial blackcurrant juice they sold in supermarkets.

Pamela and Christine had changed into jeans and blouses when they reappeared carrying trays – with plates, knives and napkins on one, pâté, olives, cherry tomatoes and a fresh baguette on the other. The Baron uncorked his champagne, poured a splash of cassis into each glass and then filled them carefully with the wine.

'Next time, you must let me partner you, Bruno,' said

Christine. 'Unless the Baron would like to help me take our revenge.'

'I'm not changing a winning team,' laughed Pamela. 'I'll stick with Bruno.'

'We are at your disposal, ladies,' said the Baron. 'Perhaps we might invite you to play at our club tournament later this summer. You would do very well, partnering each other or in the mixed doubles.'

'Sorry, but I only have until the end of May,' said Christine. 'Then it's back to England to write up my research before the end of my sabbatical.'

'Perhaps we could tempt you back for a week or so in August,' the Baron persisted.

'No room at the inn, I'm afraid,' Christine said. 'Pamela lives for the rest of the year on renting out her place in the high season, and August is the busiest month.'

'Well, you now have lots of other friends you might stay with. My modest *chartreuse* is at your disposal, and since my daughters come down from Paris for the tournament, you would be well chaperoned.'

'*Chartreuse*?' enquired Pamela. 'I thought that was a charterhouse, where monks lived.'

'That is so, for monks of the Carthusian order. But it has also come to mean an isolated country house or manor, and in this part of the world it usually refers to a certain kind of building, rather long and thin, just one room deep and with a long corridor. Grander than a farmhouse, but not so grand as a chateau,' the Baron explained. 'It has been in my family for a long time.'

'That's very kind of you, but I don't think I shall be able to get away in August,' Christine said. 'I really have to get this book finished before the next academic year.'

'That reminds me,' said Bruno. 'You know something of the archives here and the local wartime history. How would I go about researching a soccer team in Marseilles, around 1939?'

'Start with the local newspapers, *le Marseillais* or *le Provençal*, or the sports paper, *l'Équipe*,' Christine said. 'Contact the local sports federation to see if they have any records. If you have the names of the players, or of the team, it should be quite straightforward.'

'I only have one player's name, but not the name of the team nor any other information. The team played in an amateur youth league, and won a championship in 1940 but I think their coach had been a professional player. I have his name, Villanova.'

'It could be a long search, Bruno,' Christine said. 'Regional papers like *le Marseillais* tend to keep microfiche records, but I'd be surprised if they have been digitised and so you can't do an electronic search. You may have to go through all the issues for 1940. But if they won a championship, that would probably be at the end of the season, in the springtime, March or April. You might try just looking for those months. Is this to do with that murder inquiry you refused to tell us about when you were last here? We saw the reports in *Sud-Ouest*.'

'Yes, poor old Hamid, as you know, was the victim, and nothing seems to have been taken except his wartime medal and this old photo, so I'm curious to see if it might shed some light on the affair. It's just a chance – he may have taken the things down from the wall himself or thrown them away. We might be following a false trail, but so far we don't have much to go on.'

'I thought I heard on Radio Périgord that some suspects had been detained, in Lalinde, was it not?' asked Pamela. 'They didn't give any names.'

'No, if they're under eighteen, they're juveniles and their names cannot be released. Some local youngsters involved in the *Front National* have been the subject of police inquiries, but so far there's no real evidence to connect them to Hamid's killing, or even to connect them with Hamid.'

'I don't know many young people around here,' said Pamela thoughtfully. 'Perhaps I should. Some of my guests here have teenage children and it might be a good thing to introduce them to some young locals. We did that a bit last summer with a young French couple who played tennis on the court here. Rick and Jackie, I think they were called.'

'Rick and Jackie?' Bruno said sharply. 'Could that have been Richard and Jacqueline?'

Pamela shrugged. 'I just knew them by those names. An attractive young couple, about sixteen or seventeen. She's a pretty thing, blonde hair, a very good tennis player. He's slim, maybe sixty kilos. I think he said his father is a doctor around here. Why? Do you know them?'

'How did you meet them, Pamela? And when was this, exactly?'

'They said they'd been walking in the woods and noticed my tennis court. They said they'd never played on grass before and asked if they could give it a try. I had an English family with some teenage children and they spent the afternoon playing tennis. They seemed very pleasant and polite, but I got the impression they had been courting pretty energetically in the woods, rather than just walking. It must have been late August, maybe early September last year. Rick and Jackie came two or three times. I think she had a car, but I haven't seen them this year.'

'You say they came out of the woods and down to your property. Which woods, exactly?'

'Those over that hill.' She pointed. 'Over towards Hamid's place. From the hill, you can see both my place and his.'

'Did they ever mention Hamid, or meet him, or see him here when he came to tell you how to prune your roses?'

'Not that I can recall.'

'When they came to visit you again, did they come the same way, from the woods?'

'No, they came up the road by car. I remember it well because she drove too fast and I had to tell her to slow down.'

'Did they go walking off into the woods again while they were here?'

'Yes, I think they did, teenage passion and all that. You're sounding very policeman-like and serious, Bruno. Do you think they could be connected to Hamid's murder?'

'I don't know, but it suggests that they may have known the old man, or seen him, or at least had the opportunity to do so, and other than that there is nothing to connect them with Hamid.'

'They didn't seem like *Front National* types. They weren't skinheads or thuggish in any way. They seemed pretty well educated and had good manners, always saying please and thank you. They even brought me some flowers once. They spoke quite a bit of English, got on well with the English kids. They were really very pleasant – I enjoyed meeting them.'

'Well, it may be nothing, but since we have so few leads, we have to follow them all. So I must say thank you for the game and get back to work. But I'd better stroll up to those woods and see whatever's to be seen before I go.'

'Can we come too?' asked Christine. 'I have never seen a real policeman at work.'

'I'm not a real policeman, not in that sense,' Bruno laughed. 'I won't be like your Sherlock Holmes with his memory for a hundred different kinds of cigar ash and his magnifying glass. I just want to take a look. Do come along if you like.'

It turned into a gentle Sunday stroll up to the top of the rise, perhaps a kilometre to the first thin trees. Another hundred metres through the woods and over the ridge line, and there was Hamid's cottage, five hundred metres or so away and the only building in sight. They walked along the fringe of the woods and found a small clearing of soft turf, sheltered and private but with a glorious view over the plateau – a perfect place for a romantic rendezvous in the open air, thought Bruno. He looked carefully around and found some old cigarette stubs and a broken wine glass under a bush. He would have to send the forensics team up here.

They walked back to Pamela's house mostly in silence, and quickly drank what was left of the champagne. Then the Baron and Bruno took their leave. The pleasant atmosphere after the tennis had become sombre. They made no plans to play together again, but Bruno decided he could always call. Now would not be a good time, not with the shadow of a neighbour's murder hanging over Pamela's house and the knowledge that the suspects had visited her, enjoyed her hospitality, and played on the same tennis court where they had spent such an agreeable morning.

CHAPTER 15

The *Juge-magistrat*, a dapper and visibly ambitious young Parisian named Lucien Tavernier who might just have reached the age of thirty, had arrived on the early morning flight down to Périgueux airport. Bruno took an instant dislike to the man when he noticed the predatory way he looked at Inspector Isabelle at the first meeting of the investigative team. It was just after eight a.m. and Isabelle had woken him with a phone call at midnight to say his presence would be required. Bruno had not wanted to go; he had a parade to organise for midday and he was not a member of the investigative team, but J-J had specially asked him to be there to explain the new evidence that put Richard Gelletreau and Jacqueline Courtemine in the vicinity of Hamid's cottage. Without Bruno's phone call to J-J on the previous day, Richard would already have been released.

'What he said is that he used to go to the woods to have sex, and he hadn't even noticed Hamid's cottage since he had other matters on his mind,' said J-J. With his hair awry and his shirt collar undone, he looked as if he'd barely slept as he gulped thirstily at the dreadful coffee they served at the police station. After one sip, Bruno had abandoned his plastic cup and was drinking bottled water instead. There was a bottle, a notepad, a pencil and a report on J-J's last interrogation sessions in front of each person at the conference table, except for Tavernier who had pushed these local courtesies aside.

'Neither Richard nor Jacqueline have any alibi for the afternoon of the killing except one another, and they claim to have been in bed at her house in Lalinde,' J-J went on. 'But we now know that she used her credit card to fill her car at a garage just outside St Denis at eleven forty in the morning. So first, they're both lying, and second, she at least could have been at the murder scene. This strengthens the evidence from the tyre tracks on the way to Hamid's cottage, and we're awaiting the forensic report on the cigarette butts and wine glass and the used condoms found in the woods. But there's still no clear evidence from the cottage itself to demonstrate that they ever went into the place. So far, it's only circumstantial evidence, but in my view it points clearly to them. They were in the vicinity, if not necessarily at the murder scene. I should add that we have no traces of blood on their clothes nor in her car. But I think we have enough cause to continue to detain them.'

'I agree. We have a clear political motive, and the opportunity, and they are lying – quite apart from the drugs,' said Tavernier briskly, looking at them all through his large and obviously expensive black spectacles. His equally expensive suit was black, as was his knitted silk tie, and he wore a shirt with thick purple and white stripes. He looked as if he were going to a funeral. Lined up neatly on the conference table before him were a black leather-bound notebook and a matching Mont Blanc pen, the slimmest cell phone that Bruno had ever seen, and a computer small enough to fit into his shirt pocket that seemed to deliver his e-mails. Phone and computer had come from discreet black leather pouches on his belt. To Bruno, Tavernier looked like an emissary from an advanced and probably hostile civilisation.

'That's quite a strong case,' Tavernier continued. 'We have no other suspects at all, and my Minister says it is clearly in the national interest that we resolve this case quickly. So if the forensic evidence from the woods places them there, I think we might be able to file formal charges – unless there are any objections?'

He looked severely around the table, as if daring any of those present to challenge him. J-J was pouring more coffee, Isabelle was quietly studying her notes. A police secretary was taking minutes. Another bright young thing from the Prefecture was nodding sagely, and the media specialist from Police HQ in Paris, a smart young woman with blonde streaks in her hair and sunglasses pushed back above her brow, raised a hand.

'I can schedule a press conference to announce the charges, but we'd better fix the timing to catch the eight p.m. news. Then we have the anti-racism demonstration in St Denis at noon. You'll want to be there, Lucien?'

'Have you confirmed that the Minister will be there?' he asked.

She shook her head. 'Just the Prefect and a couple of deputies from the National Assembly, so far. The Minister of Justice is stuck with meetings in Paris, but I'm awaiting a call from the Interior Ministry. The Minister has a speech in Bordeaux this evening, so there's a suggestion he might fly here first.'

'He will,' said Tavernier, a note of triumph in his voice at being first with the news. 'I just received an e-mail from a colleague in the Minister's office. He's flying into Bergerac and plans to be at the Mayor's office in St Denis at eleven thirty. I'd better be there.' He looked at J-J. 'You have a car and driver ready for me?' He turned to Isabelle with a smile. 'Perhaps this charming Inspector of yours?'

'An unmarked police car and a specialist gendarme driver are at your disposal for the length of your stay. Inspector Perrault will be engaged in other duties,' J-J replied, his tone studiously neutral. J-J had been bitter when he rang Bruno's mobile earlier in the morning, as Bruno was driving up from St Denis. The young hot-shot, as J-J called him, had only been *Juge-magistrat* for three months. The son of a senior Airbus executive who had been

184

at the *École Nationale d'Administration* at the same time as the new Minister of the Interior, young Lucien had gone straight from law school to work on the Minister's private staff for two years and was already on the executive committee of the youth wing of the Minister's political party. A glittering career evidently loomed. He would want this case prosecuted, tried and convicted with maximum dispatch and to his Minister's entire satisfaction.

'I'm heading back to St Denis after this meeting, so I could give you a lift,' offered Bruno.

Tavernier looked at him, the only person there wearing police uniform, as if not sure what Bruno was doing in his presence.

'And you are?'

'Benoît Courrèges, *Chef de Police* of St Denis. I'm attached to the inquiry at the request of the *Police Nationale*,' he replied.

'Ah yes, our worthy *garde-champêtre*,' Tavernier said, using the ancient term for the *Police Municipale*, dating back to the days when country constables had patrolled rural France on horseback. 'You people have cars now, do you?'

'The Commune of St Denis is larger than the city of Paris,' said Bruno. 'We need them. You're welcome to a ride. It might help your inquiries if I briefed you on the local background, and on some of the odd features about this case.'

'It looks very straightforward to me,' said Tavernier, picking up his little computer and flicking his thumb on a small knob as he studied the screen.

'Well, there's the question of the missing items, the military medal and the photograph of Hamid's old football team,' said Bruno. 'They disappeared from the wall of the cottage where they'd always been kept. It might be important to find out where they went or who took them.'

'Ah yes, our brave Arab's *Croix de Guerre*,' Tavernier said, still studying his screen. 'I see my minister is bringing some brass hats from the Defence Ministry with him.' He looked up and focused on Bruno and, adopting a patient and kindly tone as if he were addressing someone of limited intelligence, said, 'It's the *Croix de Guerre* that persuades me that we have the right suspects. These young fascists from the *Front National* would detest the idea of an Arab being a hero of France. They probably threw it away in a river somewhere.'

'But why take the photo of the old football team?' Bruno persisted.

'Who knows how these little Nazis think,' Tavernier said airily. 'A souvenir, perhaps, or just something else they wanted to destroy.'

'If it were a souvenir, they'd have kept it and we'd have found it by now,' said J-J.

'I'm sure you would,' drawled Tavernier. 'Now, when do

we get the forensic report on that little love nest in the woods?'

'They promise to have it by the end of today,' said Isabelle.

'Ah yes, Inspector Perrault,' said Tavernier, turning to give her a wide smile. 'How do *you* feel about our two prime suspects? Any doubts?'

'Well, I haven't attended all the questioning, but they look very strong candidates to me,' Isabelle said firmly, looking directly at Tavernier. Bruno felt a small bud of jealousy begin to uncurl inside him. Isabelle would not have a difficult choice to make between a lowly country cop and a glittering scion of the Parisian establishment. 'Naturally I'd like some firm evidence, or a confession, I'm sure we all would. They both come from backgrounds that can afford good lawyers, so the more evidence we have, the better. And maybe we should also be looking hard at those thugs from the *Service d'Ordre*, the security squad of the *Front National*. They are no strangers to violence. But again, we need evidence.'

'Quite right,' said Tavernier with enthusiasm. 'That's why I'd like the forensics people to take a second look at the murder scene and at the clothes and belongings of our two suspects. Could you arrange that please, Mademoiselle? Now that they know what they are looking for, the forensics types might come up with something that puts them at the killing ground. Wouldn't that calm your doubts about circumstantial evidence, Superintendent? Or would you like me to call down some experts from Paris?'

J-J nodded. 'Some of my doubts, yes it would. But our forensics team is very competent. I doubt that they'll have missed anything.'

'You have other doubts?' Tavernier's question was silkily put, but there was irritation behind it.

'I don't quite get the motive,' J-J said. 'I see the obvious political motive, but why kill this Arab, at this particular time, in this particular way, tying up and butchering the old man as if he were a pig?'

'Why kill this one? Because he was there,' said Tavernier. 'Because he was alone and isolated and too old to put up much resistance and it was a remote and safe place to commit this ritual slaughter. Look at your Nazi psychology, Superintendent. And then they took his medal to demonstrate that their victim was not really French at all. Yes, I think I have their measure. Now it's time for me to question these two young fascists myself. I'll have what, two hours with them before I have to leave for this little town called – what is it? – ah yes, St Denis. Not the prettiest or most unusual of names, but I'm quite sure the Minister and I shall both be thoroughly charmed.'

J-J's office was in spartan contrast to the man. J-J was overweight and looked scruffy inside his crumpled suit, but his desk was clean, his books and documents all neatly filed, and his newspaper precisely aligned with the edges of the low table where they sat, drinking some decent coffee that Isabelle had made in her own adjoining room. J-J had kicked off his shoes and smoothed his hair, and was riffling through a slim file that Isabelle had brought him. She looked cool and very efficient in a dark trouser suit with a red scarf at her neck, and what looked like expensive and surprisingly elegant black training shoes with flat heels and laces. She looked at Bruno levelly, with a very faint and disinterested smile, and he felt a touch of embarrassment at the fantasies of her he had conjured up after she left his cottage.

'There's something odd about this military record of the victim,' said J-J. 'It says he came onto the strength of the First French Army for pay and rations on 28 August 1944, listed as a member of the *Commandos d'Afrique*. That unit was part of something called Romeo Force, who had taken part in the initial landings in southern France on 14 August 1944, and they seized a place called Cap Nègre. Our man is not, apparently, listed as a member of the original assault force for the invasion. He just appears on the strength, out of nowhere, on 28 August at a place called Brignolles.'

'I called the military archives and spoke to one of the resident staff,' Isabelle took up the story. 'He told me that it wasn't uncommon for members of Resistance groups to join up with the French forces and stay with them throughout the war. The *Commandos d'Afrique* were a Colonial Army unit, originally from Algeria, and most of the rank and file were Algerians. They'd taken heavy casualties at a place called Draguignan, and were keen to bring their numbers back up to strength with local Resistance volunteers. Since our Hamid was Algerian, he was signed up and stayed with them for the rest of the war. In the fighting in the Vosges mountains in the winter, he was promoted to corporal, where he was wounded and spent two months in hospital. And then, when they got into Germany, he was promoted to sergeant in April of 1945, just before the German surrender.'

'And he stayed in the Army after the war?' Bruno asked.

'Indeed he did,' said J-J, reading from the file. 'He transferred to the twelfth regiment of the *Chasseurs d'Afrique*, with whom he served in Vietnam, where he won his *Croix de Guerre* in the failed attempt to rescue the garrison at Dien Bien Phu. His unit was then posted to Algeria until the war ended in 1962 and the *Chasseurs d'Afrique* were wound up. But before that, along with some of the other long-serving sergeants and warrant officers, he was transferred to the training battalion of the regular *Chasseurs*, where he remained until he was demobilised in 1975 after thirty-five years' service. He was hired as a caretaker at the military college at Soissons after one of his old officers became the commander.'

'So what's so strange about it, J-J?' Bruno asked.

'We can't find any trace of him in the Resistance groups around Toulon, where he was supposed to be before joining the Commandos. Isabelle checked with the Resistance records. Since it was useful after the war to be able to claim a fighting record in the Resistance, most of the unit lists were pretty thorough. And there's no Hamid al-Bakr.'

'It might not mean much,' Isabelle said. 'There aren't many Arab names in any of the Resistance groups – and not many Spanish names either, although Spanish refugees from their civil war played a big part in the Resistance. But the records for the two main groups, the *Armée Secrète* and the *Franc-Tireurs et Partisans*, tend to be fairly reliable. He could have been in another group or he may have slipped through the net. He might even have used another name in the Resistance – it wasn't uncommon.'

'It just nags at me a bit, like a loose tooth,' said J-J. 'Once Hamid was in the Army, the records are impeccable, but we can't track him before that. It's as if he just turned up out of nowhere.'

'Wartime,' Bruno shrugged. 'An invasion, bombing, records get lost or destroyed. And I can tell you one thing from my own military service. The official records may all look very neat and complete because that's how they have to be and how the company clerks file them. But a lot of the paperwork is pure invention, or just making sure the books balance and the numbers add up. What we know is that he served for thirty-five years and fought in three wars. His offi-cers respected him enough to take care of him and he was a good soldier.'

'Yes, I know all that,' said J-J. 'So Isabelle tried to look back a bit further.'

'We asked the Marseilles and Toulon police to run a check, but there's not much left of the files before 1944 and they had nothing,' Isabelle said. 'The date and place of birth that he listed in Army records was back in Oran in Algeria on 14 July 1923. The chap at the archives said a lot of the Algerian troops listed that birth date because they didn't know their real birthday and that was the easiest date to remember. Birth registers for Algerians were pretty hit and miss in those days, even if we could get access to the Algerian records. And we don't have a date for his arrival in France. As far as we can tell, he had no official existence until he turns up with the *Commandos d'Afrique*.'

'I've been pushing this because I'm not sure about our two suspects,' said J-J. 'I talked with each of them sepa-rately for a long time, and I just don't feel confident that they did it. Call it a hunch. So I had Isabelle check back into Hamid's history to see if there were any clues there that might open other possibilities.'

'Tavernier seems happy to go ahead and press charges,' Bruno said.

'Yes, and I'm not comfortable with that, not with the evidence we have so far,' said J-J.

'As I said in the meeting, I'd also like more evidence,' said Isabelle.

'That makes three of us,' said Bruno, 'but there doesn't seem to be much other evidence of any kind, either to incriminate them or to steer us anywhere else.'

'See if you can get anything more on our mystery man from his own family. He must have told them something about his childhood and growing up,' said J-J. 'Otherwise, we're stuck.'

CHAPTER 16

The Mayor was quietly furious. Less than an hour remained before the event began and two of his most reliable standard bearers had decided they would boycott it. This was bad enough, but it was the first time in living memory they had turned him down, which made it even worse. To reject a mayoral request in St Denis was unheard of, and to decline his invitation when a Minister of the Republic and two generals were to grace the town's proceedings was close to revolution.

'You'll have to carry the flag of France, Bruno,' the Mayor said testily. 'Old Bachelot and Jean-Pierre refuse to take part in your little ceremony. They made it quite clear that they don't approve of Muslims, Algerians or immigrants in general and do not intend to honour them.'

Bruno noted the 'your'. If his idea of making the anti-racism march into a patriotic commemoration of a French war veteran went wrong, it would be his fault.

'What will Montsouris be carrying?' Bruno asked. 'We

can't have the red flag since there is no sign that Hamid had any politics at all, least of all Communist.'

'I think he's planning an Algerian flag,' said the Mayor, sounding rather tired of it all. 'You know we have the Interior Minister coming with a couple of generals? I've already had to do two interviews this morning, including a long one with France-Inter, and there's a woman from *Le Monde* who wants to see me this afternoon. The only one staying in town is a chap from *Libération*, who probably can't afford to join the rest of them at the *Vieux Logis*. Funny how these media types always seem to sniff out the best hotels to stay at. All this attention, of the worst possible kind. I don't like it all, Bruno. And now you say the *Juge-magistrat* seems convinced that young Richard is going to be formally charged with murder?'

'Tavernier is his name, very modern, very go-ahead, very determined,' said Bruno. 'And very well connected.'

'Yes, I think I knew his father from the *Polytechnique*.' Bruno was not much surprised. The Mayor seemed to know everybody who mattered in Paris. 'And his mother wrote one of those dreadful books about the New Woman when feminism was all the fashion. I'll be interested to see how the boy turned out. Now you'd better go and make sure that everything is organised for midday. We don't want chaos in front of all these media types. Quiet and dignified, that's the style.'

Outside in the town square, two TV cameras were taking

shots of the *Mairie* and the bridge, and a knot of what Bruno assumed were reporters had taken over two outdoor tables at Fauquet's café, all interviewing each other. At the bar inside were some burly men drinking beer, probably Montsouris's friends from the trade union. Bruno waved away a reporter who thrust a tape recorder towards him as he climbed into his van, and drove off to the college where the march was to begin, noting some coaches parked in the lot in front of the bank. Montsouris must have organised a bigger turnout than expected.

Rollo had half the school lined up in the courtyard already, some of them leaning on homemade placards that said 'No to Racism' and 'France Belongs to All of Us'. Rollo wore a small button in his lapel that read *Touche Pas à Mon Pote*, Hands Off My Buddy, a slogan that Bruno vaguely recalled from some other anti-racist movement of twenty years ago. Some of his tennis pupils called out '*Bonjour*, Bruno' and he waved at them as they stood in line, chatting and looking reasonably well-behaved and soberly dressed for a bunch of teenagers. Or perhaps they were intimidated by the presence of the entire St Denis rugby squad, both the first and the A team, about thirty big lads in uniform tracksuits who were there for Karim's sake, and as a guarantee against trouble.

Bruno looked around, but there was no sign of Montsouris, the man who had come up with this idea of the solidarity march. He would probably be in the bar with his friends from the union, but Montsouris's dragon of a wife was there in the schoolyard with Momu, and Ahmed from the Public Works, carrying a large Algerian flag. Just about all the immigrant families in town had turned out, and to Bruno's surprise, several of the women were wearing head scarves, something he had not seen before. He supposed it was a symbol of solidarity for the march. He hoped it was no more than that.

'We'll leave here at eleven forty, and that'll get us to the *Mairie* in time for midday,' said Rollo. 'It's all arranged. Ten or fifteen minutes for a couple of speeches and then we march to the war memorial with the town band, which gives us time to give the children lunch before classes start again this afternoon.'

'There may be more speeches than we expected. The Minister of the Interior is turning up, and with all these TV cameras he'll certainly want to say a few words,' said Bruno. 'And you'll have to carry the *tricolore*. Bachelot and Jean-Pierre have decided to boycott the event since they have apparently developed rather strong feelings about immigrants.'

'The bastards,' snapped Madame Montsouris, who had somewhere found a rather small flag that Bruno assumed was the national emblem of Algeria. 'And that bastard Minister of the Interior. He's as bad as the *Front National*. What right does he have to be here? Who invited him?'

'I think it was arranged with the Mayor,' Bruno told her

calmly, 'but the programme does not change. We want an orderly commemoration of an old war hero, along with a show of solidarity with our neighbours against racism and violence. Quiet and dignified, the Mayor says.'

'We want a stronger statement than that.' Madame Montsouris spoke again, loudly now so that the other teachers and schoolchildren could hear her. 'We have to stop this racist violence now, once and for all, and make it clear that there's no place for fascist murderers round here.'

'Save it for the speeches,' Bruno said. He turned to Momu. 'Where's Karim? He ought to be here by now.'

'On his way,' said Momu. 'He's borrowing a *Croix de Guerre* from old Colonel Duclos so he can carry the medal on a cushion at the war memorial. He'll be here in a moment.'

'Don't worry, Bruno,' said Rollo. 'We're all here and everything's under control. We'll start as soon as Karim arrives.'

And no sooner had he said it than Karim's little Citroën turned into the parking lot in front of the college and he came out in his rugby club tracksuit, holding a velvet cushion in one hand and brandishing the small bronze medal in the other. Rollo formed them up, Momu and Karim and the family at the front with half a dozen of the rugby team, and then the school students in columns of three, each class led by a teacher and all flanked by the rest of the rugby team. Rollo shepherded a schoolboy with a small drum on a sash around his neck into the column beside him, and the lad started to beat out the cadence of a march with single taps of his drumstick.

Bruno stood back to let them get started and then went out to the main road to stop traffic. They made, he thought, a brave and dignified parade, until Montsouris's wife produced a bullhorn from her bag and began chanting 'No to racism, no to fascism.' Fine sentiments, but not quite the tone that had been planned. He was about to intervene when he saw Momu step back to have a word with her. She stopped her chanting and put the bullhorn away.

Two TV cameras were filming them as they marched along the Rue de la République, past the supermarket and the Farmers' Co-op, past the big branch of the Crédit Agricole and over the bridge, lined on both sides with townspeople, to the town square and the *Mairie*. There, the Mayor and some other dignitaries stood waiting on the low platform that was normally used for the music festival. With irritation, Bruno noticed that the town's small force of gendarmes was lined up with Captain Duroc in front of the podium. He had asked Duroc to post his men in twos at different spots around the square as a precaution. As the church bells began to ring out noon, the siren on top of the *Mairie* sounded, and the entire parade squeezed into the remaining space. There was already quite a crowd, the bar was empty, and a third TV camera had joined the media group. The siren faded away and the Mayor stepped forward.

'Citizens of St Denis, *Monsieur le Ministre, mes Généraux*, friends and neighbours,' the Mayor began, his practised politician's voice carrying easily over the square. 'We are here to show our sympathy with the family of our local teacher Mohammed al-Bakr at the tragic death of his father Hamid. We are here to give salute to Hamid as a fellow citizen, as a neighbour, and as a war hero who fought for our dear native land. We all know the heavy circumstances of his death, and the forces of order are working tirelessly to bring justice to his family, just as we in our community are here to show our revulsion against all forms of racism and hatred of others for their origin or their religion. And now I have the honour to present Monsieur the Minister of the Interior, who has joined us today to bring the condolences and support of our government.'

'Send the Muslim bastards back where they came from,' came a shout from somewhere at the back, and everybody turned to look as the Minister stood uncertainly at the microphone. Bruno began to move through the crowd, looking for whichever idiot had called out.

'Send them back! Send them back! Send them back!' The chant began and with a sinking heart Bruno saw three flags of the *Front National* lift themselves from the crowd and began to wave. *Putain!* Those coaches he'd seen were not Montsouris's union friends at all. He felt a flurry at both sides of him and two knots of rugby men with Karim at their head began pushing their way through towards the flags.

Then came a howl from a bullhorn and another amplified chant began of 'Arabs go home! Arabs go home!' Montsouris's wife joined in with her own bullhorn calling 'No to Racism!' and the first volley of rotten fruit, eggs and vegetables began sailing through the air towards the stage. This has been well organised, thought Bruno grimly. He had seen three coaches in the car park, say thirty or forty men in each, so there were probably as many as a hundred of them here – and only thirty lads from the rugby club and a handful of Montsouris's union toughs to stop them. This could be very nasty, and all on national television. One of the *Front National* flags went down as the rugby men reached it, and groups of men began punching each other as women started to scream and run away.

Bruno stopped. There was not much a lone policeman could do here. He began pushing his way back towards the stage. His priority now was to get the schoolchildren clear. He'd leave the gendarmes to look after the dignitaries. A sudden charge by some burly men, Montsouris among them, nearly knocked him down, and as he scrambled for balance, a cabbage hit the back of his head and knocked his cap off. Quickly he bent to grab it, otherwise the schoolchildren might not know who he was. Shaking his head to clear it, he found Rollo already trying to steer the children into the shelter of the covered market. A handful of the older boys slipped aside and joined in the charge against the groups of *Front National* supporters.

Amplified howls of 'Send them back! Send them back!' fought bullhorn slogans of 'No to racism! No to fascism!' as the dignitaries put their hands over their heads against the volleys of tomatoes, and scampered into the *Mairie* past a protective gauntlet of otherwise useless gendarmes. Captain Duroc went into the *Mairie* with the Mayor, the Minister and the two generals, the gold braid of whose dress uniforms looked the worse for the barrage of old fruit and eggshells.

They managed to get the schoolchildren into the market. Shouting to making himself heard over the din of shouting protestors, Bruno told Rollo and Momu to get the youngest children into the café and tell old Fauquet to make sure the door was locked and the shutters down; then to call the *pompiers* and tell them to get their engines into the square now, with their sirens going and their water hoses ready to send out some high pressure jets to clear the area.

Bruno took in the scene around him. In the confused melee in front of the hotel, flags and placards were being turned into clubs and lances. Another smaller fight was under way beside the steps that led to the old town, and a group of St Denis women, Pamela and Christine among them, were trying to get away up the steps as some skinheads grabbed at them. The crowd was thinning and Bruno pushed his way through, seizing the first of the thugs by the collar, kicking his feet from under him and shoving him into the legs of two of his cronies. That made enough space for himself to reach the foot of the steps and get between the thugs and the women.

'Get away, get out of here!' he shouted at the women as the thugs closed in, trying to grab him. He felt the old training come back, his body moving automatically into a fighting stance, his eyes scanning the scene for threats and targets. He dropped his arms, ducked and rammed his head into the stomach of his nearest assailant, seized the leg of another and pulled him off balance, and then thumped his fist into the throat of the next, who sank to his knees, choking.

That stopped the first rush, and suddenly time began to move slowly and the instincts that had been drilled into him took over. A fierce joy began to grip him, the adrenalin of combat, the self-confidence of a man trained for battle. Now was the time to attack, when they had lost their momentum. Bracing himself on the steps, he jumped at one youth who was brandishing a length of wood, with a *Front National* poster attached, as thought it were a spear. He slammed the heel of one hand into the base of the youth's nose, then pirouetted to ram a vicious elbow into the solar plexus of another. He used the turn to kick yet another on the side of his knee and he was back at the base of the steps, three men down before him.

One of the women stepped up beside Bruno and deliberately kicked the choking skinhead in the testicles. Surprised, he registered that it was Pamela, who was drawing back her foot to do it again. He stretched out his arms to hold her back and keep the thugs away from the rest of the women when he felt a thudding blow on the side of his face. Then he was punched hard in the kidneys and kicked in the knee and someone else was hauling on his ankle. He knew that the first rule of brawling was to stay on your feet, but he was dazed and he felt himself start to go down. He forced himself to turn, to brace his arm against the stone wall, but someone was holding tight onto his leg and two more were coming at him. He flailed at the first one and stamped hard on the man holding his leg, hauling hard on his hair, and the grip on his ankle slackened. But there were too many ...

And then something extraordinary happened: a whirlwind appeared. It was a slim, slight whirlwind, but one that knew martial arts and leaped into the air, kicking out one lethal foot aimed straight at the belly of the man in front of Bruno. The whirlwind dropped, pirouetted and launched a second high kick into the throat of another thug, and then landed and delivered two hard, short punches to the nose of the man holding Bruno's ankle. Suddenly free to move, he turned to where the first blow to his head had come from and saw a middle-aged stranger backing away from the whirlwind with his hands in the air. Bruno grabbed an arm and twirled the man, seizing the back of his jacket and hauling it upwards to imprison his arms, then tripped him and planted his boot hard on the back of his prisoner's neck. Suddenly a great calm seemed to settle over him, even as the bullhorns continued to roar out their warring battle cries. The women were disappearing up the steps and, in front of him, the whirlwind had stopped fighting. At which point he saw with profound admiration that it was Inspector Isabelle.

'Thank you,' he said. She smiled and nodded and darted off to the brawl still under way in front of the hotel. Bruno released his foot from his prisoner. The man groaned, shook his head and began to crawl away. Bruno ignored him.

He almost followed Isabelle, but stopped himself. He climbed the steps to get a clearer view, and saw what he had to do next. He trotted back to the small squad of gendarmes dithering outside the *Mairie*. As he heard the sound of windows being smashed he shouted, 'Follow me – and start blowing your whistles,' although he was not entirely sure where he would lead them.

The *Front National* bullhorn seemed to be near the tossing

flags, just in front of the hotel, and that was where he headed. Four or five men were down on the cobbles, and a few dozen were still milling around, but the rugby men knew what they were doing. They had organised themselves into pairs, and fought back to back. Karim had picked up a heavy metal litter bin, which he raised over his head and threw with force into the knot of men guarding the *Front National* flags. The 'Send them back!' bullhorn seemed to hiccup in pain and stopped transmitting. Then Bruno led the gendarmes into the resulting confusion and started handcuffing the ones on the ground. All of a sudden, it appeared to be over. Men were still running, but running away.

Bruno shouted to the burliest of the gendarmes, a decent man he had known for years. 'Jean-Luc! There are three coaches in the bank car park. Go and immobilise them – that's what these bastards came in and that's how they'll try to get out. Take a couple of your mates with you and handcuff the drivers if you have to – or get some cars to form a blockade to keep the coaches in.'

Then the fire trucks arrived, two of them taking up most of the square, and the *pompiers* climbed out and began to help. The first casualty they found was Ahmed, their fellow volunteer fireman. He was unconscious, his face bloodied from a smashed nose, and one of his front teeth was kicked in. A smaller red command truck then screeched to a halt beside Bruno, its siren wailing, and

Morisot, the professional fireman who ran the local station, asked Bruno what his men could do.

'Start with first aid for those who need it, then round up anyone you don't recognise and lock them in your truck,' Bruno instructed. 'We'll sort it all out later at the *Gendarmerie*.'

Then he bent to check on young Roussel, a fast winger on the rugby team but too slim and small for this kind of punch-up. He was dazed and winded and would have a magnificent black eye, but was okay. Beside him, Lespinasse the prop forward, short and squat and tough as they come, was on his knees and retching. 'Bastards kicked me in the balls,' he grunted. Suddenly a TV camera and a microphone were in Bruno's face, and a concerned voice asked him what was happening.

Before he could think, and probably from sheer relief that none of his people had been seriously hurt, Bruno said angrily, 'We were attacked in our home town by a bunch of outside extremists. That's what happened.'

He took a breath and calmed himself, half-remembering some tedious lecture on media relations at the Police Academy, which taught that the most important thing was to get your side of the story out first because that would define the subsequent coverage.

'We were holding a quiet and peaceful parade and a meeting at the war memorial to commemorate a dead war hero and these swines began chanting racist taunts and throwing missiles and beating people up,' he said. 'It was mainly schoolchildren gathered here in our town square, but these extremists didn't seem to care. They had organised this attack. They hired coaches to get here and brought their banners and bullhorns and they came with one intention – to wreck our town and our parade. But they didn't reckon with the people of St Denis.'

'What about casualties?' came the next question, another camera this time.

'We are still counting.'

'What about your own injuries?' he was asked. 'That blood all over your face?'

He put his hand to his face and it did indeed come away bloody. '*Mon Dieu*,' he exclaimed. 'I hadn't noticed.'

The cameras turned away as an ambulance blared its way into the square. In front of the smashed plate glass window of the *Hôtel St Denis*, Doctor Gelletreau was kneeling beside one of the prone bodies.

'A couple of broken legs, a cracked collar bone and a few broken noses. Nothing much worse than a good rugby match,' Gelletreau said.

Bruno looked around his town square. He saw fire engines and ambulances, broken windows, cobbles littered with smashed fruit, eggs and vegetables – and frightened young faces peering from behind the stone pillars of the market. He glanced up to the windows of the *Mairie* and spotted some shadowed faces peering out from the banqueting chamber. So much for today's lunch, he thought, and began organising the transfer of those arrested over to the *Gendarmerie*. Bloody Duroc, thought Bruno; this is *his* job.

## CHAPTER 17

Dougal, Bruno's Scottish chum from the tennis club, never usually interfered in the official business of St Denis, even though the Mayor had twice asked him to join his list of candidates for election to the local council. After selling his own small construction company in Glasgow and taking early retirement in St Denis, Dougal had become bored and started a company called Delightful Dordogne that specialised in renting out houses and *gîtes* to tourists in the high season. A lot of the foreign residents had signed up with him, taking their own holidays away elsewhere in July and August and showing a handsome profit from the tenants to whom Dougal rented their homes. With the handymen, cleaners, gardeners and swimming pool maintenance staff that he hired to service the holiday homes, Dougal had become a significant local employer. Bruno thought it made sense, with so many foreigners moving into the district, to have one of them on the council to represent their views. Dougal had always declined, pleading that he was too busy and his

French too flawed, but the day after the disturbances he was in the council chamber with the rest of the delegation of local businessmen. Speaking an angry but serviceable French, he explained how bad the TV news reports of the previous evening had been.

'I've had three cancellations today, all from good and regular customers, and I'm expecting more. It even made the English papers. Look at this,' he said, and tossed a stack of newspapers onto the table. Everybody had already seen the headlines, and photos of the riot in the town square, but Bruno winced as Dougal brandished the copy of *Sud-Ouest* with Bruno's picture on the front page. He had been photographed standing with his arms outstretched to protect two cowering women from a group of attackers, and the headline read 'St Denis – the front line'. It was the moment when he had tried to shelter Pamela and Christine and the other women, just before he had been struck down. The photo should have been of Isabelle, he thought. She had been the real heroine.

'All credit to you, Bruno, you did a great job, but this is very bad for business,' Dougal said. And the rest of them chimed in. Everybody was worried about the coming season: the hotel, the restaurants, the camp sites, the amusement park manager.

'How long is this going to go on?' demanded Jerome, who ran the small theme park of French history where Joan of Arc was burned at the stake twice a day and Marie

Antoinette was guillotined every hour, with medieval jousting in between. 'It is up to the police to end this quickly, arrest somebody and get it over with. This business of interviewing suspects with no real result is going to spark more trouble from the right and more counter-demonstrations from the left and more bad publicity on TV. It will just ruin our season.'

'We all know that and we all agree. But what do you propose we do about it?' the Mayor asked. 'We can't ban all demonstrations, that's against the law, and as a town council we have no authority to intervene with the judicial authorities. There's been a hideous racist murder and passions have been aroused on both left and right. We've been assigned extra gendarmes to keep order and we have over forty people charged with riot and assault, so they're unlikely to bother us again. This is an isolated event. It may well hurt our business this year, but the effects won't last. We just have to grit our teeth and wait this process out.'

'I'm not sure I'll still be in business next year,' said gloomy Franc Duhamel from the camp site. He said this every year, but this time he might be proved right. 'I borrowed a lot of money from the bank to finance that big expansion and the new swimming pool, and if I have a bad season I'm in real trouble. If it hadn't been for that group booking by the Dutch lads who came down for the Motor-Cross Rally, I'd have been in trouble already.' Bruno nodded, recalling the traffic chaos the event had caused the weekend before Hamid's murder, with hundreds of motorbikes and supporters filling the town and surrounding roads.

'I've talked to the regional managers of the banks,' said the Mayor. 'They understand that this is a temporary problem, and they won't be closing anybody down – not if they want to get any business from this Commune again. And not unless they want to make an enemy of the Minister of the Interior. You all saw the report of his speech last night, about the whole of France standing firmly with the brave citizens of St Denis and our stout policeman.'

Bruno felt himself squirm. The politician had just been trying to put the best possible face on what had for him been a humiliation, shouted down from speaking and pelted with fruit and eggs. To be seen on TV presiding helplessly over a riot was not a good image for a Minister of the Interior, so naturally he had tried to spin it differently in his scheduled speech in Bordeaux. Bruno doubted very much that he would lift a finger to help any troubled businessman falling behind on his bank loans. He would never be able to hear of St Denis again without an instinctive shiver of distaste. But such assurances were what the businessmen needed to hear from their Mayor, and Bruno told himself he should be sufficiently astute to understand that by now.

'What we want is a breathing space,' said Philippe, the

manager of the *Hôtel St Denis*, who usually acted as spokesman for the town's business community. 'We need some temporary tax relief for this year to help us get through this bad patch. We know taxes have to be paid, but we want the council to agree to give us some time, so that rather than pay in June, we agree to pay in October when the season is over and we can show you our books. If we go down, the whole town goes down, so we see this as a sort of investment by the town in its own future.'

'That's a useful idea,' said the Mayor. 'I'll put it to the council, but we'll probably need to be sure such a delay would be legal.'

'The other thing on our minds is that new head of the gendarmes,' said Duhamel. 'He was useless, totally useless. If it hadn't been for Bruno taking charge it could have been a lot worse. We'd like you to ask for *Capitaine* Duroc to be transferred. Nobody in town has any respect for him after yesterday.'

'I'm not sure that's fair,' said Bruno. He had felt a great deal better about Duroc when he arrived at the bank car park after the riot and saw the three coaches blocked by a dozen gendarme motorbikes, a burly cop standing guard at each door, and the lanky Captain taking the names and addresses of the forty-odd men detained inside. Two blue *Gendarmerie* vans were parked beside the coaches. The reinforcements had finally arrived, and the policemen were doing their job.

'His immediate reaction was to ensure that the Mayor and distinguished guests were secure,' Bruno went on. 'Then he called for reinforcements and took personal charge of the arrests of the rioters who invaded our town. I found him in the car park, where he had forty of them under lock and key in their own coaches. And his men behaved well. Although he is obviously new in the town and a bit short of experience, I'm not sure we have anything to reproach him with.'

'Bruno could be right,' the Mayor chimed in. 'I'd rather we used the sympathy we now have in official circles to get some financial help through this rough patch than squander whatever influence we have in a fight with the Defence Ministry to get the *Capitaine* removed. And after those two generals got egg and tomato all over their uniforms, I'm not sure St Denis is very popular with the Defence Ministry this week.'

That was clever, Bruno thought. The local businessmen had perked up at the prospect of financial aid, and then the joke about the generals had got them all smiling. Every time he watched the Mayor in action, he felt he learned something.

'Thank you for coming to share your concerns, my friends,' the Mayor continued, rising from his seat at the head of the table. 'The council will do what we can to help. And while we're here, I am sure you'll want to join me in expressing thanks to our new local hero, our own *Chef de*

*Police*, for his outstanding service yesterday. That statement he made about our town being invaded and defending ourselves was admirable. The Minister of the Interior was particularly warm in his praise – probably because you took the potentially damaging attention away from him.'

Bruno almost blushed as they all grunted approval and some of them reached across to shake his hand. He still expected the Mayor to dress him down in private for that too-too clever idea about taking over Montsouris's protest march. But for the moment, his little speech to the TV cameras and the press coverage had become his protection.

'I do have one proposal to make,' Bruno said. 'I think it was Napoleon who said that when you're under pressure, it's always better to attack than to sit back and wait for the worst. I heard of something they've started doing in the tourist centres of Brittany that might help us here. They organise *Marchés Nocturnes* – evening markets. It's quite simple. We invite some of the regular stall holders to sell their produce in the evening, but products that can be eaten on the spot – pâté, cheese, olives, bread and salads, fruit and wine. We set up some tables and benches, provide some simple entertainment like the local jazz club, and we ask the town restaurants and *traiteurs* to provide simple hot foods like *pommes frites* and *saucisses* and pizza. There isn't a lot to do in the evenings round here and many people – particularly in the camp sites – can't afford to eat out at restaurants every night. So this would be a cheap evening out in the middle of town, as well as a new source of income for local businesses. And of course the town would charge a small fee to the stallholders. It might help bring people back to St Denis despite this latest publicity.'

'I like it,' said Dougal. 'It's just the kind of thing tourists love, and people will stay on and buy drinks at the bars after they eat. I could advertise it in all the houses we let.'

'It may be alright for you, but I make my living by keeping the customers inside my camp site, spending their money at my bar and in my café,' grumbled Duhamel. But Philippe from the hotel was enthusiastic, and they all felt better at the thought of taking some action to restore the town's fortunes. The delegation took their leave in a far better mood than when they had arrived.

'That could have gone a lot more disagreeably, so thank you for that very useful idea,' said the Mayor when he and Bruno were left alone. 'Are you sure you should be at work? You looked pretty bad on TV last night with that blood running down your face. You took some nasty knocks.'

'You should see the other guys,' said Bruno lightly, relieved that he seemed to have got away without a reprimand. 'And besides, I used to get worse on the rugby field every week.'

'Yes,' the Mayor said drily. 'Like all the rest of France, I watched you say that on TV. Very heroic, Bruno, but I also saw you getting beaten up and it looked very nasty from where I was watching. Half the women of St Denis have been telling me that you saved them from the mob. Seriously, I thought you were in for it when that gang attacked you by the steps.'

'So you saw our delightful Inspector Perrault come to my rescue? Not to mention that well-aimed kick from Pamela Nelson.'

'We all did. The Minister of the Interior was most impressed with their martial skills. I suspect the Inspector will find herself promoted back to a staff job in his Paris office quite soon with that karate black belt of hers, or whatever it is she has. An elegant and very dangerous woman – they love that sort of thing in Paris. That's why I think we'll have some help from the Ministry if we need it with the banks.'

The Mayor smiled at Bruno with the affectionate but slightly superior look of a schoolmaster realising how much his favourite pupil had yet to learn. 'I noticed your dubious look when I told our businessmen that we might be able to apply some pressure on the banks. Always remember, Bruno, that the people who really apply political pressure are seldom the politicians themselves. They prefer to let their staff do it for them and I think I'll make you a bet that the shapely Inspector Perrault will soon be in a position to help us if needed.'

'I'm not sure that she'd take such a job if it were offered. She's an independent sort of woman.'

'Spoken with feeling. Almost as if your advances had been spurned.'

'No advances have been made, Sir,' Bruno replied coolly.

'More fool you, Bruno. Now, I must answer all the phone calls I asked Mireille to hold during the meeting. Meanwhile, you'd better check on the progress of those thugs that were arrested. I assume that's being handled by the *Police Nationale* in Périgueux?'

'It should be, but our local chaps here were the arresting officers so I'll check with them first.'

Bruno had barely got back to his own office and opened his mail when the Mayor bustled in, muttering, 'That fool woman ... one of the phone calls that Mireille sat on was from the *Café des Sports*. I told her to interrupt me for anything urgent. Your *Capitaine* Duroc came along this morning and arrested Karim for assault. Can you find out what's going on?'

'Assault? It was self-defence.' But then he had a mental image of Karim, probably the biggest man in the entire square, picking up the litter bin and hurling it at the knot of *Front National* men with their flags. He winced. It had seemed a good idea at the time, but Bruno knew that he himself would have trouble even lifting the thing, let alone lifting it over his head and throwing it. And if that crucial moment of the brawl had been caught by the TV cameras, Karim could be in trouble.

'Do you remember seeing Karim throw the litter bin?' he asked the Mayor.

'Yes, it was the act that turned the tide; that and your Inspector Perrault. It was a considerable feat of strength. One of the generals said it was magnificent. Oh dear, I think I understand. That could be seen as assault with a weapon. Well, I think the Minister and the generals and I could stand as witnesses that Karim did the right thing.'

'Yes, but there's another witness – the TV cameras. And those *Front National* types have access to clever lawyers and they would relish filing a complaint against an Arab, which is how they see Karim. Even if the police decide not to file charges, the victims could do so.'

'*Putain!*' exploded the Mayor, and slammed a fist into the palm of his other hand. He never normally swore and Bruno could not remember the last time he'd seen his friend lose his temper. The Mayor paced back and forth before Bruno's desk, then stopped and fixed him with an angry eye. 'How do we fix this?'

'Well, I'll see what I can do with the police in Périgueux. But if there's a *Juge-magistrat* being assigned to lay charges against the *Front National* thugs, he'd also be the one to decide about charges against Karim, and that's way above my head. If that's the case, you'll probably have to see what influence you can bring to bear. It'll be a local

*Juge-magistrat*, so you might be able to get the Prefect to have a quiet word. A lot will depend on the statements taken by the police, so some depositions by you and the Minister and the generals would be very useful.'

The Mayor took a pad and pen from Bruno's desk and began to scribble some notes.

'The first thing is to find out exactly on what grounds the gendarmes arrested him, and whether charges have been filed by the *Front*,' Bruno said. 'I'll do that.'

'Is it possible that these swine are trying to set up a deal?' the Mayor asked, looking up from his notes. 'You know the sort of thing – if we drop the charges against them, they'll drop the charges against Karim. They're politicians, so they can hardly like the idea of forty of their militants getting charged with riotous assembly; and certainly not after members of their security squad are being charged with drug trafficking.'

'Maybe. I don't know. I've never been involved in that kind of legal deal-making. I'll go and see what I can find out at the *Gendarmerie*,' he said, grabbing his cap and heading for the stairs.

'And I'd better go and see if there's anything we can do for Rashida at the café, and we'd better call Momu. He may not know about this yet,' said the Mayor.

'I'm worried that this could be really serious for Karim,' Bruno said from the top of the stairs. 'If he's convicted of violent assault he's likely to lose his tobacco licence, and that means the end of his café and probably bankruptcy. If those bastards insist on a deal where we have to drop all charges against them, we may not have a lot of choice but to agree.'

## CHAPTER 18

A long stroll along the Rue de Paris, the main shopping street of St Denis, always calmed Bruno by forcing him to adapt to the slow and timeless ways of his town no matter what the urgency of his mission. But today, they slowed him down even more because everybody wanted to talk about the riot. He had to shake the hands of all the old men filling out their horse-racing bets at the *Café de la Renaissance*, though he refused their offers of a *petit blanc*. The women standing in line at the butcher's shop all wanted to kiss him and tell him they were proud of him. More women wanted to do the same at the *patisserie*, and Monique insisted on giving him one of his favourite *tartes au citron* as a token of her renewed esteem. He walked on, munching happily, shaking hands at the barber's shop and again at Fabien's *Rendez-vous des Chasseurs* where Bruno bought his shotgun cartridges.

Fabien wanted his opinion on a new lure he was inventing to tempt the fish in that fiendish corner of the river where only the most perfectly cast fly could evade the trees and boulders. Jean-Pierre was tinkering with a bike in front of his shop and raised an oily hand in salute. Not to be outdone, Bachelot darted from his shoe shop, nails still gripped between his lips and carrying a small hammer, to shake Bruno's hand warmly. Pascal came out from the *Maison de la Presse* to make sure Bruno had seen the newspapers and to assure him that at least three small boys had bought scrapbooks to record the sudden fame of their local policeman, and he was joined by the ladies in the flower shop and Colette from the dry cleaner's. By the time he'd reached the open ground in front of the *Gendarmerie* and greeted the two rugby forwards who were making a success of their *Bar des Amateurs* with its new snack lunches, sadly refusing their offer of a beer, he felt restored by the familiar rhythm of the town and its people.

Francine was at the desk in the *Gendarmerie*, and she had been stationed in St Denis long enough to understand Karim's importance to the town as its star rugby player, which had to be the reason for Bruno's visit. After he kissed her cheeks in greeting, she jerked a thumb towards the closed door of Duroc's office and rolled her eyes to signal her own view of Karim's arrest. She beckoned him closer and spoke very quietly.

'He's in there with Karim and a *juge-magistrat* from Périgueux who just turned up this morning with a couple of videotapes,' she whispered. 'He's the one behind this arrest, Bruno. Duroc is just obeying orders.'

'Did you recognise the guy from Périgueux?'

She shook her head. 'He's a new one on me, but a very fancy dresser. And he came in a car with a driver, parked over there by the vet's office. He made the driver carry in the video machine.'

'*Merde,*' muttered Bruno. It must be Tavernier, already armed with the TV film of Karim's part in the brawl. He thanked Francine and strolled out to the trees that shaded the old house that was the office for Dougal's Delightful Dordogne. There he pulled out his mobile and called the Mayor to warn him that Tavernier was now the problem.

'I'm with Rashida at the café and she's in hysterics,' the Mayor said. Bruno could hear Rashida in the background. 'I called Momu's house to get Karim's mother over here,' he went on, 'but she then rang Momu at school and he's heading for the *Gendarmerie*. You'd better make sure he does nothing foolish, Bruno, and I'll have to tackle Tavernier. The moment you have Momu calmed down, get hold of Tavernier and say that I want to see him urgently, as an old friend of his father.'

'Do you have a plan?' Bruno asked.

'Not yet, but I'll think of something. Is there a lawyer in there with Karim?'

'Not yet. Can you call Brosseil? He's on the board of the rugby club.'

'Brosseil is just a notary. Karim will need a real lawyer.'

'We can get a real lawyer later. We just want Brosseil to

go in there, tell Karim to say absolutely nothing, and insist that anything he *has* said so far is struck from the record since he was denied legal representation.'

'That's not French law, Bruno.'

'It doesn't matter. It buys us time and it will certainly shut Karim up. And it is European law, and Tavernier won't want to run foul of that – Brosseil has to keep on saying so. Do you have the deposition yet from the Minister or those two generals on what they saw in the square?'

'From the generals, yes. They faxed it. Nothing yet from the Minister.'

'Tavernier won't know that, Sir. If he thought that his prosecution of Karim called into question the deposition of his Minister, not to mention two senior figures in the Defence Ministry, he might have second thoughts.'

'Good thinking, Bruno. We'll try it. But first you had better stop Momu.'

That depended on whether Momu came by car, in which case he would have to come past the infants' school and the post office, or on foot or by bicycle through the pedestrian precinct, which would bring him along the Rue de Paris. Bruno could not be in both places at once. He poked his head in around the door and told Francine to block Momu at all costs and to ring him as soon as Momu appeared. Then he stationed himself at the end of the Rue de Paris just in time to catch Momu pedalling furiously towards him.

'Hold it, Momu,' he said with his hand up. 'Let me and the Mayor take care of this.'

But Momu ignored him. 'Out of my way, Bruno,' he shouted angrily, steering round him and thrusting out a powerful arm to push him away. Bruno hung on to his arm and the bike began to topple. Momu was stuck, his feet on the ground, his bike between his legs and his arm still in Bruno's firm grip.

'Get off, Bruno,' he roared. 'We'll fix you. The rugby boys are on their way, along with half the school. We can't have them rounding people up like this. It's a damn *rafle* and we've had enough.'

*Rafle* was the term the Algerians had used for the mass round-ups staged by the French police during the Algerian war, and before that to refer to the Gestapo raids against French civilians in the war. A *rafle* stood for brutality and a police state.

'It's not a *rafle*, Momu,' Bruno said urgently.

'The Nazis kill my father and leave him like a piece of butchered meat and now you take my son into your dungeons. Out of my way, Bruno! I've had it with you and your French justice.'

'It's not a *rafle*, Momu,' Bruno repeated, trying to catch the man's eyes with his own. He let go of Momu's arm and gripped his handlebars instead. 'It's Karim answering some questions and the Mayor and I are on your side, like the whole of the town. We have a lawyer coming and we're going to do this right. If you go charging in there you'll make things worse for Karim and do yourself no good. Believe me, Momu.'

'Believe you?' Momu scoffed. 'In that uniform? It was French police who killed hundreds of us in those *rafles* back during the war. Police like you rounded up Algerians and bound them hand and foot and threw them in the River Seine. Never again, Bruno. Never again. Now out of my way.'

A crowd was gathering, led by Gilbert and René from the *Bar des Amateurs*.

'Have you heard?' Momu cried. 'The gendarmes arrested Karim. He's in there. I have to get to him.'

'What's this, Bruno?' asked Gilbert suspiciously. 'Is this right?'

'Calm down, everybody,' Bruno said. 'It's true. The gendarmes came and picked him up and there's a magistrate now questioning him about the brawl in the square with those *Front National* types. The Mayor and I are trying to get things fixed. We have a lawyer coming and we're standing by Karim, just as we expect you all to do. We can't have people charging into the *Gendarmerie* – it will just make things worse.'

'What's Karim supposed to have done?' René wanted to know.

'Nothing, nothing,' exploded Momu. 'He's done nothing. He was defending himself against those Nazi bastards, defending you.'

'We don't know yet,' said Bruno, keeping firm hold of Momu's handlebars. At least Momu wasn't trying to knock him down or storm past him. 'It looks as if they are considering a charge of assault. You remember when Karim threw that litter bin.'

'Bruno, Bruno,' shouted a new voice, and Brosseil the *Notaire* came bustling up, tightening the knot of his tie. 'The Mayor just rang me, said I'd find you here.'

'We want you to go in and insist on seeing Karim as his legal representative, and tell him to say nothing and sign nothing. No statements. And then you say you demand anything he has said should be struck from the record because it was said while Karim was denied a lawyer. Then you tell them you will be filing a formal complaint in the European Court of Justice for denial of legal representation, and suing *Capitaine* Duroc personally.'

'Can I do that?' Brosseil asked. He was usually a self-important and rather pompous man but he suddenly looked deflated.

'It's European law, and it holds good in France. They might try to deny it, but just bluster and shout and threaten, and above all stop Karim from saying anything and we'll get a criminal lawyer here as soon as we can. Just refuse to take no for an answer. And remember, the whole town is counting on you. And so is Karim.'

Brosseil, whose main work was to draw up wills and

notarise sales of property, squared his shoulders like a soldier and marched off to the *Gendarmerie*.

'You have to trust me, Momu. I have to go in there now and try to help sort things out and I can't have an angry mob shouting outside or forcing their way in.' He let go of Momu's handlebars and gave him his own mobile. 'Call the Mayor. It's on speed dial so just hit number one and then press the green button and you'll reach him. The Mayor and I are following the strategy we've planned. Talk with him, and stay here and help calm people down. René, Gilbert – I rely on you to keep things under control here.' With that, Bruno followed Brosseil.

The door to Duroc's office was wide open and the shouts of angry men mingled with the soundtrack of the riot from the video playing on the TV. Duroc was standing beside his desk roaring at Brosseil to get out but the little *Notaire* was standing his ground and roaring back with dire threats about the European Court. Tavernier was sitting calmly behind Duroc's desk, watching the confrontation with an air of amusement. Karim sat, hunched and baffled, before the desk. Bruno sized up the situation, then moved to the TV and switched it off. Brosseil and Duroc stopped shouting in surprise.

'Gentlemen, if you please,' he said. 'I have an urgent message for the *Juge-magistrat*. A confidential matter.' He turned to Duroc, shook him warmly by the hand and began steering him out of the door. '*Mon Capitaine*, dear colleague, if you would be so kind, the courtesy of your office, just a brief moment, so grateful ...' Bruno kept murmuring smooth platitudes while his other hand grabbed Brosseil's coat and tugged him along until he had them both in the hallway. He extricated himself, told Karim to join his lawyer in the hall and closed the door. He leaned his back against it and scrutinised Tavernier, whose face wore a sardonic expression.

'We meet again, *Monsieur le Chef de Police*,' Tavernier said mockingly. 'Such a pleasure. You bring a message for me?'

'An old friend and classmate of your father, Senator Mangin, requests the pleasure of your company,' said Bruno.

'Ah yes, the Mayor of St Denis, making up for the disappointments of his political career in Paris by running the affairs of this turbulent little town. My father tells amusing stories of his old classmate. Apparently he was out of his depth even then. Please convey my sincere respects to the Mayor, but I am for the moment detained on judicial business. I shall be happy to call on him after my business here is concluded, probably towards the end of the day.'

'I think the Mayor's business is rather more urgent, *Monsieur le Juge-magistrat*,' Bruno said.

'Sadly, you must remind your Mayor that the law waits for no man. Please send the others back in when you leave, but you can take that ridiculous little *Notaire* away with you.'

'You are right about the law,' Bruno said. 'That's why we wasted no time in getting the depositions from our illustrious guests who happened to witness that act of aggression by outside agitators. Depositions from both generals, and the Minister. I think the Mayor wishes to discuss them with you before any further judicial decisions are made.'

'Very clever,' said Tavernier after a long silence. 'And I am sure the depositions are very flattering about the role of our hulking Arab, and of the town's *Chef de Police*.'

'I wouldn't know, Monsieur. I haven't seen them. I only know the Mayor wishes to discuss them with you, in the interest of furnishing all possible assistance to the judicial authorities.'

'In rather the same way that somebody sent that silly little *Notaire* in here spouting about the European Court of Justice. Was that your doing?'

'I don't know what you're talking about, Monsieur. I do know that no responsible policeman would stand in the way of allowing someone the benefit of legal advice if they're being questioned. I'm sure you and *Capitaine* Duroc would agree.'

'A country policeman who follows the judgments of the European Court of Justice,' Tavernier sneered. 'How very impressive.'

'And the European Court of Human Rights,' Bruno said. 'It is the duty of a policeman to pay attention to the laws he is sworn to uphold.'

'The law is even-handed, *Monsieur le Chef de Police*. The outside agitators involved in the riot are facing prosecution, and so are the local townspeople who reacted with undue force. And we are still seeking to establish who was responsible for starting the violence.'

'Then, Monsieur, I am sure you will want to waste no time in consulting the depositions of such eminent witnesses as the generals and the Minister, as the Mayor invites you to do.'

A long silence ensued as Tavernier kept his eyes fixed on Bruno's, and Bruno could only guess at the calculations of personal and political ambition that were taking place behind the young man's calm features. He kept his own face similarly immobile.

'You may inform the Mayor that I shall wait upon him in his office within thirty minutes,' Tavernier said finally, and turned his gaze away.

'The Mayor and I will both stand surety for the young man you were questioning before this regrettable interruption,' Bruno said. 'We guarantee that he will be available to you at any time for further questioning, along with a suitable legal representative.'

'Very well,' said Tavernier. 'You may take your violent Arab along for the moment. I think we have all the evidence we need.' He waved a languid hand at the video.

'He's as French as you or me, but I'll remember you said that.' Bruno turned on his heel and walked out. He collected

Karim and Brosseil on the way, and Duroc started to protest. Bruno simply looked at him and pointed back to the closed door of Duroc's office and said, 'Check with the boy wonder in there.'

And then they were down the steps and into the open air, and a cheer came up from the crowd that had gathered at the corner of the Rue de Paris as Momu trotted forward joyfully to embrace Karim. Half the town seemed to be present, including the two old enemies from the Resistance, Bachelot and Jean-Pierre, both of them beaming. Bruno thanked Brosseil, who was jaunty with pride at his own part in the proceedings and too excited even to think about whether he might send someone a bill for his services. This surprised Bruno, who wondered how long Brosseil's forgetfulness would last. He slapped Karim on the back, and Momu came up apologetically to shake his hand.

'Was that true what you said about the *rafles*, throwing people in the River Seine?' Bruno asked.

'Yes, in 1961, October. Over two hundred of us. It's history. You can look it up. They even made a TV programme about it.'

Bruno shook his head, not in disbelief but with weary sadness at the endless march of human folly.

'I'm very sorry,' he said.

'It was the war,' said Momu. 'And at times like this I get worried that it isn't over.' He looked across to where

234

Karim was being led into the *Bar des Amateurs* for a cele-bratory beer. 'I'd better make sure he just has the one and gets back to comfort Rashida. Thanks for bringing him out. And I'm sorry I pushed you, Bruno. I was very worked up.'

'I understand. It's a hard time for you with your father and now this. But you know the whole town is with you.'

'I know,' Momu nodded. 'I taught half of them how to count. They are decent people. Thanks again.'

'Give my respects to Rashida,' Bruno said, and walked off alone up the Rue de Paris to brief the Mayor.

## CHAPTER 19

Bruno dressed for dinner. He had pondered what to wear while feeding his chickens, and he thought a pair of chinos and casual shirt, with a jacket, would be suitable. A tie would be too much. He also took a bottle of his unlabelled Lalande de Pomerol from the cellar and put it on the seat of his car beside the bunch of flowers he had bought, so that he would not forget. He showered, shaved and dressed, fed Gigi and then drove off, wondering what the mad Englishwoman and her friend were going to feed him. He had heard much of English cooking, none of it reassuring, although Pamela was clearly a civilised woman with the excellent taste to live in Périgord. But still, he was nervous, and not only for his stomach. The invitation had come by hand-delivered note to his office, and was addressed 'To our Defender'. The tongues of the women in the *Mairie* had not stopped wagging since.

It had been a tiresome day, with half the newspapers and TV stations in France wanting to interview 'the lone cop of St Denis', as *France-Soir* had called him. He turned them all down, except for his favourite, Radio Périgord, who seemed disappointed when he said that a lone cop would have been knocked silly and it was the presence of Inspector Isabelle Perrault that had made the difference. Isabelle had then called him to complain that *Paris-Match* wanted to photograph her in her karate fighting suit and the damn female media expert at Police HQ was insisting she submit. But she accepted his invitation to dinner the following evening, only – she said – because she wanted to get a good look at his black eye and bruises.

It was still fully light outside as Bruno parked at Pamela's, yet there were lights blazing throughout the house, an old oil lamp glowing softly on the table in the courtyard, and some gentle jazz music playing. An English voice called out, 'He's here,' and Pamela appeared, looking formal in a long dress and her hair piled high. She was carrying a tray with a bottle of what looked like Veuve Clicquot and three glasses.

'Our hero,' she said, putting the tray down on the table and kissing him soundly on both cheeks.

'After seeing what you did to that young skinhead I'm not sure I ought to get any closer,' he said, smiling as she took his flowers and wine, laid them on the table, and then took both his hands in hers.

'That's one of the best black eyes I've ever seen, Bruno,' she said. 'And stitches! I didn't know you'd have stitches, but I'm not surprised after seeing that club he hit you with.' She turned as Christine appeared. 'Just look at Bruno's stitches.'

Christine came up, kissed him on both cheeks and hugged him tightly, bathing him in her perfume. 'Thank you, Bruno. Truly, thank you for coming to our rescue.'

He thought of replying that there were other women there to be defended, or that he would have made a poor job of it but for Isabelle's presence, or that the whole damned event was probably his own fault. But none of it seemed quite right so he remained silent and beamed at them both.

'We heard you on the radio this afternoon,' Christine said. 'And we bought all the newspapers.'

'I'm just sorry you got caught up in it, and sorry too that St Denis now has this dreadful reputation for fighting and racial troubles,' he said. 'Some of the tourist businesses have had cancellations, so I hope it won't hurt your rentals this summer, Pamela. I was told there was something in the English newspapers.'

'And on the BBC,' said Christine.

'I should be fine,' Pamela said, handing him the champagne to open. 'I don't use St Denis in the address of this place, only the postal code. I just give the name of the house, then the name of the little hamlet of St Thomas et Brillamont, and then Vallée de la Vézère. It sounds so much more French to the English ear.'

'I didn't know the house had a name,' he said, gently tapping the hollow at the base of the bottle to prevent the foam from overflowing.

'It didn't before I christened it *Les Peupliers*, the poplars.'

'I think you would call that *le marketing*,' laughed Christine as he began pouring the wine. She too was wearing a long dark skirt and blouse, but her hair had been freshly curled. They had dressed up for him and he began to regret not wearing a tie.

'So perhaps you'd tell me what this *English* dinner you've kindly invited me to will be?'

'It's a surprise,' said Pamela.

'A surprise for me as well,' said Christine. 'I don't know what Pamela has cooked, but she does cook very well. My contribution was to spend the day on the computer on your behalf, researching into your Arab football team.'

'I tried the sports editor of *le Marseillais* today,' said Bruno. 'He was very helpful when he realised I was the same St Denis cop whose picture was in his newspaper, but there was nothing in their files. He said he would ask some of the retired journalists if they knew of anything in the old archives. He even looked through the back issues of those months in 1940, but he said they didn't seem to cover amateur leagues.'

'Well, I have something,' Christine said. 'I decided to check the thesis data base. You know there are all these new graduate studies in areas like sports and immigration history? Well, they all have to write theses, and I found two that could be useful. One of them is titled: "Sport and Integration; Immigrant football leagues in France, 1919–1940", and the other is called "Re-making society in a new land: Algerian social organisations in France". I couldn't get the texts from the internet, but I did get the name of the authors, and I tracked down the first one. He teaches sport history at the University of Montpellier, and he thinks he knows about your team. There was an amateur league in Marseilles called *Les Maghrébins*, and the team that won the championship in 1940 was called Oran, after the town in Algiers where most of the players came from. And here is his telephone number. He sounded very nice on the phone.'

'This is amazing,' Bruno marvelled. 'You got all that from your computer?'

'Yes, and I now have a copy of his thesis all printed out and ready for you. He emailed it to me.'

'This is very kind,' said Bruno. 'It'll be my bedtime reading. But for now, the night is young and our glasses are filled with champagne. I'm in the company of two beautiful women and I'm looking forward to my English cuisine, so no more talk of crime and violence. Let's enjoy the evening.'

'First tell us what you expect of English cooking,' said Pamela. 'Let us know the worst.'

'Roast beef that is overcooked, mustard that is too hot,

sausages made of bread, fish covered in soggy thick batter and vegetables that have been cooked so long they turn to mush. Oh yes, and some strange spiced sauce from a brown bottle to drown all the tastes. That's what we had when we all went over to Twickenham for the rugby international. We all liked the big egg and bacon breakfasts but I have to say the rest of the food was terrible,' he said. 'Except now I hear that your new national dish is supposed to be some curry from India.'

'Well, Pamela's cooking will change your mind,' said Christine. 'But first, what did you think of the champagne?'

'Excellent.'

'It's from England.' Pamela turned the bottle so that he could see the label. 'It has beaten French champagnes in blind tastings. The Queen serves it, and Christine brought me a bottle so it seemed a good time to serve it. I should confess that the winemaker is a Frenchman from the Champagne district.'

'I'm still impressed. It reminds me that the English are full of surprises, especially to us French.'

Bruno felt more than a little uncomfortable, not knowing what to expect of the evening, or what was expected of him. It was the first time he had dined in an English home and the first time he had dined alone with two handsome women. Dining alone with either one would have been easier, on the familiar territory of flirtation and discovery. Two against one left him feeling not so much outnumbered as unbalanced, and the ritual jokes about the English and the French would hardly suffice to carry an entire evening. But it was their occasion, he told himself, and up to them to guide the proceedings. And the evening had already more than justified itself, thanks to the news of Christine's researches.

The women led him indoors, and Bruno looked around with interest to see what the English would do with a French farmhouse. He was in a large, long room with a high ceiling that went all the way to the roof, and a small balustraded gallery on the upper floor. There was a vast old fireplace at the end of the room, two sets of French windows, an entire wall filled with books, and half a dozen large and evidently comfortable armchairs, some of leather and some covered in chintz.

'I like this room,' he said. 'But it wasn't like this when you arrived here, I imagine?'

'No. I had to repair the roof and some of the beams, so I decided to do away with half the upper floor and make this high ceiling. Come through to the dining room.'

This was a smaller, more intimate room, painted a colour somewhere between gold and orange, with a large oval table of dark and ancient-looking wood and eight chairs. Three places were set at one end, with glasses for both red and white wine. On one wall was a carefully spaced array of old prints. The flowers he had brought had been placed in a large pottery vase on the table. As in the larger living room, the floor was laid with terracotta tiles, scattered with rugs of rich reds and golds that glowed in the soft light of the table lamps and the two candelabras on the table. On the long wall hung a large oil portrait of a woman with auburn hair and startlingly white shoulders, wearing an evening dress from an earlier era. She looked very like Pamela

'My grandmother,' Pamela said. 'She was from Scotland, which helps explain the one part of the meal where I cheated, just a little. I'll explain later, but do sit down and we'll begin.'

She went to the kitchen and returned with a large white tureen of steaming soup. 'Leek and potato soup,' she announced. 'With my own bread, and a glass of another English wine, a Riesling from a place called Tenterden.'

The bread was thick and brown, with a solid, chewy texture that Bruno decided he liked, and it went well with the filling soup. The wine tasted like something from Alsace, so he declared himself impressed again.

'Now comes the bit where I cheated,' said Pamela. 'The fish course is smoked salmon from Scotland, so it isn't quite English, but Christine and I agreed that it still counts. The butter and the lemons are French, and the black pepper comes from heaven knows where.'

'This is very good *saumon fumé*, paler than the kind we usually have here and a most delicate flavour. Delicious!' Bruno raised his glass to the women.

Pamela cleared the plates, then brought in a large tray that held warmed plates, a carafe of red wine, two covered vegetable dishes and a steaming hot pie with golden pastry.

'Here you are, Bruno. The great classic of English cuisine: steak and kidney pie. The young peas and the carrots are from the garden, and the red wine is from the Camel Valley in Cornwall. They used to say you could never make good red wine in an English climate but this proves them wrong. And now, prepare for the most heavenly cooking smell I know. Come on, lean forward, and get ready for when I cut the pie.'

Bruno dutifully obeyed, and as Pamela lifted the first slice of pastry he took a deep breath, savouring the rich and meaty aroma. '*Magnifique*,' he said, peering into the pie. 'Why so dark?'

'Black stout,' said Pamela. 'I would normally use Guinness, but that's Irish, so I used an English version. And beefsteak and *rognons*, some onions and a little garlic.' She piled Bruno's plate high, then Christine served the peas and carrots. Pamela poured the wine and sat back to observe his reaction.

He took a small cube of meat from the rich sauce and then tried a piece of kidney. Excellent. The pastry was light and crumbly and infused with the taste of the meat. The young peas in their pods were cooked to perfection and the carrots were equally right. It was splendid food, solid and tasty and traditional, like something a French grandmother might have prepared. Now for the wine. He sniffed, enjoying the fruity bouquet, and twirled the glass in the candlelight, watching the crown where the wine fell away from the sides of the glass as it levelled. He took a sip. It was heavier than the kind of red Gamay from the Loire that he had expected, his only experience of red wine grown that far to the north, and it had a pleasantly solid aftertaste. A good wine, reminding him slightly of a Burgundy, and with the body to balance the meat on his plate. He laid down his knife and fork, took up his glass, sipped again, and then looked at the two women.

'I take back everything I've said about English food. So long as you prepare it, Pamela, I'll eat any English food you put before me. And this pie, you must tell me how to make it. It's not a kind of dish we know in French cuisine. You must come to my house next time and let me cook for you.'

'Yes!' exclaimed Christine, and to his surprise, the Englishwomen raised their right hands, palms forward, and slapped them together in celebration. A curious English custom, he presumed, smiling at them and addressing himself once more to his Cornwall wine. Cornwall, he reminded himself, was known in French as *Cornouailles*, and he knew from school that the traditional language was very like the Breton spoken on France's Brittany peninsula, so they were therefore really French in origin. That explained the wine.

Even the name for Pamela's country, *Grande Bretagne*, simply meant larger Brittany.

The salad, the ingredients again from Pamela's garden, was excellent and fresh, although crisp lettuce mixed with *roquette* did not seem particularly English to Bruno. But the cheese, a fat cylinder of Stilton brought from England by Christine, was rich and splendid. Finally, Pamela served a home-made ice cream made with her own strawberries, and Bruno confessed himself full, and wholly converted to English food.

'So why do you keep this a secret?' he asked. 'Why do you serve such bad food most of the time in England, and why is its reputation so terrible?'

The women each spoke at once. 'The industrial revolution,' said Christine. 'The war and rationing,' said Pamela, and they both laughed.

'You explain your theory, Christine, while I get the final treat.'

'It's pretty obvious, really,' explained Christine. 'Britain was the first country to experience both the agricultural and the industrial revolutions of the eighteenth century, and they very nearly destroyed the peasantry. Small farming was replaced by sheep farming because the sheep needed less care, just as better ploughs and farming techniques needed less labour and more investment. So small farmers and farm labourers were pushed off the land, while the new factories needed workers. Britain became an urban, industrial country very fast, and the mass urban markets needed foods that could be easily transported and stored and quickly prepared because so many women were working in the mills and factories. Then the new farm lands of North America and Argentina were opened, and with its doctrine of free trade Britain found its own farmers beaten on price and became a massive importer of cheap foreign food. It came in the form of tinned meat and mass-produced breads. And this happened just as the old traditions of peasant cooking that were handed down through the generations were disappearing, because families dispersed into the new industrial housing.'

'Some would say that similar forces are at work now in France,' Bruno observed. He turned to Pamela, who brought to the table a small tray with a large dark bottle, a jug of water and three small glasses. 'What of your theory about the war being responsible, Pamela?'

'Hold on a minute, Bruno,' said Christine. 'It was you French who invented tinned food back in the Napoleonic wars, and wars were what spread the system. The Crimean War of the 1850s, the American Civil War of the 1860s and the Franco-Prussian War of 1870 were all run on tinned food, because that was the only way to feed mass armies. Just the other day in your local supermarket here I saw cans of Fray Bentos – do you know how that got its name?'

Bruno shook his head, but leaned forward, suddenly fascinated by this conversation. Of course the huge conscript armies would need tinned food. The First World War in the trenches could probably not have been fought without it.

'Fray Bentos is a town in Argentina that began exporting meat extract to Europe in the 1860s, to use up the surplus meat from all the animals that were killed for the Argentine leather trade. And pretty soon the meat trade was far bigger than the leather.'

'Amazing,' said Bruno. 'I knew you were a historian of France, but not of food.'

'It's how I teach my students about globalisation,' said Christine. 'You have to show them that history means something to their lives, and there's no easier way than to talk about the history of food.'

'I wish I'd had teachers like you. Our history lessons were all kings and queens and popes and Napoleon's battles,' said Bruno. 'I'd never thought of it like this.'

'I agree with all that Christine says about the history,' Pamela said. 'But World War Two and rationing, which continued for nearly ten years after the war, made everything worse. After depending so long on cheap imported food, Britain was nearly starved by the German submarine campaign. People were limited to one egg a week, and hardly any meat or bacon or imported fruits. Even the tradition of better cooking in restaurants nearly died because there was a very low limit on how much they could charge for a meal. It took a generation to recover and to get people travelling again and enjoying foreign food, and to have the money to go to restaurants and buy cookbooks.' She lifted the dark bottle off the tray. 'And now I want you to try this as your *digestif* instead of cognac. It's a Scotch malt whisky, which is to ordinary whisky what a great chateau wine is to *vin ordinaire*. This one is called Lagavullin, and it comes from the island where my grandmother was born, so it has a taste of peat and the sea.'

'You sip it like cognac?'

'My father brought me up to sniff it first, a really long sniff, then to take the tiniest sip and roll it around your mouth until it evaporates, and then take a deep breath through your mouth so you feel the flavour all down your throat. Then you take a proper sip.'

'It feels warm all the way down,' said Bruno, after taking his deep breath. 'That's very good indeed,' he said, after a long sip. 'A most unusual smoky taste, but a very satisfying *digestif* after a wonderful meal and a great conversation. I feel that I've learned a lot. Thank you both.'

He raised his glass to them, trying to decide which of the two he found the most attractive. He knew that they'd been teasing a little throughout the evening, and he might try some teasing in return.

'So let me sum up,' he said, ' by asking whether I've really had English cuisine this evening?' Pamela looked slightly disconcerted. 'I've had Scotch malt whisky and Scotch salmon, wine from Cornwall, French beef and French kidney, French salad and vegetables and strawberries, and French-style champagne that was made in England. The only wholly English part of this meal was the cheese. And it was all wonderfully cooked by an Englishwoman with the very good taste to live in the Périgord.'

With the taste of the whisky still lingering pleasantly in his mouth, Bruno cruised to the end of Pamela's drive. He stopped on the brow of a hill where the signal would be better, took out his mobile and checked the time. Just after ten thirty. Not too late. He called Jean-Luc, a brawny man who was a strong supporter of the rugby club and his best friend among the local cops. A woman's voice answered.

'Francine, it's Bruno. Are they out tonight?'

'Hi, Bruno. You'd better take care. *Capitaine* Duroc has the boys out just about every night these days. The bastard wants to break the record for drunk-driving arrests. Hold on, I'll get Jean-Luc.'

'Out drinking again, Bruno?' said his friend, his voice a little blurred with wine. 'You ought to set a better example. Yes, the bastard sent the lads out again. He had me and Vorin on the Périgueux road last night, and he took the road junction that goes off to Les Eyzies – with young Françoise. I think he might be a bit sweet on her but she can't stand the sod. Neither can any of us. He's got us on alternate night shifts and we're all getting fed up with him. I tell you what. Young Jacques is out on patrol tonight. I'll call him and see where he's stationed and call you back.'

Bruno waited and let his thoughts linger on the two women with whom he'd spent the evening. Christine was conventionally pretty, a dark-eyed brunette of the kind he always liked, and her liveliness and quick intelligence made her seem somehow familiar. Aside from her accent, she could almost be French. But Pamela was different, handsome rather than pretty, and with that wide and graceful stride of hers and her upright posture and strong nose, she could only be English. There was something rather splendid about her, though, he reflected. Serene and self-confident, she was a woman out of the ordinary, and a very fine cook. Now what should he cook for them? They had probably had more than enough Périgord cuisine, and he certainly had, so he could forget the *touraine* soup and the *foie gras*, and the various ways with duck, but he still had some truffles stored in oil so a risotto with truffles and mushrooms would be interesting. The two women would be standing gracefully at the counter in his kitchen while he stirred it, and—

His phone rang, jolting him out of his reverie. 'Bruno, it's Jean-Luc. I rang Jacques and he's on the bridge. He said Duroc has gone out to the junction at Les Eyzies again. Apparently he found good pickings there. Where are you? Up near the cave? Well, you could come back by the bridge and give a wave to Jacques as you pass, he knows your car. Or you could go around by the water tower and have a clear run home. Is it just you or are some of the rest of the lads out tonight?'

'Just me, Jean-Luc, and thanks. I owe you a beer.'

He took the long way home, down to the narrow bridge and up the ridge to the water tower, smiling grimly at all the things about St Denis that Duroc would never know, and wondering if the man would ever learn that the rules were rather different in rural France. It was interesting to hear that he had his eye on young Françoise, a plumpish blonde from Alsace with a sweet face and generous hips, who was said to have a small tattoo on her rump. It was listed in her personal file as an identifying mark, according to Jean-Luc. There were a series of private bets among the other gendarmes over what it might be; a spider or a cross, a heart or a boyfriend's name. Bruno's bet was a cockerel, the symbol of France. Nobody had yet claimed the prize and Bruno hoped it would not be Duroc who succeeded in uncovering Françoise and her secret, although perhaps an affair was just what Duroc needed. But the man went so carefully by the book that he would never break the strict *Gendarmerie* rule against romantic attachments with junior ranks. Or would he? If the others suspected he was smitten with Françoise, he was getting into risky territory already. Bruno filed the thought away as his car climbed the hill to his cottage.

Turning the corner, he saw the faithful Gigi sitting guard at his door.

He took the printout of the thesis with him to bed, turning first to the back for the chapter headings, and frowning slightly as he saw there was no index. This could take longer than he thought, but there was an entire chapter on Marseilles and the Maghreb League, which from its name was presumably composed of teams and players from North Africa. He lay back and began to read, or at least he tried to. This was like no prose he had ever read before. The first two pages were entirely about what previous scholars had written about North African life in Marseilles and about the theory of sports integration. When he had read the paragraph three times, he thought he understood it to say that integration took place when teams of different ethnic groups played one another, but not when they just played between themselves. That made sense, so why didn't the man say so?

He battled on. The Maghreb League had been founded in 1937, the year after Leon Blum's Popular Front government came to power with its commitment to social policy, paid holidays and the forty-hour week. He remembered learning about that in school. Blum had been Jewish and a Socialist, and his government depended on Communist votes. There had been a slogan among the rich – 'Better Hitler than Blum'.

The Maghreb League was one of several sporting organisations that had been started by a group of social workers employed by Blum's Ministry of Youth and Sport. There was also a Catholic Youth League, a Young Socialists league, a *Ligue des Syndicats* for the trade unions, and even an Italian League because south-east France from Nice to the Italian border had been part of the Italian kingdom of Savoy until 1860. Then the Emperor Louis Napoleon had taken the land as his reward for going to war against Austria in support of a unified Italy. Again, Bruno vaguely remembered that from school. But the Young Catholics, Young Socialists and young trade union members did not want to play against the North Africans. Only the Italians agreed to play them and this was encouraged by the Ministry of Sport as a way to integrate both minorities. Some things haven't changed, he thought glumly. But then he caught himself: yes they had. Look at the French national soccer team that won the World Cup in 1998, captained by Zidane, a Frenchman from North Africa. And he allowed himself a small glow of satisfaction at the way the young sportsmen of St Denis had grown out of this nonsense and played happily with blacks, browns and even young English boys.

The *Maghrébins* were enthusiastic players but not very skilful, and invariably lost to the teams of young Italians. So, in the interests of getting better games the Italians offered to help the North Africans with some coaching. Very decent of them, thought Bruno. And the main coach for the Italian League was a player for the Marseilles team called Giulio Villanova.

Bruno sat up in bed. Villanova was the name of the man that Momu had remembered. This was Momu's father's team! Bruno read on avidly. In those days of amateur teams before football players could dream of commanding the fantastic salaries they earned these days, Villanova was happy to coach the Maghreb League in return for a modest wage from Leon Blum's Ministry of Sport. Sounds like somebody back then had a good idea, thought Bruno, and it would be very pleasant if somebody were to pay him even a token stipend for all the training he did with the tennis and rugby *minimes*. Dream on, Bruno, and besides, you enjoy it.

Under Villanova's coaching, the Maghreb teams became better and better, and some of them began to win matches. The best team of all was the *Oraniens*, the boys from Oran, who won their League championship in March 1940, just before the German invasion that led to France's defeat in June and the end of organised sports for the young North Africans. The chapter went on to analyse the possibility that, had the war not intervened, the success of the *Oraniens* and the Maghreb League might have secured them the chance to play the Catholic and Socialist Youth and thus begin the process of assimilation.

But Villanova, the social workers, and the players over the age of eighteen had already been conscripted into the

Army. The young Arabs that were left began to play among themselves informally and the Maghreb League collapsed, leaving only a memory. Bruno thumbed quickly through the rest of the thesis, looking for photos or lists of the players' names or more references to the *Oraniens* or Villanova, but there was nothing. Still, he had the phone number of the author of the thesis, and that was a lead to be followed up in the morning. Well fed, well pleased with finding the name of Hamid's team, and deeply satisfied at having evaded Duroc's trap for motorists, Bruno turned out his lamp.

He rang the author as soon as he got into his office in the morning. The teacher of sports history at Montpellier University was intrigued by Bruno's question, delighted that his thesis had turned out to be useful to someone other than himself and his teaching career, and declared himself eager to help. Bruno explained that he was involved in a murder inquiry following the death of an elderly North African called Hamid al-Bakr, who had kept on his wall a photograph of a football team dated 1940. The police were very interested to learn more about this, he said. The victim's son believed that he had played in the team and had been coached by Villanova, and since the victim had been holding the ball when the photo was taken, he was either the captain or the star of the team. Was there any more information?

'Well, I think I have a list of team names in my research notes,' said the teacher. 'I wanted to check whether any of the players became famous after the war, but none of them seemed to make it into the professional teams in France. They may have done so back in North Africa, but I had no funds to take my researches over there.'

'Can you find the team list for the *Oraniens* in 1940? And do you have any team photos?' Bruno asked. 'Or anything more on Villanova – that seems to be the only name we have.'

'I'll have to check, but it won't be until I get home this evening. My research notes are stored there and I have to teach all day. I do have some photos, but I'm not sure if they'd be relevant. I'll check. And Villanova seems to have dropped out of sporting life during the war. He doesn't reappear on any team lists that I came across, nor at the Ministry of Sports when it re-opened in 1945. I'll call you back this evening. Okay?'

Bruno hung up, telling himself he was probably following a false trail. Still, the disappearance of that photo was one of the only clues they had and he thought J-J and Isabelle would be impressed if he could come up with some new evidence. And, being honest with himself, Bruno knew it was Isabelle whom he wanted to please.

The inquiry had made little real progress that Bruno knew of. The tyre tracks had matched, but only confirmed what they already knew, that both young Gelletreau and Jacqueline had been in the clearing in the woods over-looking Hamid's cottage. In any case, they had admitted going there at various times to make love, while firmly denying seeing Hamid or visiting his cottage, and even a second forensic sweep had failed to produce any new evidence that could break their story. The one big hole in their case was Jacqueline's lie about being in St Denis on the day of the killing. She had first claimed that she had simply come to pick up Richard to take him back to her house, but she was lying again. Playing truant from his *lycée*, Richard would have stayed at her home in Lalinde. Under separate questioning, the boy had firmly denied being in St Denis at all that day but, even when caught in the lie, Jacqueline stuck to her story. J-J and Isabelle assumed that her jaunt probably had something to do with the drugs, making a pickup or a delivery, and she was more frightened of the drug dealers than she was of the police.

Bruno had a sudden thought. Most of the Ecstasy pills in Europe were said to come from Holland. He picked up the phone and rang Franc Duhamel at the big camp site on the river bend below the town.

'*Bonjour*, Franc, it's Bruno and I have a question for you. Those Dutch lads who stayed at your site for the Motor-Cross rally, how long did they stay?'

'*Salut*, Bruno. They stayed the whole week. They came

down late on the Friday night, stayed the week and went back the next Sunday. There were about thirty of them, a couple of those big camping vans, a couple of cars and the rest on motorbikes. Along with the camping vans for some of the teams that were competing, I was nearly full that weekend. It was just what I needed to start the season.'

'Franc, I know you have that wooden pole across the entrance and a night watchman, but do you run security during the day? Take note of car registration numbers and all that?'

'Certainly. The insurance requires it. Every vehicle that comes in gets recorded in the book.'

'Even visitors, even local cars from round here?'

'Everybody. Visitors, delivery trucks, even you.'

'Do me a favour. Look up the visitors' book for May the eleventh, and see if you have a listing for a local car with a twenty-four registration.' He gave Franc the number of Jacqueline's car, and waited, listening to the rustling of pages.

'Hello, Bruno? Yes, I found it. The car came in at twelve and left at three-thirty. It looks like whoever it was, they came for a good lunch.'

'Any idea who was driving the car, or who they visited?'

'No, just the number.'

'Do you have the names of the Dutch lads who were staying with you?'

'Certainly. Names, addresses, car and bike registrations, and some credit cards. Mostly they paid cash, but some paid with cards.' Franc spoke hesitantly, and Bruno smiled to himself at Franc's new dilemma, whether he would now have to declare to the taxman even the cash income he had taken from the Dutchmen.

'Don't worry, Franc. This is about the Dutchmen and their visitor, nothing to do with you or taxes. Can you get the paperwork together with the names and addresses and all the information you have on them and I'll be down in twenty minutes to make copies.'

'Can you tell me what this is about, Bruno? It's not involved with the murder of that Arab, is it?'

'It's just a hunch, Franc, but we're investigating the way some drugs have been getting into the area, that's all. Twenty minutes.'

With Franc's paperwork in hand, Bruno thought he had better tie up another loose end and drove on through the town to Lespinasse's garage on the main road to Bergerac. It was a Total filling station, slightly more expensive than the petrol at the supermarket but well-placed for the tourist trade, and it was where Jacqueline had filled her car. Lespinasse's sister ran the pumps, while he and his son and a cousin tinkered happily with engines and gearboxes and bodywork in the vast hangar of their garage. Lespinasse liked all cars, but he loved old Citroëns, from

261

the 1940s *Model Sept* with the sweeping running boards and the doors that opened forwards to the humble but serviceable *Deux-Chevaux* and the '60s beauties that were known as the gorgeous goddesses – the aerodynamic models called the DS that when said aloud sounded like the French word for goddess – *déesse*.

As always, he found Lespinasse under a car, chewing on a matchstick and singing to himself. He called out and the plump, jovial man wheeled himself out on the small board on which he lay and rolled off to greet Bruno, presenting his forearm to be shaken rather than cover Bruno's palm with oil.

'We saw you in the newspaper,' said Lespinasse. 'And on TV. A proper celebrity you are now, Bruno. Everybody says you did a great job with those bastards.'

'I'm here on police business, Jean-Louis, about one of your credit card customers. I need to look at your fuel sales records for May the eleventh.'

'The eleventh? That would have been Kati's day off, so the boy would have been running the pumps.' He looked back into the garage and whistled, and young Edouard came out, waving cheerfully. He was the image of his father but for a full set of teeth. The boy was eighteen now but he had known Bruno ever since he'd first learned to play rugby, so he came and kissed Bruno on both cheeks.

'You still write down the registration numbers on the credit card slips?' Bruno asked.

'Always, except for the locals that we know,' said Edouard.

Bruno gave him the number of Jacqueline's car, and Edouard leafed through the file to the right day.

'Here we are,' he said. 'Thirty-two euros and sixty centimes at eleven forty in the morning. *Carte Bleu*. I remember her, she was a real looker. Blonde. When she came back she was with a bunch of guys, though.'

'She came back?'

'Yes, after lunch, in one of those big camper vans with a bunch of Hollanders. I filled them up. Here it is, eighty euros exactly at two forty in the afternoon, paid with a Visa card and here's the registration number,' said Edouard. Bruno checked his own list. It was one of the numbers listed at the camp site.

'And there were a couple of them on motor bikes at the same time and I filled them too,' Edouard went on. 'They must have paid cash. I remember asking myself what a nice French girl like that was doing with a bunch of foreigners. Tough-looking guys, they were. I saw her in the back of the van with them when the guy that paid opened the back door to get his jacket with the wallet. I don't think we saw them again, and I'd have remembered if we'd seen her.'

'If you hadn't given up playing tennis you might have met her at the tournament last year. She came and played at the club.'

'Well, it was either tennis or rugby so maybe I made the wrong choice,' said Edouard. 'But you know me, I was always better at rugby and I like the lads in the team.'

## CHAPTER 21

Bruno left the garage feeling rather proud of himself and went directly to see Isabelle in her temporary office above the tourist board. Trying not to show that he felt like some ancient warrior returning with trophies from the battlefield, he went straight to her desk, laid down three thin files and announced, 'New evidence.'

Isabelle, in dark trousers and a white shirt of masculine cut, sat pensively at her desk with a pencil in her hand and wearing earphones. She looked startled to see him at first, and then pleased. She took off the earphones and switched off a small machine that Bruno could not identify, then rose and kissed him in greeting.

'Sorry,' she said. 'I was listening to the tape of the last round of interrogation. J-J emailed it to me. You said there was new evidence?'

'First, I've identified the missing photo,' he said, trying to sound matter-of-fact rather than pompous. 'It's of a team called *les Oraniens* who won the Maghreb League trophy in Marseilles in 1940. They were coached by a professional player called Giulio Villanova. By this evening we should have a full list of the team, thanks to this man, a sports historian, who wrote a thesis on it. Here are my notes and his phone number.' He pushed out one of the files he had brought.

'Second, I've traced Jacqueline's movements on the day in question.' He put his finger on the next file, which contained the list of Dutch names and credit card numbers and a photocopy of the camp site's visitors' book with Jacqueline's registration number. It also contained the numbers of the vehicles that had left the camp site while Jacqueline's car was there.

'Third, we can put Jacqueline in the company of the visiting Dutch boys for almost all of the time that we think the murder was committed. This third file has photocopies of the credit card they used to buy diesel, and the name of an eye witness who saw her with them, and who earlier saw her fill up her own car.'

Isabelle poured him some of her own coffee before returning to her desk and looking through the files Bruno had brought. 'So why would she not explain to us that she was simply visiting some Dutch boys at the camp site?' she asked.

'My question exactly. And you know you thought it might be drug-related, and she was frightened of her suppliers if she talked? Well, the Dutch produce most of the Ecstasy pills, and a bunch of Hollanders were staying at the camp site when she visited. They came down in cars, camper vans and bikes, mainly for the Motor-Cross rally but they stayed on – not a bad cover for distributing drugs. I have a list of names here, some of them with credit card numbers, and I thought you might want to see if any of them are known to your Dutch colleagues or to any of those Europol cooperation agencies.'

'This is good work, but it's the murder we're supposed to be dealing with here, Bruno, not another drugs ring,' she said. 'Our elegant young Monsieur Tavernier seems mainly interested in the drugs charges as a way to put pressure on Jacqueline and keep detaining her. That and the politics, discrediting the *Front National* boys.'

'It's all crime, and I get worried at the thought of serious drugs in St Denis,' said Bruno. 'And it's strange to me that Jacqueline would rather be the main suspect in a murder inquiry than cover herself by admitting she visited some Dutch men at a camp site.'

She nodded. 'I'll brief J-J and send off a report to Tavernier. We'll need J-J's signature to send the request to the Dutch police. I presume the Dutchmen have all left St Denis, so they're out of our reach?' He nodded, still standing before her desk. 'And I presume you also realise that this could give the girl an alibi for the period when the murder was committed?'

'Maybe,' he said. 'It looks as if she left her car at the camp site and then went out in one of the Dutch vans.

Look at the page of the visitors' book, and the times of various vehicles coming and going while her car was there. You might want to ask the Dutch police to check whether any of those lads had connections with the extreme right.'

'You sure you want to remain in the *Police Municipale*, Bruno? We could use someone like you in the real police.' She put her hand to her mouth. 'Sorry, I didn't mean that the way it came out. It's not that I think you are not a real cop, it's just that it's clear that you have talents that could be used at a national level. You're a natural, and J-J thinks the same.'

'Yes, and every time I see him J-J tells me how much he envies my life here,' Bruno protested, laughing to take any sting out of it. 'I'm just useful for my local knowledge, you know that.'

'He just says that. He thinks the world of you, but J-J loves his work. He's dedicated to what he does, even when there are things about the work that he hates.'

'Like Tavernier, you mean? And the politicking?'

'Don't change the subject, Bruno. Why not transfer to the *Police Nationale*? Make a career of it. I won't say you're wasted here, but look at this new evidence you brought in about the camp site. Nobody else thought of that. And then tracking down the photo. You ought to be in the detectives. We need people like you.'

He heard something like urgency in her voice. This was not light banter. Bruno paused for thought, studying the pent-up energy in her pose. She was sitting squarely, her back forward from her chair, her arms on the desk and her jaw slightly tilted. She was making him an invitation, he thought, and not necessarily about police careers. So how could he answer her without sounding defensive or complacent?

'I'm happy here, Isabelle,' he said slowly, not knowing if she would understand. 'I'm busy, I think that I'm useful, and I live in a place that I love among a lot of people that I like. It's a way of life that pleases me and I can understand why J-J feels wistful whenever he sees me. I like him, but I would not want his life.'

'You don't want more?'

'More what? More money? I have enough to live as I please and I even manage to save a little. More friends? I have many. More satisfaction in my work? I have that.' Bruno stopped himself, knowing from the look on Isabelle's face that he was not saying this well. This was a strange conversation to be having in a police office. He started again. 'Let me tell you what I think, Isabelle. I think there are two kinds of people in this world. There are those who do their work for eight hours a day and they don't enjoy it and don't respect themselves very much for what they do. And then there are those who don't see much difference between their work and the rest of their lives because the two fit happily together. What they do to earn their living doesn't seem like drudgery to them. Around here there are a lot of people who live like that.'

'And you're saying that I don't?' she challenged, looking at him intently.

'You're able and ambitious and you want to follow your talents as far as they will take you. You like challenges. That's your nature and I admire it.' He meant it.

'But we're different people with different priorities and our lives will take different trajectories. That is what you're saying. Am I right?'

'Trajectories? Now there's a word. Our careers will probably take different trajectories because you have that kind of drive.' He got the feeling he had suddenly been drawn into a different kind of conversation altogether, where the language was different and the meanings had shifted.

'Drive for what?' she persisted. He noticed her fingers were clenched around her pencil.

'To get to the centre of things, to fulfil your talents.'

'You mean I want power?' She was looking almost fierce. He threw up his hands.

'Isabelle, Isabelle. This is me, Bruno, and yet from my side this feels like an interrogation. You're putting words into my mouth and I like you too much to get into a confrontation.' Her fingers seemed to relax on the pencil. 'What I'm saying is that you're a dynamo, Isabelle, you're full of energy and ideas and you want to shape things, to change things. I'm the kind of person who likes to keep them the same, but I have been around long enough to know that people like you are needed, probably more than people like me. But we have our uses too. That's how *le bon Dieu* made us.'

'All right, Bruno. Interrogation over,' she said, smiling and laying the pencil down on the desk. 'You promised to take me to dinner, remember?'

'Of course I remember. Around here we have a choice of bistro, pizza, not very good Chinese food, several restaurants serving the Périgord cuisine you are probably tired of by now, and a couple of places with a Michelin star, but we would have to drive to those. Your choice.'

'I was thinking of something less formal, more in the open air like a picnic. I liked your cooking.'

'Are you free this evening?' She nodded, suddenly looking happy and very young. 'I'll pick you up at seven. Here, or at your hotel?'

'The hotel. I'd like to bathe and change.'

'Okay. Don't dress up. Picnic-style it will be.'

He had to rush, and Bruno hated that. There were the final details to clear with the company that had the contract for the three firework displays of St Denis – the June eighteenth event that really launched the season, the usual national celebration on the fourteenth of July, and the feast day of St Denis at the end of August, which the town celebrated as its birthday. The company had wanted

60,000 euros for the three events, but with a little trimming of the display and a lot of negotiation he managed to reduce the bill to 48,000, which was just short of his 50,000 euro budget. That meant more money for the sports club fund. Then he had to call all the local businessmen to persuade them to take out their usual ads in the tournament brochure for the tennis club, and each had to grumble about the bad season and cancellations, but finally it was done. A tourist had lost a purse and he had to take a statement. He had to brief the Mayor on the latest developments in the murder case, fend off two interview requests, and check over the Mayor's deposition describing the riot. He just had time to get to the tennis club at four o'clock and change for his *minimes* class of five-year-olds.

By now the kids could hold a racquet, and were starting to put together the hand-eye coordination that allowed most of them to hit the balls most of the time. He lined them up at the far end of the court, and with the big wire basket of balls beside him at the net, he tossed a gentle bounce to each of the kids, who ran forward in turn to try and hit the ball back towards him. If they were lucky enough to send the ball his way, he would tap it back gently with his racquet and the child was entitled to another hit. Two was usually all they could manage, but in every class there would be one or two who were naturals, who struck the ball surely, and these were the ones he kept his eye on. But for the young mothers, who stood watching in the shade of the plane trees, each child was a future champion, to be cheered on before hitting the ball and applauded after it. He was used to it, and to their complaints that he was throwing the ball at their little angel too hard or too high, or too low or too out of reach. When they became too strident he would suggest it was time for them to start preparing the milk and cookies that ended each session of the *minimes*.

Young Freddie Duhamel, whose father ran the camp site, got the ball back to him four times and was looking like a natural, and so was Rafiq, one of Ahmed's sons. The other was a natural rugby player. And Amélie, the daughter of Pascal the insurance broker, was even able to play a backhand shot. Her father must have been teaching her. The kids went round ten times. They all counted carefully, and knew that after three rounds there would be no more balls in the wire basket and they could scamper around the court to pick them all up and replace them. Sometimes he thought that was one of the parts they most enjoyed. The other favourite moment came at the end of the ninth round when, by tradition, he would declare the session over and they would all shout that Bruno couldn't count and they had the tenth round to go. Then he could count off each of his fingers and admit that they were right, and give them each another round.

The final part of the class was what he called the game, knowing the kids were desperate to play against one another. There were three open courts, so he stationed four children at one end of each court, each child in its own little square and responsible for balls that landed in his or her territory. By this time, he had sent the mothers into the clubhouse to prepare the snack, or they would have become impossible in their partisanship. He started the game at each court by hitting a ball high into the air, and the game began when it bounced.

He had just hit the ball to launch the game in the second court when he noticed that one of the mothers was still watching, but when he turned to look he saw that it was Christine. He started the game in the third court and then strolled across to the fence to say *bonjour*.

'That was a wonderful dinner last night,' he began, wondering what had brought her here. She looked dressed for a walk, in strong shoes, loose slacks and a polo shirt.

'That was Pamela's cooking, not me,' she said. 'This is very strange after seeing you fight the way you did in the square, and now here you are like every kid's favourite uncle. You French police have a remarkable range of skills. I didn't know that tennis lessons were part of your duties as a country policeman.'

'It isn't exactly a duty, more a tradition, and I enjoy it. It also means I get to know every kid in the town long before they start getting to be teenagers and ripe for trouble, so that counts as crime prevention. And while we talk of crime, that thesis you found for me was very useful indeed. It was exactly what I needed to track down the missing photo.'

'Good, I'm pleased. Look, I didn't mean to interrupt. I didn't know you would be here, and I think your children need you.'

He had already turned, alerted by the sound of infant howls from the second court where a ball had bounced on the centre line and two children each claimed it. He sorted that out, and then saw a similar tussle looming on the third court so he went and stood silently by the net to make sure they stayed calm. From the corner of his eye he saw Christine still hovering on the far side of the fence. He looked at his watch and held up a finger; one moment.

At five p.m. he blew his whistle and the children collected the balls and ran into the clubhouse for their snack.

'Sorry,' he said to Christine. 'I have to go and join them soon.'

'That's fine. I was just passing by and saw the courts and thought I'd take a look. I didn't know you'd be here, but since you are, is there anything specific you'd like me to look up in Bordeaux? I'm going there for a couple of days on Thursday, to that Centre Jean Moulin I told you about, you remember? Resistance research.'

He nodded. 'Let me think about it and get back to you

tomorrow. I don't really know what I'm looking for. More information on Hamid, I suppose, and which group he was with before he joined the Army down near Toulon in 1944. If I get the rest of the names of his team, maybe we could see if any of them crop up. And then there's this Giulio Villanova.'

'I think I know what to look for. I read the thesis. You'd better go to your children. You're very good with them; you'd make quite a father.' She blew him a kiss and sauntered off slowly towards the road that led to the cave, now and then bending to pick a wild flower. He watched her for a moment, enjoying the swing of her hips. She turned and saw him, and waved. Twice she had used the phrase 'your children' and Bruno did not think it was accidental from a woman with no children herself. He waved back and went into the clubhouse to be greeted by the usual bedlam of a score of five-year-olds and as many mothers. The latter eyed him gleefully, giggling like a pack of schoolgirls as they rolled their eyes and asked about his new lady friend.

## CHAPTER 22

In the low light of the hotel lobby, Isabelle looked striking and almost mannish. Her hair, evidently still wet from her shower, was slicked back from her brow, and she was dressed entirely in black. Flat black shoes, black slacks and blouse and a black leather jacket slung over one shoulder, all set off by a bold crimson suede belt at her waist.

'You look lovely,' he said, kissing her cheeks. She had on the merest hint of eye make-up, lipstick to match her sash, and no perfume but the fresh scent of her shampoo. He led her to his van, which he had cleaned out specially, at least the front seat. As he showed her in, Gigi looked up from sniffing at the large cool box that was strapped on top of the spare wheel. He put his head over the front seat and licked Isabelle's ear. Bruno set off over the bridge.

'This isn't the way to your place,' she said. 'Where are you taking me?'

'It's a surprise picnic,' he said. 'A place you probably do not know, but you should. And it's a pretty drive.' He had thought carefully about this dinner and toyed with the idea of taking her home, but decided on balance against it. They had been together frequently enough and clearly liked one another so there was going to be sexual tension in their evening anyway. It would be all the more loaded if they were on his territory, his bedroom just a few steps away. Isabelle, he judged, was a woman who would decide for herself whether and when and where to take a lover, and yet it would feel odd to him – and probably to her – if he did not make an advance on his own turf. Neutral ground was called for, and the lady wanted a picnic, so a picnic it would be.

He drove up the long hill past the water tower and out onto the plateau that gave the best views along the bank of the river, and Isabelle made suitably appreciative noises. At a road so small it looked like a track, he turned off. They climbed another low hill, and came to the foot of a high and almost vertical cliff where he parked on a small patch of ancient gravel, opened her door for her and then released Gigi. He took a small picnic bag from the cool box and she heard the tinkling of glasses.

'I want you to meet a friend of mine,' he said. He led her up a track, round a corner and there, nestling into the base of the cliff, was a small house. It had a door, two windows, and its roof was the great rock itself. A small stream flowed from the base of the house through a gutter to tumble down the hill with a soft sound. In front of the house was a narrow terrace, with an old metal table and three chairs, and beyond it was a small vegetable garden. A black and white mongrel dog was tied to a hook screwed into the doorpost, and growled when it first saw Gigi . But Bruno's dog knew his manners and approached slowly and humbly, his tail wagging as if asking permission, and the two dogs sniffed each other courteously.

'They're old friends,' Bruno explained. 'We go hunting together.'

The door opened and a small elderly man poked his head into the open. 'Ah Bruno,' he said, as if they had last met a few minutes ago. 'Welcome, welcome, and who is your friend?'

'Isabelle Perrault, this is Maurice Duchêne, owner and keeper of the sorcerer's cave, who was born in this cliff house and has lived here all his life. Maurice Duchêne, meet Inspector Isabelle of the *Police Nationale*, a colleague but also a good friend.'

'My home is honoured to receive you, my dear Mademoiselle.' The old man, terribly bent with age, came forward to shake her hand. He had to cock his head sideways to peer up at her, but Bruno noticed his glance was keen and almost roguish.

'A beauty, my dear Bruno, you have brought a real beauty to my home, and my magnificent Gigi, prince among hunting dogs. This is a pleasure, such a pleasure.'

'Come, sit and have a drink with us, Maurice, and then with your permission I'd like to show Isabelle the cave.

And could you bring us some of your water? Isabelle is from Paris and she will never have tasted anything like it so we must take care of her education.'

'Gladly, gladly, my dears. Sit down and I shall be with you immediately.' He turned and hobbled back into the house. Isabelle sat, and Bruno took a dark wine bottle with no label from his bag and three small wine glasses, and poured. Isabelle sat back and turned to look at the view, a vast sweep of the valley with trees marking the river's meandering course and more cliffs on its far side.

'Here we are, here we are, the finest water of mother nature and father Périgord,' said the old man, coming out with a tray and a jug of water and three tumblers that were opaque with age. 'Straight from the rock, straight into my kitchen and bathroom, always running water. It never runs dry. And Bruno has brought my favourite aper-itif. He makes it himself, you know, every year on St Catherine's day. This must be last year's vintage.'

'No, Maurice, in your honour, and for Isabelle, I have brought the '99 that you like. Here, let us drink a toast to friendship, but first, Isabelle, I should tell you that this is *vin de noix*, made from our local green walnuts and Bergerac wine and *eau de vie* from my own peaches. You won't find this in Paris.'

'Delicious,' she said. 'And what a magnificent view you have, Monsieur Duchêne. But is it not cold up here in win-ter?'

'Cold? Never. The water never freezes and the rocks keep me dry. I have plenty of wood and my stove is all I need, even on the coldest nights when there's snow on the ground. Now you must try my famous water, my dear. If there were much more of it, I'd call it a source and bottle it and become richer than Monsieur Perrier.'

She took a sip. It was cool, so lightly *pétillant* that she could barely taste the bubbles, and without any of the chalky taste of some mountain waters. She liked it and took some more, swirling it around her mouth.

'It tastes like freshness itself,' she said, and the old man rocked back and forth with glee.

'Freshness itself. Yes, that's a good one,' he said. 'Yes, we shall remember that. You think they would like that in Paris, Mademoiselle?'

'Paris, New York, London – they would love it everywhere,' she said. Bruno was touched by her enthusiasm.

'May I show her the cave, Maurice?' he asked. 'I have brought two torches. And the *vin de noix* is for you, old friend, along with some pâté I made this Spring.' He took a large glass jar with a rubber seal from his bag and placed it on the table, and the old man handed Bruno an ancient key and poured himself another glass of Bruno's drink.

They walked on past the vegetable garden, along an increasingly narrow winding track, where only a flimsy rope fence protected them from the drop, and then around a steep buttress in the cliff. They came to a patch of brilliant green turf that led to an ancient iron-bound door in the rock. Bruno opened it with the key, gave Isabelle a torch, and told her to watch her footing. He took her arm to guide her in, and they stood for a moment to let their eyes get accustomed to the darkness. Gigi stayed at the entrance, backing away from the cave's black interior and growling softly. Bruno was very conscious of Isabelle's closeness as he steered her forward, his feet carefully feeling their way over the rough rock.

'They call this the Cave of the Sorcerer, but hardly anyone knows about it and even fewer come to see it,' he said. 'Maurice prefers it that way, so he puts up no signs and will not let the tourist board advertise it. But it has something very rare among the cave paintings of this district.'

He stopped, turned her slightly towards him and saw her give a small start, and then lean slightly towards him as if she expected to be kissed, but he shone his torch high and told her to look carefully. As she followed the movement of the torch beam she suddenly saw that he was illuminating the outlines of a creature, crouching and heavy and somehow touched with power and menace.

'Is it a bear?' she asked, but the torch was moving on. And there, next to it, was another image, but now Bruno was playing the torch beam up and down along a strange curve that seemed at first sight to be part of the rock. Bruno let her take in the dark painted shape.

'It's a mammoth!' she said, marvelling. 'I see the tusks, and that's a trunk, and those massive legs.'

'Twenty thousand years old,' said Bruno softly, and shone the beam further along to a small creature on all fours, its face turned towards them.

'Its face is so human,' Isabelle said. 'Is it a monkey, an ape?'

'No tail,' said Bruno, moving the torch to the rump. 'This is just about unique, the only identified humanoid face in all the Périgord cave engravings that are known. Look: the eyes, the curve of the jaw and shape of the head, and the gap that seems to be an open mouth.'

'It's wonderful, but it looks almost evil.'

'That's why Maurice calls it the Sorcerer. See that bag that he seems to clutch in one hand? Maurice says that's his magic tricks.' He paused, and she shone her own torch around the cave, up to the jagged, sloping roof and back to the mammoths. 'There's one more thing I want to show you, something I find very moving,' he said, and steered her around a pillar of rock and into a smaller cave, his torch darting back and forth at waist height before he found what he was looking for. Then the beam focused on a tiny hand, the print of a child's palm and fingers, so clear and precise that it could have been made yesterday.

'Oh, Bruno,' she said, clutching at his hand and squeezing it. 'A child's hand print. That's so touching, it's marvellous.'

'Can't you just see the little one at play? While his parents are painting mammoths and sorcerers, the child puts a hand in the paint and then makes a mark that lasts for ever.'

'Twenty thousand years,' she whispered, then impulsively reached up and touched his cheek and kissed him. She let her mouth linger on his as the light from their torches darted aimlessly around the cave. Bruno responded, tasting the wine on her lips, until she moved her hand up to stroke his cheek. She drew back, her eyes glinting in the torchlight and smiling questioningly, as if asking herself whether he had brought any other women to this cave, and whether it had worked the same magic on them.

They bade farewell to Maurice and his dog, and the sun was still an hour or more from sinking as they returned to the car, hand in hand.

'Now what?' she asked.

'Now for your picnic,' he said firmly, and drove on up the narrow, winding road. They came out on a wide plateau formed by the cliff that harboured the cave. He drove on towards a small hillock topped with a ruined building, but the distance was deceptive. The hillock was far larger than it seemed at first sight, and the ruined building was tall and imposing.

'It's a ruined castle,' exclaimed Isabelle with delight.

'Welcome to the old castle of Brillamont, seat of the

Seigneurs of St Denis, built eight hundred years ago. It was twice taken by the English and twice recaptured and sacked, and ruined over four hundred years ago by fellow Frenchmen in the religious wars. It boasts the best view in France and the best place I know for your picnic. You have a look around with Gigi while I organise our meal. Just don't climb the walls or the staircase – it's not safe.'

Bruno watched as Gigi bounded ahead, occasionally glancing back to see what took this human so long, and Isabelle climbed the hill past the crumbled castle walls to a large sloping expanse of turf dominated by a central tower. Three of its walls still stood, but the whole of the interior was open to her view. A stone staircase that looked solid enough climbed up the interior of all three walls. Bruno glanced up from the fire he was making as she paced the exterior walls and looked out over the plateau, where the view was even grander than it had been from the cave, with the River Vézère flowing into the Dordogne as it came from an adjoining valley.

Swifts and swallows were darting above Isabelle as she rejoined Bruno. He had built a small fire inside a nest of stones and laid across it a metal grill he had brought with him. Two freshly gutted fish were steaming gently above the coals. He had spread a large rug and some cushions on the ground, and two champagne glasses stood on a large tray. He'd put a fresh baguette ready, with a hefty wedge of Cantal cheese and a block of pâté on a wooden board.

As she knelt on a cushion, he reached into the cool box and pulled out a half bottle of champagne.

'Now there's a responsible policeman. Only drinking a half-bottle because he has to drive,' she said, sinking to her knees on the rug. 'This looks even better than I could possibly have dreamed when I asked for a picnic, Bruno. Where did you get the fish?'

'From my friend the Baron. He caught those trout less than half an hour before I met you at the hotel.'

'What would you have done if he hadn't caught anything?'

'You don't know the Baron; he's a born fisherman. The fish stand in line for the honour of taking his bait. But just in case you're still hungry after the fish, a couple of my homemade sausages from the pig we killed in February are in the cool box.'

'Can we have one of those as well?' she asked, clapping her hands. 'Just so I can try them? I don't think I have ever had a homemade sausage before.'

'Certainly, anything for the lovely lady of Brillamont,' he said, handing her a glass of champagne, and then diving into his giant cool box to bring out a long skein of sausage which he laid carefully over the coals.'

'That's far too much. I just want a little taste.'

'Yes, but Gigi has to eat too.' He raised his glass. 'I drink a toast to my rescuer, with my deepest appreciation. Thank you for saving me from a real beating back there in the square. Some day you must tell me where you learned to fight like that.'

'My toast is to you and your wonderful imagination. I can't think of a better evening or a better picnic, and there's no one I'd rather enjoy it with.' She leaned forward and kissed him briefly, letting her tongue dart out between his lips, then sat back, smiling almost shyly.

'I'm glad,' he said, and poured the rest of the champagne into their glasses. 'Drink up, before the sun goes down and it gets too dark to see what we're eating.'

'Knowing you, Bruno, you'll have thought of that, and some elderly retainers will march out from the castle ruins holding flaming torches.'

'I think I'd prefer the privacy,' he laughed, and handed her a tin plate from his picnic box. He moved across to the fire to turn the fish and sausage, and looked back briefly. 'Help yourself to the pâté and break me off some bread, please.' He turned back to his cool box, and came out with two fresh glasses and a bottle of rosé. 'This is why we only had the half-bottle of champagne.'

'Tell me about this pâté – the softer stuff in the middle and the dark bits.'

'That's how I like to make it. It's a duck pâté, and then the circular bit in the middle is *foie gras*, and the dark bits are truffles.'

'It's delicious. Did you learn to make this from your mother?'

'No, from friends here in St Denis,' he said quickly. He paused a moment. How should he go on? 'I learned how to do this from my predecessor in this job, old Joe. He taught me a lot about food and cooking, and about being a country policeman. In fact, between them, he and the Mayor and the Baron probably taught me everything I know. I didn't have a family of my own, so my family is here in St Denis. That's why I love it.'

The fish were just right, the blackened skin falling away from the flesh and the backbone pulling easily free. She saw thin slivers of garlic that he had placed inside the belly of the trout, and he handed her half a lemon to squeeze onto the pink-white flesh, and a small side plate with potato salad studded with tiny *lardons* of bacon.

'I couldn't make a feast like this in a fully fitted kitchen, and you produce it in the middle of nowhere,' she said.

'I think they probably had very grand banquets up here in the castle in the old days. The sausage looks about ready, and we still have another hour of twilight after the sun goes down.'

'I wonder what the cave people ate,' she mused, picking up a piece of sausage with her fingers. 'This is delicious but I'm getting full.' She put her plate down, and when Gigi came up to sniff it, the dog looked enquiringly at Bruno. He put the plate down in front of his dog and stroked its head, giving Gigi permission to eat.

'We know what they ate from the archaeologists,' he

said. 'They ate reindeer. There were glaciers up in Paris in those days. It was the ice age, and reindeer were plentiful. The archaeologists found some of their rubbish heaps and it was almost all reindeer bones, and some fish. They didn't live inside the caves – they saved them for painting. Apparently they lived in huts made of skin, probably like the American Indians in their tepees.'

He tossed the fishbones into the fire and put their plates and the cutlery into a plastic bag. This went into his cool box after he'd brought out a small punnet of strawberries and placed it beside the cheese.

'This is it, the last course, but no picnic is complete without strawberries.' Then he put some more sticks onto the fire, which blazed up as they lay on their sides on the rug, the strawberries between them, and the sun just about to touch the horizon.

'It's a lovely sunset,' Isabelle said. 'I want to watch it go down.' She pushed the strawberries aside and turned to lie close to him, her back against his chest and her buttocks nestled into him. He blew softly against her neck. Over on the far side of the fire, Gigi was discreetly asleep. Bruno put his arm around her waist and she snuggled into him more tightly. As the sun finally sank she took his hand and slipped it inside her blouse and onto her breast.

## CHAPTER 23

Bruno woke up in his own bed, still glowing from what had happened the night before. He reached across for the enchantingly new female body that had filled his dreams and, for a moment, the emptiness of his bed surprised him. Then, with his eyes still closed, he smiled broadly at the memory of the previous evening by the fire before, reluctantly, they had dressed and Bruno had driven Isabelle back to her demure hotel, stopping the car every few hundred yards to kiss again as if they could never taste one another enough.

He sprang from his bed and into his familiar exercises, his mind fresh and alert and alive with energy as he ducked into the shower, turned on the radio and dressed to go outside and delight in the newness of the day. He fed himself, his dog and his chickens, and then pondered the list of names he had scribbled down from his telephone call the previous evening to the teacher of sports history at Montpellier.

He read them through again, even though he had made

the lecturer spell out each one, letter by letter, so that there would be no more mistakes. The complete list should already be on his fax machine at the *Mairie*, and he would have to check it again, but clearly there was some error somewhere. How else to explain why the final list of the *Oraniens* championship team contained no Hamid al-Bakr, when the young man had pride of place in the official photograph? Unless of course he had changed his name?

His phone rang and he leaped towards it, a lover's intuition persuading him that it was Isabelle.

'I just woke up,' she said. 'And it's so unfair that you are not here. I miss you already.'

'And I miss you,' he said, and they exchanged the delightful nothings of lovers, content just to hear the other's voice in the electronic intimacy of a telephone wire. In the background of her room, another phone rang. 'That'll be J-J on my mobile for the morning report. I think I'll have to go to Bergerac for the drugs case.'

'This evening?' he asked.

'I'm yours, until then.'

He gazed out over his garden, suddenly noting that it must have rained in the night while he slept. At least the rain had held off for them, and he felt himself smiling once more. But the list was still there by his telephone, nagging at him, and he looked at the name that was listed as the team captain: Hocine Boudiaf. Beside the word

Hocine, Bruno had written in brackets 'Hussein', which the Montpellier lecturer said was an alternative spelling and which looked more familiar. He had not been able to come up with a team photograph, but he promised to fax Bruno another photo that included Boudiaf, which might help solve the puzzle. He checked his watch. Momu would not yet have left for school. He called him at home.

'Bruno, I want to apologise again, to apologise and thank you,' Momu began almost at once.

'Forget it, Momu, it's alright. Listen, I have a question. It comes from trying to track down your father's missing photograph. Have you ever heard the name Boudiaf, Hussein Boudiaf? Could he have been a friend of your father?'

'The Boudiaf family were cousins, back in Algeria,' Momu replied. 'They were the only family my father stayed in touch with, but not closely. I think there might have been some letters when I went through the stuff in his cottage, just family news – deaths and weddings and children being born. I suppose I should write and tell them, but I've never been in touch. My father felt he could never go back to Algeria after the war.'

'Did you know any of his friends from his youth, football friends or team-mates? Do you remember any names?'

'Not really, but try me.'

Bruno read down the list of the *Oraniens* team. Most got no response, but he put a small cross beside two of the names that Momu said sounded vaguely familiar. He rang off and called Isabelle again.

'I knew it was you,' she laughed happily. 'I am just out of the shower and thinking of you.'

'Sorry, my beauty, but this is a business question. That helpful man you spoke to in the Military Archives. If you have his number, would he speak to me? I have the list of the *Oraniens* team and the mystery is that Hamid's name is not on it. I want to see if we can trace any of the other team members. One or two might still be alive.'

She gave him the number. 'If you don't get very far, I can try him. I think he was an old man who liked talking to a young woman.'

'Who could blame him, Isabelle? I'll call your mobile if I need help. Until this evening.'

As Bruno had expected, the faxes from Montpellier had already arrived at his office when he got in. He checked the list. The names were the same, and then he looked at the photo, grainy and not too clear. It had come from an unidentified newspaper and showed three men in football gear. In the centre was Villanova with his arms around two young North Africans, one of them named as Hussein Boudiaf and the other as Massili Barakine, one of the names that Momu had half remembered. Now he felt he was getting somewhere. He rang the Military Archives number that Isabelle had given him, and a quavering voice answered.

'This is Chief of Police Courrèges from St Denis in Dordogne, Monsieur. I need your help in relation to an inquiry where you've already been very helpful to my colleague Inspector Isabelle Perrault.'

'Are you the policeman that I saw on TV, young man, in that riot?'

'Yes, Sir. I think that must have been me.'

'Then I'm at your entire disposal, Monsieur, and you have the admiration of a veteran, *sous-officier* Arnaud Marignan, of the seventy-second of the line. What can I do for you?'

Bruno explained the situation, gave the names, and reminded Marignan of the connection with the *Commandos d'Afrique* who had landed near Toulon in 1944. And did the archives have a photograph of the young Hamid al-Bakr?

'Yes, I remember. And we should have an identity photo on the copy of his pay book, if not for the *Commandos d'Afrique* then certainly after his transfer. Give me your phone number and I'll call back, and a fax so I can send a copy of the pay book photo. I'm afraid we can't send the original. And please convey my regards to your charming colleague.'

Bruno smiled at the effect Isabelle seemed to have on the telephone, and began thinking what other lines to pursue. He was about to ring Pamela's number when he suddenly caught himself, took a piece of notepaper from his desk and wrote a swift letter of thanks for his English dinner. He put the envelope in his Out tray, then rang Pamela, exchanged amiable courtesies, and asked for Christine. He gave her the new names for her researches in Bordeaux, made sure they had one another's mobile numbers and rang off. Instantly the phone rang again. It was J-J.

'Bruno, I want to thank you for that good work on Jacqueline's movements,' he began. 'It turns out those Dutch lads she was with are well known up there. Drugs, porn, hot cars – you name it, they're into it. From what I see of their convictions, in France we'd have locked them up and thrown away the key, but you know how the Dutch are on prisons. To get to the point, we showed Jacqueline the evidence you collected and she cracked last night. I tried to reach Isabelle late last night to tell her but she was out of contact; bad mobile service out there in the country, I suppose. Anyway, we have a full confession on the drugs, but she's still saying nothing on the murder.'

'That's great as far as it goes, J-J. What about Richard? Was he involved in the drugs?'

'She says not, so I don't think we can still hold him. We can't shake his story, and now that she's come clean on the drugs I'm inclined to believe her on the killing. If it were up to me, Richard would be out today, but that decision is up to Tavernier. By the way, what did you guys do to him yesterday? He came back steaming and spent hours on the phone to Paris.'

'I think our Mayor gave him a talking to, as an old friend of his father's. You know he got the gendarmes to pull an arrest on Karim, the young man who found his grandfather's body. For assault, after Karim charged into those *Front National* bastards in the riot.'

'He did what? He must be out of his mind. Half of France saw that riot and they all think you St Denis lads are heroes.'

'Not Tavernier. He said the law had to be even-handed.'

'Even-handed, between a bunch of thugs and some law-abiding citizens? He must be mad. Anyway, you seem to have sorted it out. Anything else?'

'We seem to be making a bit of progress on that photo of the football team. I'll keep you posted.'

'It's a bit of a sub-plot, Bruno, but keep at it. We're still looking for a killer, and we don't have any other leads.'

As he rang off, Bruno heard Mireille's voice in the corridor greeting Momu. Should he not be at school at this hour? He looked out into the hallway and saw Momu about to go into the office of Roberte, who looked after the *Sécu*, the social security paperwork. He waved and Momu came over to shake his hand.

'I can't stop,' he said. 'I just came up in the morning break to sign these papers closing down my father's *Sécu*. But it's good to see you.'

'Give me ten seconds, Momu. I have a picture to show you.' He went and got the fax from his desk, without much conviction that Momu might recognise any of them, but since he happened to be here …

'Where in heaven's name did you get this?' Momu demanded. 'That's my father as a young man, or his identical twin. What's the name?' He pulled out his reading glasses. 'Hussein Boudiaf, Massili Barakine and Giulio Villanova. The Boudiafs are our cousins, so I suppose it's a family likeness, but that's an extraordinary resemblance. And Barakine? I recall that name from somewhere. Villanova is the coach he talked about. But that Hussein Boudiaf – I'd almost swear it was my father as a young man.'

Bruno sighed as he opened his mail and read three more anonymous denunciations of neighbours. It was the least pleasant aspect of the citizens of St Denis, and of every other Commune in France, that they were so ready to settle old scores by denouncing one another to the authorities. Usually the letters went to the tax office, but Bruno got his share. The first was a regular letter from an elderly lady who liked to report half the young women of the town for 'immorality'. He knew the old woman well, a former housekeeper for Father Sentout who was probably torn between religious mania and acute sexual jealousy. The second letter was a complaint that a neighbour was putting a new window into an old barn without planning permission, and in such a way that it would overlook other houses in the village.

The third letter, however, was potentially serious. It concerned that incorrigible drunk Léon, who had been fired from the amusement park for misplacing Marie-Antoinette on the guillotine and cutting her in half rather than just decapitating her, much to the horror of the watching tourists. They were even more appalled when he fell drunkenly on top of her. Now Léon was reported to be working *au noir* for one of the English families who had bought an old ruin and had been persuaded that Léon could restore it for them, payment in cash and no taxes or insurance.

He sighed. He wasn't sure whether to warn Léon that somebody was probably reporting him to the tax office, or to warn the English family that they were wasting their money. Probably he'd do both, and tell the English about the system whereby they could pay a part-time worker legally and cheaply, and still have the benefit of workers' insurance. Léon had a family to support, so Bruno had better get him onto the right side of the *Sécu*. He checked the address where he was supposedly working, out in the tiny hamlet of St Félix, where he had had a report of cheeses being stolen from a farmer's barn.

He looked again at the letter about the offending window. That was St Félix as well; *mon Dieu*, he thought, a crime wave in a hamlet of twenty-four people. He sighed, grabbed his hat, phone and notebook, plus a leaflet on the legal employment of part-time workers, and went off to spend the rest of the day in the routine work of a country policeman. Halfway down the stairs he remembered that he would need his camera to photograph the window. Fully burdened, he went out to his van, thinking glumly that Isabelle would not be very impressed if she knew how he usually spent his days.

Three hours later he was back. The English family spoke almost no French, and his English was limited, but he impressed upon them the importance of paying Léon legally. He would leave it to them to discover the man's limitations. The owner of the allegedly offending window had not been at home, but Bruno took his photographs and made his notes for a routine report to the Planning Office. The affair of the stolen cheeses had taken most of his time, because the old farmer insisted that somebody was destroying his livelihood. Bruno had to explain repeatedly that since the cheeses were homemade in the farmhouse, which fell well short of the standards required by the European Union, they could not be legally sold, and thus they had to be listed as cheeses for domestic consumption in his formal complaint of a crime. Then he had to explain it all over again to the farmer's wife. She finally understood when he pointed out that the insurance company would seize the chance to refuse to pay for the theft of illegal cheeses.

In his office, the phone was ringing. He lunged and caught it just as camera, keys and notebook tumbled from his grip onto the table. It was the *sous-officier* from the Military Archives.

'This name Boudiaf,' the old man said. 'The name you gave me was Hussein, and for that we have no trace. But we do have a Mohammed Boudiaf in the *Commandos d'Afrique* and his file. He was a corporal, enlisted in the city of Constantine in 1941, joining the *Tirailleurs*. He then volunteered for the Commando unit in '43, and on the recommendation of his commanding officer he was accepted. He took part in the Liberation, and was killed in action at Besançon in October of 1944. No spouse or children listed, but a pension was paid to his widowed mother in Oran until her death in 1953. That's all we have, I'm afraid. Does that help?'

'Yes, indeed,' said Bruno automatically. 'Does the file list any siblings or other relatives?'

'No, only the mother. But I think we might assume that Corporal Mohammed Boudiaf was a relative of your Hussein Boudiaf. Now I know it's Hamid al-Bakr that you are interested in, but there is a coincidence here. Al-Bakr joins the unit in August '44 in an irregular way, a unit where his acceptance would have been made a lot easier by Corporal Mohammed. Is there a possibility of a name change here? It's just speculation, but in cases like this we often find that the new recruit had some good reason to want to change his name when he enlisted. They do it all the time in the Legion, of course, but it's not uncommon in other branches of the service. If your man al-Bakr was originally called Boudiaf and wanted to change his name, no easer way than to join a unit where his brother or his cousin was already well installed.'

'Right, thank you very much. If we need copies of this for the judicial proceedings, may I contact you again?'

'Of course, young man. Now, did you receive my fax of the pay book photo?' Bruno checked the fax machine. It was there, the first two pages of an Army pay book, featuring a passport-sized photo of a young man known to the French Army as Hamid al-Bakr. Beneath it were two thumbprints, an Army stamp, and on the previous page the details of name, address, date and place of birth. The address was listed as Rue des Poissoniers, in the *Vieux Port* of Marseilles, and the date of birth was given as 14 July 1923.

'Yes, it's here. Thank you.'

'Good. And again, well done in that brawl of yours. We need more policemen like you. I presume you are an old soldier.'

'Not that old, I hope. But yes, I was in the combat engineers.'

'You were in that nasty business in Bosnia?'

'That's right. How did you guess?'

'I couldn't resist looking up your file. You did well, young man.'

'I was lucky. A lot of the lads were not.'

'Feel free to call on me any time, Sergeant Courrèges. Goodbye.'

His ear was damp with sweat when he removed the phone. He focused on the notepad in front of him and the two photos. Hamid al-Bakr of the French Army was the spitting image of Hussein Boudiaf, the footballer. Could they be one and the same person? That would explain Momu's surprise at the photograph and Momu's surprise had been real. If Hamid had changed his name, why had he done so? What was he so intent on covering up that he hid his real name from his own son? And could this secret of the past explain Hamid's murder, nearly sixty years after the young football player decided to join the Army and change his name?

He could talk this through with Isabelle this evening, he thought, smiling at the prospect, then admitting to himself that there probably wouldn't be a lot of time spent talking about crime and theories – or talking about anything. He remembered the way she had kissed him in the cave, just a millisecond before he was going to kiss her, and then that sweet and trusting way she had slipped his hand onto her warm breast ... The phone broke into his reverie.

'Bruno? It's Christine, calling from Bordeaux. I'm at the Moulin archive and I think you had better get down here yourself. There's nothing about Hamid al-Bakr that I could find, but we have certainly tracked your Villanova and that new name you gave me, Hussein Boudiaf. It's dynamite, Bruno.'

'What do you mean, dynamite?'

'Have you ever heard of a military unit called the *Force Mobile*?'

'No.'

'Look, Bruno, you're not going to believe it unless you come and see this stuff for yourself. Your men Villanova and Boudiaf were war criminals.'

'War criminals? Where? How do you mean?'

'It's too complicated to explain on the phone. There's so much background. What I suggest is that you go to Pamela's house and ask her to give you a couple of my books that she'll find on the desk in my room. Have you a pen? I'll give you the titles. Look up the *Force Mobile* in the indexes. The first one is *Histoire de la Résistance en Périgord* by Guy Penaud, and the other one is *1944 en Dordogne* by Jacques Lagrange. I'll call Pamela and get her to look them out for you, but you have to read the bits about the *Force Mobile* and call me back. I— Dammit, my phone's running out of juice. I'll recharge it and wait for your call. And my hotel in Bordeaux is the *Hotel d'Angleterre*, easy to remember. Believe me, you have to come here.'

## CHAPTER 24

In Pamela's large sitting room, where the walls were glowing gold in the sunlight and her grandmother's portrait stared serenely down at him, Bruno plunged back nearly sixty years into the horror of war and occupation in this valley of the Vézère. The smell of burning and cordite seemed to rise from the austere pages of Christine's books, and the history of times long before he was born suddenly seemed intimately, terribly close.

The *Force Mobile*, he read, was a special unit formed by the *Milice*, the much-feared police of the Vichy regime that administered France under the German Occupation after 1940. Under German orders, transmitted and endorsed by French officials of the Vichy government, the *Milice* rounded up Jews for the death camps and young Frenchmen who were conscripted into forced labour in German factories. As the tide of war turned against Germany after 1942, the Resistance grew, and its ranks were swollen by tens of thousands of young Frenchmen fleeing to the hills to escape the STO, the *Service de Travail*

*Obligatoire*. They hid out in the countryside, where they were recruited by the Resistance and took the name Maquis, from the word for the impenetrable brush of the hills of Corsica.

To this raw material, the Maquis, came the parachute drops of arms and radio operators, medical supplies, spies and military instructors from Britain. Some came from the Free French led by de Gaulle, some from Britain's Special Operations Executive and others from British Intelligence, MI6. The British wanted the Maquis to disrupt the German Occupation, or, in the words of Winston Churchill's order establishing the SOE, 'to set Europe ablaze'. But as the invasion neared, the prime British objective was to disrupt military communications in France, and to force German troops away from defending the beaches against an Allied invasion, and drive them into operations against the Maquis deep inside France. The Gaullists wanted to arm the Maquis and to build the Resistance into a force that could claim to have liberated France, thus saving France's honour after the humiliation of defeat and Occupation. But the Gaullists also wanted to mould the Resistance into a political movement that would be able to govern France after the war and prevent a seizure of power by their rivals, the Communist Party. On occasion, Gaullists and Communists fought it out with guns, usually in disputes over parachute drops.

The *Milice* and their German masters crafted a new

strategy to crush the Resistance in key areas. Specialist German troops, anti-partisan units, were shipped in from the Russian front, and from Yugoslavia where they had become experienced at battling similar guerrilla forces. But the real key to the new strategy was to starve out the Resistance by terrorising the farmers and rural people on whom the Maquis depended for their food. Rural families whose sons had disappeared were raided, beaten, sometimes killed and the women raped. Crops and livestock were confiscated, farms and barns were burned. This reign of terror in the countryside was carried out by a unit specially recruited for the task, the *Force Mobile*. In the Périgord, it was based in Périgueux.

Sitting in Pamela's peaceful home, Bruno read on, rapt and appalled. He knew that the Occupation had been rough, that many in the Resistance were killed, and that the Vichy regime became engaged in a civil war of Frenchmen killing Frenchmen. He knew about atrocities like Oradour-sur-Glane, the village to the north where German troops, in reprisal for the death of a German officer, had locked hundreds of women and children into the church and set it on fire, machine-gunning any who tried to escape the flames. He knew of the small memorials dotted around his region: a plaque to a handful of young Frenchmen who died defending a bridge to delay German troop movements; a small obelisk with the names of those shot *pour la Patrie*. But he had never known about the *Force*

*Mobile*, or the wave of deliberate brutality inflicted on this countryside he thought he knew so well.

The *Force Mobile* in Périgord was commanded by a former professional footballer from Marseilles called Villanova. Oh, sweet Jesus, Bruno thought as he read the name he'd so recently come to know. Villanova brought a new refinement to the rural terror. He believed that the French peasants would be even more effectively intimidated if the reprisals and rapes and farm burnings were carried out by North Africans, specially recruited for the job with promises of extra pay and rations, and all the women and loot they could take from the farms they raided. Villanova found his recruits in the immigrant slums of Marseilles and Toulon, where unemployment and poverty had provoked desperation, and where he had many acquaintances in the local football teams that included young Arab immigrants.

Bruno shivered as he realised where this was leading. He would have to pursue the hypothesis that his murder victim, Hamid al-Bakr, war hero of France, had also been Hussein Boudiaf, war criminal and terroriser of Frenchmen. Christine was right. He would have to go to Bordeaux in the morning, and gather the evidence about the *Force Mobile*, Villanova, Boudiaf, and other members. This theory, which had seemed as obvious to Christine as it now did to him, was indeed dynamite. The evidence for it would have to be complete and unassailable. They would also have to research the names of the victims of the *Force Mobile* in order to identify the families who had suffered – and who had every reason to want vengeance against any of Villanova's North African troops still living. They would certainly have the motive to kill an old Arab whom they recognised from those dark days of the war.

And what of Momu? What would it do to Momu, to Karim and Rashida, if they were to learn that their beloved father and grandfather had been a war criminal, a terrorist in the employ of the puppet Vichy state, acting under Nazi orders? What kind of shock would it be to learn that the man you respected as a war hero, as the brave immigrant who established his family as Frenchmen with education and prospects and family pride, had in reality been a beast who spent the rest of his life living a lie? How could the family stay in St Denis with that knowledge hanging over them? How would the rest of the little North African community in St Denis react to this revelation?

Bruno could scarcely bring himself to think about the French public reaction to the North Africans once all this became known, or to imagine by how many hundred votes the *Front National* vote would swell. He bent forwards in his chair, his head in his hands, biting his lip as he tried to cudgel his brain into rational thought. He had to make some plans, talk to the Mayor, brief J-J and Isabelle, and arrange to go to Bordeaux in the morning. He must talk to Christine, get some advice on how on earth he could pre-pare his town for a bombshell such as this.

'Are you all right, Bruno?' Pamela had come in to the room. 'Christine said you would have some pretty grim news and you would need a very stiff drink, but you look quite devastated. You're as white as a sheet. Here, have some whisky – it's not that Lagavullin you tried the other night. It's plain Scotch, so take a big gulp.'

'Thanks, Pamela.' He took a hefty gulp, and almost gagged on the fire of it, but it made him feel better. 'Thanks for the drink, and for being normal. I'm afraid I have been in something of a nightmare, reading about these horrors of the Occupation. It's a relief to come back to the present day and to life in a pleasant home.'

'Christine said she thought it was somehow related to Hamid's murder, but she didn't give any details. It's funny how the past never quite goes away.'

'You're right. The past doesn't die. Maybe it even keeps the power to kill. Look, I have what I need now. I'll take these books and leave you in peace. I have to get back to my office and get to work.'

'Are you sure, Bruno? Don't you need some food?'

He shook his head, picked up Christine's books and took his leave. As he drove away he looked with new eyes at this placid countryside that had known such events, and known them within living memory. He thought of smoke in the sky from burning farms, blood on the ground from slaughtered fathers; he imagined French policemen giving the orders that deployed military convoys on the country roads – convoys packed with Arab mercenaries in black uniforms, with licence to rape, loot and pillage. He thought of half-starved young Frenchmen, hiding in the hills with only a handful of weapons, helplessly watching the reprisals unleashed against their families and their homes. Poor France, he thought. Poor Périgord. Poor Momu.

And, Bruno wondered, whatever can we do with the Frenchmen who took their long-delayed revenge against one of their tormentors? At least now he knew why a swastika had been carved into Hamid's chest. It signified not the politics of the killers, but the real identity of the corpse.

Once back in St Denis, Bruno drove immediately to the Mayor's house by the river on the outskirts of town, showed him Christine's books and the photograph of young Boudiaf with Villanova, and explained why he now believed their dead Arab war hero had been in the *Force Mobile*. The Mayor was swiftly convinced, but agreed the chain of evidence had to be made solid. They sat down and, from memory, composed a partial list of all the families they knew in St Denis or the surrounding region who had been part of the Resistance. They could flesh out the list the next day from the records of the *Compagnons de la Résistance* in Paris.

'So the police are now going to start investigating half the families of St Denis to see which of them might have known that Hamid had been in the *Force Mobile*. How the hell do we stop this getting out of hand, Bruno?'

'I don't know, Sir. I'm trying to think this through. They'll question the old ones first, those who might have recognised Hamid. It could take weeks, a lot of detectives, and then the media and the politicians get involved. We could have a national scandal on our hands. We may need all your political connections to get the people in Paris to realise there can be no winners in this, nothing but a political nightmare when the right-wingers make hay about French families being burned out and terrorised by Arabs in German pay. Speaking personally, I'm so outraged by it I can hardly think straight, Sir.'

'Stop calling me Sir, Bruno. We've been through too much for that and I don't know what to do any more than you do. In fact, I trust your instincts on this better than my own. I'm too much the politician.'

'Politics may be what we need to get through this. But I have to go and brief the investigation team.'

'You haven't told them yet? So they don't know anything about the *Force Mobile*?' the Mayor demanded, and then paused before continuing thoughtfully, 'So we have some time to think how much to tell them.'

311

'No time at all, Sir,' Bruno said briskly. Determined to squash whatever thoughts might be stirring in the Mayor's mind, he went on, 'They know I'm working on this and Isabelle, the Inspector, has already been delving in the military archives about Hamid's mysterious war record. They are close on that trail, and I have to go.'

Bruno left the Mayor sitting hunched and looking slightly shrunken in the rather over-decorated sitting room that was his wife's great pride, and walked out to his van to call Isabelle. They met in his office at the *Mairie* where he laid out the evidence for her. Together they rang J-J and agreed to meet in Bordeaux the next morning. He phoned Christine at her Bordeaux hotel, got from her the mobile number of the curator of the Jean Moulin archives, and arranged for the next morning's visit. He decided it was not his job to alert Tavernier. J-J could do that.

More depressed than he had ever felt, Bruno could not think of food, but Isabelle took him off to the local pizza restaurant where he ate mechanically and drank too much wine. Careless of the town's gossips, she drove him home and put him to bed. She fed his chickens, undressed and climbed into bed beside him. He awoke in the early hours, and she pushed him into the shower and put on a pot of coffee. Then she joined him under the steaming water and they made urgent love amid the soap suds, ending up passionately on the bathroom floor.

Later she brought the coffee and they went back to bed. There, they turned more gently to one another and were still engrossed in each other's bodies when the cockerel crowed to signal the dawn – which made them both laugh and Bruno realised he felt human once more. They showered again, and Bruno watered his garden and fed Gigi, then made fresh coffee while Isabelle went back to her hotel to dress. She returned with a bag of fresh croissants from Fauquet's and they took her car to Périgueux. Bruno kept his hand resting lightly on her thigh for the entire journey.

'You're a very remarkable woman,' he told her as they reached the new motorway at Niversac. 'That makes twice you've rescued me. And this time you did it even after you saw me drunk.'

'You're worth it,' she said, taking his hand, putting it between her thighs and squeezing it. 'And there's another bad moment ahead, when you have to help us make the arrest. You'd better prepare yourself for that. Whatever Hamid was or whatever he did, he was unlawfully murdered.'

'I know,' he said. 'But if it had been your family, your farm, your mother, you would have killed him yourself. That's justice.'

'It may be justice, but it's not the law,' she said. 'You know that.'

Indeed he did know it, and it saddened him. Yet his

sadness was of a different order to the despair that had gripped him the previous evening. That at least had lifted.

Bruno and Isabelle met J-J and a liaison officer from the Bordeaux police on the steps of the Centre Jean Moulin at nine a.m. Christine was already inside with the elderly French historian who ran the archives. The Centre was named after one of the most famous of France's Resistance leaders, who had sought to unify Communists, Gaullists and patriots into a common command and had been betrayed to the Gestapo. It stood in the centre of the city, an elegant neo-classical building of white stone that hid the dark history within. Best known to the public as a museum of the Resistance, it contained showcases of domestic objects: wooden shoes, wedding dresses made of flour sacks, ration cards and other realities of daily wartime life. Also on show were bicycle-driven dynamos that produced electricity for clandestine radios, and cars with giant bags on the roof that contained carbon gas made from charcoal, to use in the absence of petrol. There were displays of the different contents of the weapons containers – Sten guns and bazookas, grenades and sticky bombs – dropped by British aircraft for use by the Resistance. Underground newspapers were laid out to read. And playing in the background was a discreet but continuous soundtrack of the songs they sang, from the love songs of Charles Aznavour to the defiant heroics of the Resistance anthem, *Le Chant des Partisans*.

But Bruno discovered that the real heart of the Centre Jean Moulin was to be found on its upper floors, which contained the written and oral archives and the research staff who worked there, keeping alive the memory of this tortured period of French history.

Christine and J-J sifted through the fragmentary records of the *Force Mobile*, and established that Hussein Boudiaf and Massili Barakine had been recruited to a special unit of the *Milice* in Marseilles in December 1942. After two months of basic training, they were assigned to the *Force Mobile*, a unit of a hundred and twenty men commanded by a Captain Villanova, which specialised in what were described as 'counter-terrorist operations' in the Marseilles region. In October of 1943, after the British and Americans had invaded Italy and knocked Hitler's ally Mussolini out of the war, the Germans had spread the Occupation into the previous 'autonomous' zone run by the Vichy government, and the *Force Mobile* came under Gestapo rule. The outfit was expanded, and Villanova's unit was assigned to Périgueux in February 1944, charged with taking 'punitive measures against terrorist supporters'.

They found pay slips with Boudiaf's name, movement orders for Villanova's unit, payroll listings that included Boudiaf and Barakine, and requisitions for special equipment that included explosives and extra fuel to destroy 'terrorist support bases'. The curator, cross-checking with the records of the *Force Mobile*'s pay office, found a record of Boudiaf's promotion to squad leader in May, after one of Villanova's trucks was destroyed in a Resistance ambush. The promotion listing included a new *Milice* pay book and identity card, complete with photograph, that had never been collected by Boudiaf. The *Milice* records stopped in June 1944, with the Allied invasion of Normandy and the complete collapse of the Vichy regime.

Bruno and Isabelle went through the *Force Mobile* mission reports, the punitive sweeps – staged from the Périgueux base – north into the Limousin region, west to the wine country of St Emilion and Pomerol, east toward Brive and south into the valleys of the Vézère and the Dordogne. They hit the region around St Denis in late March of 1944, raiding farms where the sons had failed to appear for forced labour service. They hit again in early May, based on intelligence from interrogations of Resistance prisoners after a Wehrmacht anti-partisan force, the Bohmer division, had surprised and destroyed a Maquis base in the hills above Sarlat. Bruno noted the names of the interrogated prisoners, who had all been shot; the names of the families listed as having sons who failed to appear for the STO, and the names of the towns and hamlets where the *Force Mobile* had been deployed. St Denis was not among them, but the surrounding hamlets of St Félix, Bastignac, Melissou, Ponsac, St Chamassy and Tillier had all been raided.

They spread out the photographs on the curator's desk and compared them. There was no doubt that Hussein Boudiaf the footballer was also Hussein Boudiaf the newly promoted squad leader of the *Force Mobile*. And if he was not also Hamid al-Bakr then it was his double. But all bureaucracies tend to operate in the same way. The French Army pay book contained two thumb prints of al-Bakr, and the *Milice* pay book had been designed in precisely the same format and contained two thumb prints of Boudiaf. They were identical. The dates and place of birth were also identical, 14 July 1923, in Oran, Algeria. Only the addresses were different. Boudiaf's address was given as the police barracks in Périgueux, not as Marseilles.

'So that's our murder victim,' said J-J. 'The bastard.'

'Just one moment,' said the curator, and went to a large bookshelf where he removed a fat volume. He began leafing through the index, and then looked up with satisfaction. 'Yes, I thought I remembered that. Rue des Poissoniers was part of the *Vieux Port* of Marseilles that was destroyed in the bombing before the invasion, which makes it a useful address for someone who wanted to hide his true identity.'

They went back to the *Force Mobile* mission reports, signed by Villanova. The raids around St Denis on May the eighth had included squad leader Boudiaf's unit. They claimed to have destroyed fourteen 'terrorist supply bases', which meant farms. May the eighth 1944, thought Bruno, the day that France celebrated her part in the victory that came exactly a year after the *Force Mobile* raided the outlying hamlets of the Commune of St Denis. He would never think of the annual May parade at the town war memorial in quite the same way again.

Suddenly, a memory came to him in a series of distinct but clear images, almost like the frames of a comic book or a film in slow motion. This year's parade, just three days before Hamid's murder, and Hamid in the crowd with his family, proudly watching Karim carry the flag to the war memorial. Hamid, who had been a recluse, never seen in the town, never going to the shops or sitting in the café to gossip or playing *petanque* with the other old men. Hamid, who had mixed only with his own family and kept himself carefully out of sight. And then Jean-Pierre from the bicycle shop and Bachelot the shoemender, the two Resistance veterans who never spoke but who carried the flags side by side at each May the eighth parade ... In his mind's eye, he clearly saw them at this year's parade, saw that moment when he noticed them staring intently at one another in unspoken communication. He saw the Englishman's grandson playing the Last Post, remembered the tears it brought to his eyes, and recalled his conclusion that Jean-Pierre and Bachelot had connected through the music and the memory. Perhaps that was not the connection at all ...

Bruno played each scene back carefully in his mind, then he went to the interrogation reports that came from the prisoners taken by the Bohmer division. He examined the list of captured men who were to be shot. The third name was Philippe Bachelot, aged nineteen, of St Félix. Jean-Pierre's family name was Courrailler, but he found no Courrailler in the list of prisoners. There was still a branch of the Courrailler family, though, in Ponsac, where they kept a farm, and a daughter who ran the kennels, breeding Labradors. He knew the farm, because it was one of the few places new enough and wealthy enough to have installed a special barn with white tiles that met European hygiene codes. Bruno excused himself and stepped out from the Archives and down the stairs, through the museum and into the open air of the square. There he took out his mobile phone to call the Mayor.

'It's him all right, Sir,' Bruno told Gérard Mangin. 'Photograph and thumb print. Hamid al-Bakr was also Hussein Boudiaf of the *Force Mobile*, a squad leader who burned a lot of farms in our Commune in May of 1944. There's no question about it, the evidence is solid. But it gets worse. One of the farms that was hit was that of Bachelot's family, after they interrogated his elder brother. Another was in Ponsac, and I think it was the Courrailler farm, but could you get someone to check the compensation records in the *Mairie* archives? I remember that the families all got some kind of compensation after the war.'

'That's right,' said the Mayor. 'There was a lawsuit in the Courailler family about who got what after the Germans paid over a lot of money for war damages. All I recall is that half the family still doesn't speak to the other half because of the lawsuit, but I'll get hold of the full list and call you back. Is this leading where I think it is, towards Bachelot and Jean-Pierre?'

'It's too soon to say, but I'm not with the police team now. I'm taking a walk outside on my own. This part is between you and me; it's town business. When I go back into the Archives I assume we'll just collate all the evidence, make copies and get them certified by the curator. And of course we'll collect the names of families who were victimised by the *Force Mobile*. We could end up with a long list of possible suspects and it could take some time. A lot of potential witnesses have died and memories aren't what they were.'

'I understand, Bruno. You will be back in time for tomorrow's parade?'

Tomorrow was the eighteenth of June, the anniversary of the Resistance, of de Gaulle's message from London in 1940 for France to fight on, for she may have lost a battle but she had not lost the war. Bachelot and Jean-Pierre would carry the flags, just like always.

'I'll be there, Sir. And everything is in order for the fire-work display tomorrow night.'

'Let's hope those are the only fireworks we get,' said the Mayor. With a heaviness in his step but a sense of justice in his heart, Bruno went back into the building.

## CHAPTER 25

They drove back in convoy to the police headquarters in Périgueux, Bruno riding with J-J and Isabelle following behind with thick files of photocopies in the back of her car. He would have driven with Isabelle but J-J held open the passenger door of his big Renault and said, 'Get in.'

J-J waited until they were out of Bordeaux and on the autoroute before saying, 'If you screw me around on this, Bruno, I'll never forgive you.'

'I thought you would threaten to put me in jail,' Bruno said.

'If I could, I damn well would,' J-J grunted. 'I think you already know who killed the bastard, and you are pretty sure that nobody else will ever find out. That's what you went out to tell your Mayor. You and your local knowledge. Am I right?'

'No, you're *wrong*. I may have some suspicions, but I'm pretty sure neither you nor I nor anybody else is going to be able to prove it. There's no forensic evidence. If there wasn't enough to convict Richard and Jacqueline, I don't see how you're going to be able to pin this on anybody else, not without a confession. And some of these old Resistance types went through a Gestapo interrogation without talking. They won't confess to you. If this case goes public, you can imagine the lawyers who'll be standing in line to represent them for free, for patriotism. It will be an honour to stand up and defend these old heroes. Any ambitious and clever young lawyer can build a career on a case like this. You know what, J-J? Tavernier will fight tooth and nail for the privilege of representing them. He'll resign from the Magistrature, resign from the Ministry, make a big media trial and ride it all the way to the National Assembly.'

J-J grunted a kind of agreement and they drove on in silence.

'Damn it to hell, Bruno,' J-J finally burst out. 'Is that what you want? An unsolved murder? Dark suspicions of racial killing? It will poison your precious St Denis for years to come.'

'I have thought hard about that and it's a risk we have to take, a risk we have to balance against the alternative,' Bruno said. 'And there's something else that worries me. We toss this phrase around about him being a war criminal, and it was hideous what he and that *Force Mobile* did around here. But think about it a bit more. He was a kid, nineteen or twenty, living in the slums of Marseilles in the middle of a war. No job, no family, probably despised as a dirty Arab by the people around him. The only guy who ever gave him a break was his football coach, Villanova. Suddenly through Villanova he gets a job and a uniform, three square meals a day and his pay. And just for once he's somebody. He has a gun and comrades and a barracks to sleep in, and he carries out the orders he's given from a man he respects and who has all the authority of the state behind him. After the *Force Mobile* was wound up, he paid his dues. He fought for France, in our uniform this time. He fought in Vietnam. He fought in Algeria. He was in a good unit that saw a lot of combat. And he stayed on for the rest of his life in our own French army, the only place he could think of as home. So yes, a war criminal, but he did his best to make up for it. He raised a fine family, made his kids get an education so that now his son has taught every kid in St Denis how to do his sums. His grandson is a fine young man with a great-grandson on the way. Do we want to drag all that through the shit-storm this would become?'

'Shit-storm is right.'

'Anyway, this is not going to be decided by you or me, J-J,' Bruno went on. 'This is going to go all the way to the top, to Paris. They're not going to want a trial of some old Resistance heroes who executed an Arab war criminal sixty years after he burned their farms, raped their mothers and killed their brothers. Work it out. The Minister of the Interior, the Minister of Justice, the Minister of

Defence and the Prime Minister will all have to troop into the Elysée Palace and explain to the President of the Republic how the TV news and the headlines for the next few weeks are going to be about gangs of armed Arabs collaborating with the Nazis to terrorise patriotic French families. And then they evade justice by hiding out undiscovered in the French Army. And on top of all that they fool us into making them war heroes with a *Croix de Guerre*. Can you imagine how that plays out in the opinion polls, on the streets, in the next election? Tell me, what would the *Front National* do with that?'

'Those are not our decisions, Bruno. We do our work, collect the evidence, and then it is up to the judicial authorities. It's up to the law, not us.'

'Come off it, J-J. It's up to Tavernier, who'll do nothing without considering every possible political angle and checking with every minister he can reach. When we explain all this to him, he will understand instantly that this case is political suicide. In fact I'll bet you a bottle of champagne that Tavernier takes one look at all this and decides to take a prolonged leave of absence for reasons of health.'

'I don't take bets I know I'm going to lose, Bruno. Not for that little shit. But it's not just Tavernier. No matter how it gets sat on, this is going to leak out eventually, probably from that English historian woman. Is she your latest, by the way?'

'Mind your own business, J-J. But I'll tell you what I want out of today. I want to go with you into Tavernier's conference room and lay out the evidence, and then I want to drive back to St Denis with young Richard Gelletreau in the back of the car and hand him over to his parents with no charges against him. You have your drugs conviction with that nasty little Jacqueline, and you'll get bonus points for cooperation with the Dutch police when Jacqueline's evidence convicts them. You have the *Front National* thugs on narcotics charges. You and Isabelle come out smelling of roses.'

'That will be a nice farewell present for her,' J-J said. 'You know she's being transferred back to Paris? The order came in last night and I haven't had the chance to pass on the good news. We'll miss that girl in Périgueux.'

'Don't tell me,' Bruno said automatically, feeling he had just been punched in the stomach, but knowing that he would have to say something or J-J would notice. Deep down, he told himself, this was no surprise. It was inevitable. He made an effort to keep his voice level. 'The Mayor predicted that she would be assigned to the Minister's staff.'

'Who knows? But I wouldn't be surprised,' J-J said fondly. He clearly thought a lot of her. 'The orders just said she was assigned back to HQ in Paris as of September the first. But she'll go with a feather in her cap and – what was that old Napoleon phrase? – with a Marshal's baton in her knapsack. She'll probably end up as my boss in a year or two, but Isabelle will always have a soft spot in her heart for us rustics down here in Perigord. We'll just have to keep her well supplied with *foie gras*.'

Tavernier knew all about the promotion, and strode into the conference room with a cheerful smile and a comradely handshake. 'Let me be the first to congratulate you, my dear Inspector Perrault,' he said. J-J handed her the transfer order, and for the briefest and most self-indulgent of moments Bruno watched her reaction before he scolded himself and looked away. He had seen her eyes light up and that was enough.

'Now, I hear you have made a breakthrough in the case,' Tavernier said. 'New evidence from Bordeaux, they tell me. Explain.'

Bruno laid out the photocopies of the pay books from Vichy and from the French Army. Then he added the fax photo of Hussein Boudiaf with Massili Barakine and Giulio Villanova, and the *Force Mobile* action report that cited Boudiaf's role in the raids around St Denis.

'Our murder victim was a hired killer for the Vichy *Milice*, who changed his name and his identity to hide out in the French Army,' he said, and sat down. 'That is why his executioner carved the swastika onto his chest.'

Tavernier looked first at J-J, then at Isabelle and finally at Bruno, a half-smile on his face as if he were expecting someone to tell him it was all a joke and it was soon going to be time to laugh.

'I think we may have to alert our masters that they might wish to consider some of the wider national implications of this,' Isabelle said coolly. 'As far as I know, the role of North Africans being specially deployed by the Vichy regime to inflict brutal retaliations on the French population during the Occupation has not become common knowledge. It is now likely to become very well known indeed.'

Tavernier looked carefully at the papers Bruno had put out before him.

'Notice the thumb prints on the pay books,' said Isabelle. 'They match. And when the forensics team searched the cottage, they naturally took all the victim's fingerprints. Here they are.' She shoved another sheaf of papers across to Tavernier. 'It's the same man.'

'We await your guidance,' said J-J.

'Do you have any recommendation for me, any proposal on how you plan to proceed?' Tavernier asked.

'We have a list of the known Resistance families in the region, including those who were targets of the *Force Mobile*,' said Isabelle. 'Any of them would have a motive to murder their old tormentor. The obvious next step would be to question them all, about forty families altogether. That is just in the Commune of St Denis. We may have to spread our net wider.'

'Why on earth did the old fool ever come back to St Denis and run the risk of being recognised?' Tavernier asked, almost to himself.

'It was the only family he had,' Bruno said. 'He'd changed his name, abandoned his old family back in Algeria, lost his brother in the war, lost his country after the Algerian war and his wife had just died. His son found work here in St Denis, and so did his grandson, and he was about to become a great-grandfather. He was old and tired and lonely, and he took a chance.'

'And you think he was murdered by someone who recognised him from the old days?'

'Yes,' said Bruno. 'I think he was executed by someone who felt he had a right to vengeance. At least, that's how I would make the case for the defence if I were his lawyer.'

'I see,' said Tavernier. 'I'd better review these overnight. As you say, my dear Isabelle, there are a lot of implications to be considered, some consultations to be made.' He looked up at them, a determined smile on his face. 'You three have obviously had a very long day. This is brilliant research, and I must congratulate you on first-class detective work. And now perhaps you all deserve to take some time off while we decide how best to proceed. So, no questioning of the old Resistance heroes for the moment, and I suggest you go off and have the best dinner Périgueux can provide. The investigation budget will pay. You've earned it.'

With a final beaming smile, a murmured promise to call J-J when a decision had been made, and a half-bow to Isabelle, he stood up, gathered the papers and was about to leave the room.

'Just one thing,' said Bruno. 'You have to sign the release order for Richard Gelletreau, the teenage boy. He's obviously no longer a suspect.'

'Bruno is right,' said J-J. 'We have nothing on him for the drugs charges, and we still have a lot of work to do with the Dutch police to nail those suppliers. Young Jacqueline has given us all the testimony we need. It's a good result.'

'Right,' said Tavernier. 'A good result.' Bruno looked across to see Isabelle smiling at him. Tavernier took some notepaper and his seal of office from his elegant black leather attaché case. He scrawled the release order with a flourish, and then stamped it with the seal. 'Take him home, Bruno.'

Bruno awoke in his own bed with Isabelle still sleeping beside him, her hair tousled from the night and one arm flung out above the covers and resting on his chest. Gently, he crept out and tip-toed to the kitchen to make coffee, feed Gigi and his chickens, water the garden and start this day of June the eighteenth. He knew that if he turned on the radio, some announcer on France-Inter would play de Gaulle's full speech. Somewhere he had read that there was no copy of the original broadcast of 1940, and de Gaulle had recorded it all over again after the Liberation ... '*La France a perdu une bataille! Mais la France n'a pas perdu la guerre!*'

While the water boiled, he walked, still naked, out to his garden, to his compost heap at the far side of the vegetable garden and enjoyed the deep masculine pleasure of urinating in the open air. At his feet, he saw that Gigi had cocked a leg to follow his master's example. Still peeing, he heard the sound of applause and turned to see Isabelle in the doorway, clapping her hands slowly together and looking particularly fetching in the blue uniform shirt he had worn the previous day.

'*Magnifique*, Bruno,' she called, and blew him a kiss.

'The same to you,' he called back, laughing. '*Police Municipale* – it suits you.'

'Night after night away from the hotel,' she said over coffee. 'My reputation is in tatters.'

'You'd be amazed how fast the word goes around that you were on special duty in Bordeaux and Périgueux,' he assured her. 'And besides, what does it matter? You're leaving for Paris.' It was the first time he had raised this.

She stretched out her arm and put her hand on his. 'Not until September,' she said quietly. 'I have to be here for the drugs case, and with all the bureaucracy of the Dutch liaison, that's at least another month. That's the rest of June and half of July. Then I have my vacation and

that's July and half of August. Then I have my re-assign-
ment leave. That's the rest of August. You'll probably be
tired of me by then.'

He shook his head, suspecting that whatever he said
would be wrong, and leaned across and kissed her
instead.

'I saw that you'd put the photograph away, that one
of you and the blonde girl,' she said. 'You didn't have
to do that for me, not if she was important to you.
Particularly not if she was important.'

'Her name was Katarina and she was important.' He
forced himself to look at her as he spoke. 'But that was a
long time ago, a different Bruno, and it was in the middle
of a war. The rules all seemed to be different then.'

'What happened to her?' she asked, and then shook her
head. 'Sorry. You don't need to answer. It's just curiosity.'

'She died. The night that I was wounded, she was in a
Bosnian village that got attacked and burnt out. She was
among the dead. My captain went looking for her after
the battle and told me when I got out of hospital. He knew
that she meant a lot to me.'

'Captain Mangin, the son of the Mayor of St Denis,
which is how you came to be here. Captain Mangin who
was promoted to Major while you were in hospital and
then resigned his commission.'

'You knew all along?'

'J-J recognised the name, and then we talked to him in

Paris. He teaches philosophy and is a rising star in the Green Party. He'll probably be elected to the European Parliament next time. He says you were the best soldier he ever knew, and a good man, and he's proud to be your friend. He told us about rescuing the women from that Serb brothel but he didn't say anything about Katarina. At least she knew some happiness with you before she was killed.'

'Yes,' he said. 'We knew some happiness.'

Isabelle rose and came round to his side of the kitchen table. She opened the shirt she was wearing and put his head against her breast and stroked her hands through his hair. She murmured, 'I know some happiness now, with you.' She bent to kiss him.

'June the eighteenth, Resistance Day,' he said later. 'You'll be able to see all our main suspects gathered at the war memorial at midday. I have to go and make the preparations, and find time to track down a cheese thief, uncover some unemployed labourer for making some cash as a gardener, and probably rescue a lost cat from a tree. And later I have to collect the green walnuts to make this year's *vin de noix*. All in a day's work. And as a special treat because you are the guest of the local Chief of Police, you are invited to lunch in the banquet room of the *Mairie* after the ceremony, the same place from which you'll see tonight's firework display. And then tomorrow, I can show you our famous weekly market and you can help me protect the farmers from the new Gestapo of Brussels.'

'Poor old Paris will seem very flat, after all this,' she said drily, kneeling to stroke Gigi as she waved him goodbye.

When he reached the *Mairie* and parked his van, Bruno noticed Father Sentout bustling up the street from the church into the square, and heading for the building. They shook hands, and Bruno bowed to let the plump priest go first and, as a courtesy, joined him in the elevator rather than taking the stairs.

'Ah, Father, and Bruno, just the men I wanted to see,' called out the Mayor, waving them into his office. 'Now, Father, you know that under the law of 1905 separating church and state, there are strict limits on the degree to which you may participate in civic events. However, since this year we are marking the tragic recent death of an old soldier of the Republic, as well as the usual ceremonies, I wondered if you might give us a short prayer of reconciliation, forgiveness of our enemies. I don't think the Republic will fall if you do that. A very short prayer and a blessing. No more than one minute. Forgiving our enemies and we all sleep in the peace of the Lord. Can you do that? I'll have to cut you off if you go beyond a minute.'

'My dear Mayor, I shall be delighted. One minute it is, and forgiving our enemies.'

334

'And of course we shall see you afterwards, at lunch,' the Mayor added. 'I think we are having lamb again.'

'Splendid, splendid,' said the priest, bowing his way out, and visibly delighted that at last the word of the Lord had penetrated the secular temple of the Republic.

'The case is suspended until Tavernier gets his orders from Paris,' Bruno began once Father Sentout had gone. 'But I don't think that future inquiries are going to be energetically pursued.'

'Good,' said the Mayor. 'Putting those two old devils on trial would be the last thing this town needs.'

'Have you spoken to them?'

The Mayor shrugged. 'I couldn't think what to say, and nor I imagine can you. They are old men, and Father Sentout would tell you that they will soon face a far more certain justice than our own.'

'Two unhappy old men,' said Bruno. 'They fought on the same side and lived and worked opposite one another for sixty years and refused to exchange a single word because of some old political feud, and they all but poisoned their marriages by constantly suspecting their wives of betraying them. Think of it that way and the good Lord has already given them a lifetime of punishment.'

'That's very neat, Bruno. Perhaps we should tell them that. But there's something else – Momu and his family. What did you tell them?'

'I saw them both, Momu and Karim, and told them

335

that we had new evidence that convinced us that Richard and the girl could not possibly have been reponsible for Hamid's murder, and that in the absence of any other evidence, the police would now have to start work on the theory that the swastika was a distraction carved onto the corpse to mislead us. So the next line of inquiry would have to be Islamic extremists who saw the old man as a traitor.'

'Did they buy that?'

'Momu kept silent at first, but Karim said the old man had a good long life and died proud of his family and knowing that he had a great-grandson on the way. He seemed fatalistic about it. Then Momu said he'd been thinking a lot about the *rafle* of 1961 that he told me about, and how much things had changed since then. He said he was touched by the way everybody in the town came out to be sure that Karim was released by the gendarmes. He never thought he'd live to see the day that his son was a town hero. When I left, he came after me and said that as a mathematician he always knew that there were some problems beyond human solution, but none beyond human kindness.'

The Mayor shook his head, half-smiling, half-grimacing. 'I was a student in Paris at the time of the *rafle* and all we heard was rumour. But do you know who was the Prefect of Police at the time, the man responsible? It was the same man who had been Prefect of Police of Bordeaux under the Vichy regime in the war; a man who rounded up hundreds of Jews for the Nazi death camps, and had *Force Mobile* troops under his orders. Then the same man went on to be Prefect of Police in Algeria during that dreadful, dirty war – Maurice Papon. I met him once, when I was working for Chirac. The perfect public servant, who always followed orders and administered them with great efficiency whatever they were. Every regime finds such men useful. It's our dark history, Bruno, Vichy to Algeria, and now it all comes home to St Denis again, just as it did in 1944.'

The Mayor's voice was calm and measured, but tears began spilling down his cheeks as he spoke. Bruno considered: a month ago, he would have stood impotently by, not knowing what to do or say. But now, realising how much he loved this old man, he stepped forward to hand the Mayor his handkerchief, which smelled faintly of Gigi, and put his arm around his shoulder. The Mayor snorted into the handkerchief and returned the embrace.

'I think it's over,' said Bruno.

'Should we go back to Momu, do you think? Tell him the truth in private and in confidence?' The Mayor stepped back, his usual self-control restored.

'Not me,' said Bruno. 'I'm content to let it lie, which means that Momu goes on teaching the children how to count, Rashida will still make the best coffee in town and Karim continues to win our rugby games.'

'And the younger generation uses Resistance tricks with potatoes to immobilise the cars of our town's enemies.'

The Mayor smiled. 'They are our people now, three generations of them. One of the things that troubled me most was that Momu and the whole family would feel they had to leave St Denis if all this became public.'

'They don't even know that the old man was not who he claimed to be,' said Bruno. 'Maybe it's better that it stays that way.'

The Mayor donned his sash of office and Bruno polished the brim of his cap as they walked down the stairs together to the square, where the town band had already begun to gather for the parade and Captain Duroc had his gendarmes lined up to escort the march to the war memorial. Bruno called Xavier, the Deputy Mayor, and the two of them posted the *Route Barrée* signs by the bridge and brought up the flags from the basement of the *Mairie*. Montsouris and his wife approached and respectfully took the red flag, and Marie-Louise took the flag of St Denis, and Bruno smiled and hugged her closely as he remembered that the *Force Mobile* had destroyed her family's farm after she was sent to Buchenwald. He looked around, just a little nervously, but there was no sign of Bachelot and Jean-Pierre.

A crowd was beginning to gather, and he went across to the outside tables of Fauquet's café where Pamela and Christine were sharing a table with Dougal, wine glasses now empty in front of them. 'We're celebrating Waterloo day,' laughed Pamela as he kissed both women in greeting and shook Dougal warmly by the hand. Then he turned and saw Isabelle striding jauntily towards him. For the pleasure of it rather than the camouflage for the gossips, he kissed her formally on both cheeks and Christine rose to kiss her too. He supposed that Isabelle would ensure that the Englishwoman understood the need to keep the town's secrets. With a burst of cheery greetings, Monsieur Jackson and his family arrived, the grandson with his bugle brightly polished, and Pamela introduced them to Isabelle, who dutifully admired Monsieur Jackson's British flag.

It was less than five minutes to twelve when Momu arrived with Karim and his family. Bruno kissed Rashida, who looked ready to give birth there and then, and hugged Karim as he handed him the flag with the Stars and Stripes, and the Mayor came across to greet them. Bruno checked his watch. The two old men were usually here by now. The siren was about to sound, and the Mayor looked at him, one eyebrow eloquently raised.

And then Jean-Pierre and Bachelot emerged, walking slowly and almost painfully up opposite pavements from the Rue de Paris into the square, and made their separate ways to the *Mairie* to collect their flags. The two men were very old, Bruno thought, but neither one would stoop to use the assistance of a walking cane while the other walked unaided. What power of rage and vengeance had it required, he marvelled, to endow these enfeebled ancients with the strength to kill with all the passion and fury of youth?

He stared at them curiously as he handed them the flags, the *tricolore* for Jean-Pierre and the Cross of Lorraine for Bachelot the Gaullist. The two men looked at him suspiciously and then shared the briefest of glances.

'After all that you've been through together, and I include the secret you've shared for the past month, do you not think in the little time remaining to you that you two old Resistance fighters might exchange a word?' he asked them quietly.

The old men stood in grim silence, each one with his hand on a flag, each with a small *tricolore* in his lapel, each with his memory of a day in May sixty years ago when the *Force Mobile* had come to St Denis, and a day in May more recently when the story had come full circle and another life had been taken.

'What's that supposed to mean?' snapped Bachelot, and turned and looked at his old enemy, Jean-Pierre.

A look passed between them that Bruno remembered from the schoolroom, two small boys stoutly refusing to admit that there was any connection between the broken window and the catapults in their hand; a look composed of defiance and deceit that masqueraded as innocence. So much contained within a single glance, Bruno mused, so much in that initial look they had exchanged when they first saw the old Arab at the victory parade. That had been the first direct look between the two veterans in decades, a communication that had led to an understanding and then to a resolve and then to the killing.

Bruno wondered where they had agreed to meet, how that first conversation had gone, how the agreement had been reached to murder. Doubtless they would have called it an execution, a righteous act, a moment of justice too long denied.

'If you've got something to say, Bruno, then say it,' grunted Jean-Pierre. 'Our consciences are clear.' Beside him, Bachelot nodded grimly.

'Vengeance is mine, sayeth the Lord,' Bruno quoted.

This time they did not need to look at one another. They stared back at Bruno, their backs straight, their heads high, their pride visible.

'*Vive la France!*' said the two old men in unison, and marched off with their flags to lead the parade as the town band struck up the *Marseillaise*.

## ACKNOWLEDGMENTS

The author wishes to thank Gabrielle Merchez and Michael Mills for luring him to the Périgord, René for making the house so comfortable, and Julia, Kate and Fanny Walker and our basset hounds Bothwell and Benson for filling it with life. This is a work of fiction and all the characters are invented but I am indebted to the incomparable Pierrot for inspiration and for his cooking, to the Baron for his wisdom and his wines, to Raymond for his stories and his bottomless bottle of Armagnac, and to Hannes and Tine for their friendship, tennis and memorable meals. The tennis club taught me how to roast wild boar; everybody taught me how to make *vin de noix*, and those who taught me how to ensure that nothing of a pig was wasted had better remain nameless, in view of the European Union regulations. It would be invidious to name all my wonderful friends and neighbours who filled our lives with warmth and welcome but the inhabitants of the valley of the river Vézère in the Périgord rightly call it a tiny corner of paradise, and I am honoured to share it. Jane and Caroline Wood between them whipped the book into shape and I am deeply grateful.